The Traveler

Stephen R. Wilk

ISBN: 978-1-62420-431-9

Credits
Cover Design: Design by Paul Potiki
Editor: Sherry Derr-Wille

Dedication

To the Females in my Life –

My Wife, Jill,

My Daughter Carolyn Renee,

My Mother, Mary,

My Sister, Cynthia,

and My Cat Hestia

(Sorry, Hermes)

The Traveler

I first found out about the Traveler because I was playing at Nuts with The Runt. I probably would've found out about him anyway sooner or later, because The Runt doesn't know how to keep a secret, but he really was responsible, so to be honest, I have to give him credit.

We were playing Nuts on the third step from the bottom of the Temple of Venus Fortuna in the Little Forum. Up at the top, near the door of the temple, the steps are clean and swept every day, and the priests chase you off if you try to sit there. Down at the bottom, where the steps blend into the mud and the blown leaves and the ox poop, they don't care. So, the drunks sleep on the lower steps of the Temple of the Skinny Venus. The workmen sit down to rest there, and the steps are deeply scratched with names and graffiti and playing boards. That was where Publius Marcurius, that's The Runt's real name, and I were playing at Nuts. The priests wouldn't think it worthy of them to bother a couple of boys playing practically down in the dirt.

The way you played at Nuts was you took turns putting your nuts one at a time at the intersection of the lines on the board. When you put all four down, you took turns moving them, one at a time, from one intersection to the next. If you got three of them in a row, that means you won the game, and you got to keep the nuts you put down, plus you got to take all the ones your opponent put down.

We had been playing for a while. Even though The Runt started out with a whole little sack full, he really didn't know how to play, and he'd lost almost all of them. I wasn't that interested in winning all of his, but I couldn't believe anyone could play so badly. So, I kept on playing to see if he'd figure out how to put the nuts down to block me, or how to move them after they were all down. Even after I started giving him help, he still wasn't catching on. I figured it was my responsibility to keep beating him so he wouldn't be the victim of some unscrupulous person.

Finally, he was down to his last four, and he was playing as badly as ever. I even told him what to do, I even played badly myself, but it was no use. I still beat him. I took the last of his nuts and put them in my bag. I was going to smile at him and say something about teaching him how to play properly when he suddenly broke down and cried, right out there in the public square.

He was embarrassing me, and I tried to get him to shut up before one of the drunks noticed. Even so, he wouldn't quiet down. Those nuts were supposed to be his lunch. It was all his mother gave him. He couldn't go back and tell her that he'd lost them playing a game, or she'd hit him. The Runt was so honest and so timid he'd never try to sneak a wedge of bread from the baker's, like any ordinary person.

I couldn't just *give* him back the nuts. You don't do that. So, I looked him over and told him I'd give him half the nuts he lost if he'd give me that weird necklace he was wearing. It's not like I wanted the necklace, but it would be a way to let him have the nuts back and still be respectable.

It was no good. He wouldn't accept my generous offer. I thought maybe he didn't want to part with his precious necklace, but that wasn't it. He wanted ALL of the nuts back. He was afraid he'd starve without the whole lunch his mom gave him, or something. I wasn't going to give in. If I did that, I'd lose respect, you know? In the Forum, or in the Alleys, everybody knows you have to keep respect. Everybody except The Runt.

I wasn't sure what to do, but he finally quieted down and started to think. *Better late than never,* I figured. He made an offer. If I gave him all the nuts back, he'd show me something good.

What was it, I asked him?

The Runt was usually the last to know anything. If there was something worth seeing, I probably saw it already.

There was a crazy man, he said. His father saw him, and most people didn't know about him yet. He looked strange, dressed strange, and hardly spoke any Latin at all. He mostly grunted, but that might be some barbarian language. He didn't know about things, apparently.

I said I didn't know. I wasn't sure seeing a Crazy Man, even a Crazy

Barbarian, was worth it. The Runt surprised me by saying I could hold onto the nuts. I could only give him the other half after I saw the Crazy Man, and decided if he was really worth it.

He was learning. I was so proud of The Runt, I agreed on the spot. We went off to see the Crazy Man. He turned out to be at the shop of Marcus the Blacksmith. I could understand that. Marcus always needed somebody to do the heavy work, what he called the Donkey Work, lifting loads, bringing in the charcoal, working the bellows. It probably wouldn't matter if the Crazy Guy couldn't speak, or even understand a lot of words. It was usually pretty noisy in Marcus' shop anyway, with all the hammering. All Marcus would have to do was point.

We didn't just walk in there, of course. Not even The Runt was that naïve. Adults figure any child in a shop is either there to make trouble, or else is going to get in the way. They thought a child would get hurt. We snuck in, around the side, and looked in through the window. There was Marcus, and his apprentices, and somebody I didn't recognize. He had a great unwashed mop of hair, and was sweating as he worked the bellows.

There was something wrong about him, but I wasn't sure what. His clothes didn't look right. The way he moved was wrong, somehow. That was when I saw his face. It wasn't the right shape or color. His *eyes* were wrong, and looked misshapen. Maybe he was an accident of birth, like that lamb over at the Tannery that was born with five legs. I paid a copper to see that, but it was worth it. With that thought, I gave The Runt the whole bag of nuts, including the ones I didn't win from him.

Having paid, I figured I had a right to see him up close. I slipped in through the window. Everyone's attention was elsewhere, and with the noise, they couldn't hear me so it looked safe to do. If this guy was working in a shop alongside other people, and they trusted him around fire, he couldn't be too dangerous.

When The Runt saw what I was doing, he tried to stop me, but he was too late. He certainly wasn't going to come in after me. Instead, The Runt ran away, taking the nuts with him. Good.

I crept closer to the Crazy Man, who was facing away from me. I just wanted a closer look at his face, so I could see what looked wrong with it. He was so intent on his work he didn't notice me until I was really close.

In order to see, I had to work around the furnace, so there was nothing between me and him. He looked up from the bellows for a moment, and that's when he saw me.

At first, he simply looked surprised—like he was wondering where I came from when there was no door over where I was. His expression changed as he saw my necklace, the one I'd won from the Runt. It fascinated him, even more than I did. He couldn't take his eyes off it. He stopped pumping the bellows and started walking toward me, his hand outstretched toward my neck.

So, I backed up, trying to put the furnace between us. He kept coming around, and I realized I was in a dead end. Before I could get up into the window and away, he'd grab me. The only other way out was past him.

I didn't hesitate. Most adults are slow, and easy to dodge. The Crazy Man's befuddlement made him seem even slower, so I was sure I'd evade him. I was wrong. He was *fast*, and snaked out one hand to grab my arm. I responded without thinking, kicking out at his knee. That always stops the grown-ups in the alleys. While they recover, I get a chance to run away.

Not this time. The Crazy Man did something I still can't figure out. He twisted around somehow and my kick went somewhere I hadn't intended. I ended up facing sideways, his hand still gripping my arm. I was starting to get worried. At that point, he did something I didn't expect. He spoke to me.

"You...where...you...pebbles?" he asked.

I think he was asking. His voice had that lift at the end. I thought I should answer him.

"Let me go, you crazy grunt," I said. For good measure, I shouted," Marcus!"

"No!" he said. "Pebbles! Where?"

With his other hand he reached for my neck. I tried to draw back, but he was too close and too fast. Only he didn't reach for my neck. He grabbed the necklace and pulled. The string broke, and the beads he wasn't holding dropped off onto the ground. The Crazy Guy lost all interest in me. He dropped to the ground and started looking for the beads.

I started to run past him, thinking I was free. I ran right into Marcus, who's as big as one of the columns of Venus' temple.

"What are you doing here?" he growled at me. "Are you bothering my worker?"

"You, why did you stop pumping the bellows?" He addressed this last question to the Crazy Guy, who was on his hands and knees, scrabbling through the ashes for the scattered beads.

I turned away from Marcus, because I saw a clump of the beads. I picked them up and nudged the Crazy Man, because I figured that 'helping the Crazy Guy' would explain what I was doing there. He looked up at me, and I saw his eyes didn't look crazed any more. When he saw the beads in my cupped hand, he said something I couldn't understand, but his meaning was clear. He smiled at me, and nodded his head up and down.

"Tenobius!" yelled Marcus "Back to work!"

He illustrated this by pointing at the bellows and mimed pumping it up and down.

Tenobius, this must be the Crazy Guy's name, nodded his head rapidly up and down. He got up from the ground, and I thought he was going back to work, but he grabbed my hands together and pumped them up and down like a bellows. He smiled at me.

"You...more...pebbles," he said, then went back to work.

"And you," Marcus said, standing over me with his hands on his hips, "Beat it!" I did.

As I ran from Marcus' blacksmith shop, I realized I lost the nuts, and I lost the necklace. I had nothing to show for my morning, except that I saw Tenobius, the Crazy Guy, up close. If I wanted to see him again, he would be eager to see me, if only I brought more beads.

~ * ~

The next day I went to see The Runt. As usual, I climbed up on top of Horatius' vegetable stand and looked in through Publius' window, because his mother didn't want him to be hanging out with me. Fortunately, he was in, but he almost got us in trouble by shouting my name loud enough for anyone in the *domus* to hear. The shout was inspired by his surprise at seeing me alive and whole, with no visible scars, so I let it pass. I told him to make some excuse and come outside to meet me.

A little while later we were walking down the street. The Runt gave me a little bag of nuts. He felt guilty about running off with all of them the other day, even if I did give them up. He wanted to know how it was I wasn't dead, and what happened with The Crazy Guy. So, I told him the story, embellishing it just a little. He was amazed The Crazy Guy had a real name.

"Tenobius..." he said, pondering it.

"Yeah," I said. "I've been thinking about that. It bothers me. I've never heard a name like it. What do you think?"

One thing I'll give the Runt is he may not have street smarts, but he has a lot of book learning. He can read, and his parents have paid for tutors. If Tenobius was a name in any of the major kingdoms, or was a foreign word, he'd probably know about it. It was no good. He racked his brain, staring off into the distance for a long while, but when he came back to earth, he had nothing for me.

"I'll have a look through my father's books." he promised. "He has a lot of geography stored away."

We talked about Tenobius' interest in the bead necklace. Now that he had a name, it didn't seem right to call him The Crazy Guy. The Runt said it might be because they were made of glass and had metal in them, so they were shiny. Lots of animals liked shiny things, and so did a lot of barbarians. He heard that the Phoenicians used to take strings of beads when they sailed out into the Wild, to trade with the savages.

That made sense. It would explain why he got so excited when he first saw them, and how he scrabbled through the dust looking for all of them. I asked Publius if he had any more of them, so I could see if he was still excited. I wanted to go see the Stranger again, and if I did, I wanted to bring something.

Publius told me he had put together that string himself from a set of his mother's Egyptian beads that broke apart. That's why it broke apart so easily. He said there were more of them, and he'd get them for me if I told him how the Stranger reacted to them.

~ * ~

A little while later I had a bag of beads. I tried stringing some of them together, but it was a pain to run the thread a string through the tiny hole in the bead without having the string come apart, or get stuck partway through. I finally decided he seemed to like the unstrung beads that came apart, so he'd probably like a bag of unstrung beads as well as a fully assembled set.

I was almost at Marcus' shop when I had another idea. If Tenobius liked shiny beads, he might like other shiny things. I found some bits of glass in the trash at the jeweler's, and the bodies of some flies near the food stalls. I found some small pebbles, too, since Tenobius babbled about pebbles. So, I had several little bags of stuff to bring over.

Why did I do it? I wanted to see how he reacted. I liked the way his face lit up when he first found the beads, and he felt so grateful to me.

Carrying all my bags, I went to Marcus' stall. Marcus looked up, saw me, and frowned. I hadn't really considered how I was going to get past him.

"What are you doing here? Get back to your home, or I'll give you a proper whipping. I don't need any loafers here."

I decided to do something unexpected, I told him the truth. I showed him my bag of beads, and said it was for the Stranger. A queer look came over Marcus' face when I said this.

"They are, huh? You expect me to pay for them?"

"No. He was just so happy to get them yesterday, I wanted to see how he'd react if I gave him more."

He was sure there was some kind of trick in it, and he was stumped when he couldn't figure it out. Finally, I said, "Don't you want to see what he does?"

Marcus thought a couple of moments more. Then, without taking his eyes off me, he raised his voice to call into the shop.

"Tenobius! Get over here."

The Crazy Stranger was already coming before Marcus finished calling for him. He looked at Marcus, before he noticed me. There was curiosity in his face, followed by interest. I held out the bag of beads to him without saying anything. He took it gingerly and poured some of the contents out into one hand. His mouth opened in surprise, and he looked up at me, smiling broadly and nodding his head enthusiastically. He put the bag down and stirred the few he'd poured into his palm with one finer of his other hand. He carefully picked up a bead between his thumb and forefinger and examined it carefully, turning it over and over, looking down the hole in the center.

Evidently, he liked it. He babbled something in some foreign language, smiling.

I held out the other bags, and his puzzled expression was easy to understand. Was I giving him more beads? He took the other bags and, one at a time, opened them, poured some into his hand, and studied them.

He didn't care for the flies, even though their bodies shone like colored metal. He smiled crookedly and shook his head emphatically from side to side. It was evident he wasn't interested when he handed the bag back to me. He was more interested in the glass, looking through it carefully to see if here were any beads among the chips. There weren't, but he kept the bag anyway. He scrutinized the bag of metal shards carefully, and decided he would keep it, too. The bag of pebbles didn't interest him at all.

When he finished, he placed the bags he wanted in folds in his clothes. He took me by each shoulder, looked at me gratefully, and gave a formal nod of his head. He suddenly stopped, turned away, and left.

"That's it," said Marcus. "The puppet show is over. You've had your fun. Tenobius has to get back to work. Go on, out."

I looked pleadingly back up at him. Marcus had a reputation as a tough man, and I could see it in his face. I turned to go. I was almost to the street when Tenobius came panting after me, shouting something over and over. He saw me and came over, despite Marcus' protests. He had his hands together in a ball, holding something. As I watched, he dramatically opened them, revealing...a disc of some kind. It felt like a piece of horn, only flat. He grabbed my hand and carefully laid it in my hand, then closed my fingers over it. It was mine, he was saying. This was in return for the beads and other things.

He pointed to himself and said a long screel of something in barbarian talk, which ended in "Tenobi", and pointed to his chest. He pointed at me, and his face asked a question. What's your name? He was asking.

"Argus," I said, giving him the name, everyone knew me by.

"Arr—goos" he said, thoughtfully to himself. After a moment, he said to me, "*gobbledegook*, Argus" With that, he turned back to the shop, where Marcus was shouting at him.

I resisted the temptation to look at what he'd given me until I was safe in one of my hideaways. When he put it in my hand, I thought he was just giving me something shiny in return for the shiny things I'd given him. Something light and multicolored. Insect wings, maybe, or nacre from inside an oyster shell from somebody's lunch.

What he gave me was something I never saw before. Light as a feather, it was flat and perfectly round. More circular than a new denarius. You couldn't say what color it was. It was no color, and all colors. As you turned it over and moved it around it was first red, then yellow, then green. When the sunlight hit it, it reflected light up on the ceiling in a bright rainbow of colors. It was a magic mirror that colored the sunlight. I couldn't stop looking at the glory of it. Nobody ever saw anything like this before.

What in the name of the gods was this? Who was Tenobius that he had it, and would give it away for a sack full of shiny beads? What had I gotten myself into?

~ * ~

We were sitting in the Leather tree, overlooking the Little Forum. There were several forks partway up that were comfortable to sit or lie in, and gave you a view of the entire square. You could watch the Guard making its patrols, or watch the Vegetable Girls come in from the country and set up their stand. You could keep an eye on Menelaius, the very bad pickpocket trying to steal something, and make bets on how long it would take the Guard to stop him. Mostly, you could just lie comfortably above the world, like the gods in Olympus, and see it go by.

The Runt and I were up there, along with Tullius. The tree belonged to Tullius, mostly because he claimed it, and kept people he didn't like out of it. Also, because the tree was in front of his father's leatherwork shop. If you wanted to get into the tree, Tullius had to approve of you, and you had to pay tribute. Right now, Publius was up there because of me, and I was there on the strength of the disc Tenobius gave me.

When I put it into Tullius' hand, he tried not to look impressed, but he clearly was. He held it close to his eye and far away, he tried to see reflections in it. He reflected sunlight from it onto his hand and looked at all the different colors he could get. Publius had done the same things.

The excitement he felt at first ran down, and he was beginning to get used to the thing being around. He was now examining it carefully, instead of playing with it. I hadn't given it to him, he was just getting to look at it. He understood that, and I understood that. If he tried to keep it, he knew he wouldn't ever be able to come down safely from his tree. I'd be waiting for him. We were friends, and all, but you have to recognize how things stand. I was still trying to teach this to the Runt.

"It's been punched out," Tullius said, after carefully studying the edge. "Whoever made this used a punch like the one my dad uses to make holes for the harness. The edge is perfectly smooth and round. Nobody cut this out with a knife or a set of shears."

"I heard that old Marius could use a pair of shears to cut a perfect circle from vellum," I said.

"Yeah, yeah. I've heard stories like that. I don't believe them. Nobody's hand is that steady. This was punched out."

He examined it again, running his fingernail over the surface.

"This stuff it's made out of. I don't know what it is. It feels kind of like dried fish bladder. Still it's ridged, like a feather. If you hold a feather up to your eye you can sometimes see colors, you know?"

"Not like this," I answered. "Don't go trying to pull it apart to see if it is some kind of feather."

"All right, all right. Do you know where he got this?"

"He can barely speak Latin. Maybe when he learns more, I can ask him. Not now. I'm lucky I know his name."

I turned to where The Runt was perched uneasily in a crotch of the tree. He was delighted to be in Tullius' tree, but scared he might fall. I don't think he'd ever been that high off the ground without a floor under him. Between his shyness and his fear, he was uncomfortably quiet.

"Speaking of his name," I said to him, "What have you found out in those books of yours?"

"I couldn't find 'Tenobius', or anything like it. Barbarian names are all weird, but they're weird in different ways."

"Weird how?"

"They use different letters, or put them together in different ways. I think I could tell if a name is Gaulish, or Egyptian, even if I haven't heard it before. I don't know what 'Tenobius' is. I'll bet it's not really his name."

"What do you mean?" asked Tullius, looking up from the disc.

"Grown-ups change names so they sound more like Latin ones. I asked my father about foreign names, and the ones Egyptians use to each other aren't the same as the ones they use with us. We throw in more letters. We put an 's' at the end. His real name might be 'Tenobi' Maybe you can ask him."

"How is he gonna do that?" Tullius asked. "He can barely speak."

"No, no," I said. "I know how I can ask him. The problem is I don't think Marcus wants me to be around anymore. I'll have to get past him and those two apprentices he has. They'll squeal if I try to get close."

I held my hand out toward Tullius. He didn't want to give up the Rainbow Disc, but fair's fair. He'd had it long enough. He slowly extended his hand, very deliberately holding the disc between thumb and forefinger. I knew if I reached too fast for it, he'd just pull it away, and I'd look like a jerk. I couldn't look too eager. The thing to do was to hold out my hand as if I expected him to put it in my hand. I hoped The Runt was paying attention.

He was. His attention was riveted as Tullius transferred the disc to my hand.

"Argus," said Publius, "I have an idea."

"Yeah, what?" I was afraid he'd have some involved, hare-brained idea about how to get to Tenobius.

"Look at Tullius' hand." I did. It looked the same as it always did. It was a hand.

"What about it?"

"Well, look at it. It doesn't look like yours. He's got scratches and scars on it. Here's hard callus at the base of his thumb, and his fingers are thick. It's a working man's hand, even though he's a boy like us."

"Yeah. Not a girly hand like yours," bragged Tullius.

Publius turned away and hid his hand at first, but then he held it up, fingers spread.

"Yes, look," he said. "Thin fingers with no calluses. They also bend more easily. I don't swing a hammer punch or cut up hides. I write, and I play the *cithara*. You can tell what I do from the way my hand looks. Argus has hands between the way ours look. He climbs, he gathers things. He works, but not hard."

"So?" asked Tullius.

"So, what are Tenobius' hands like? I didn't get a good look, but Argus did."

"I don't know. I wasn't paying attention."

"If they were thick and callused, you'd probably have noticed."

"Okay, so say they weren't. So what?"

"So, if they weren't, maybe he wasn't pumping bellows for a long time, or shoveling charcoal. He had to eat, so what was he doing with his hands before he was at Marcus' shop?"

Tullius and I were silent. It was an interesting thought. It was interesting to think you could read a man through his hands. I thought about the draymen with their coarse fingers, and the farmers who brought their grain and vegetables to the market, where merchants with soft hands piled things up and wrote in accounts books sold them. What could Tenobius have been doing with those hands? I'd have to get a better look at them.

"So, what *was* he doing with his hands?" asked Tullius.

"He was making *that*," said Publius, indicating the disc.

Of course. It was so obvious, once he said it.

"It's just a guess, maybe he was a jeweler or a goldsmith in his own country. Some skilled trade like that."

"There's a thought," I said.

Marcus was a blacksmith and a sometime worker in bronze and tin. He'd love to elbow his way to the upper strata of silversmithing and goldsmithing, but he didn't have the knowledge. What if he had a skilled metalsmith in his shop already, just pumping the bellows? How did Tenobius feel about doing such grunt work? There were possibilities here.

~ * ~

"Beat it!" said Marcus, barely looking up at me. "I'm busy!"

I hadn't gotten any closer than the shop entrance. It was the greeting I expected, and I was ready for it. I pulled out Tenobius's disc and caught a shaft of sunlight with it, reflecting a bright patch of color right into Marcus' eye. As I rotated it, the color changed in the weird way it did with that disc. I swept red light, yellow light, green light, blue light back and forth across Marcus' face. It was actually sort of pretty.

He knew something was wrong, and acted at first as if a fly had landed on his face. He tried to brush it away, but of course he couldn't brush the color away.

Tenobius looked up, straight into the glare, and opened his mouth to yell. He realized something strange was going on when the color flooding his face kept changing. It had a miraculous effect. Marcus stopped being nasty.

"What's that you've got there?" he asked, when he realized it was me behind the flashing light.

"Something Tenobius gave me."

"Give it here," he said, motioning with his hand.

"Only if I get it back. He gave it to *me*."

Marcus nodded. I took that as agreement, and I approached him with it.

I was taking a chance, I knew. Grown-ups don't think there's anything wrong with breaking their word to a child. I was a nuisance, and he gave me more respect on account of that.

I couldn't tell you exactly why I was doing this, risking my bauble for Tenobius' account. Part of it was because I thought he deserved better. I think part of me was calculating what I could get out of it. If this worked, not only would Tenobius owe me, Marcus might think he did too. It's always good to build up a stock of obligations that you can cash in later.

"All right," Marcus said, finally, "What is it?"

"Tenobius gave it to me. Ask him."

"You know I can't..."

"Look, it's small and light and pretty. It flashes light like a cut gem. I say maybe it's part of some jewelry."

I gave him Publius' argument about Tenobius being a jeweler, with his delicate hands, and the evidence of this rainbow thing. Marcus allowed it might be true.

"Even so," he said, "How can we use this?"

"*You* can't use it, it's mine. If he gave me the one, he probably has more, or knows how to make more. You've told people you want to move into goldsmithing. This might be the way to do it."

"What? Give Tenobius a chance with the fine tools? He'll probably break them or steal them."

"What do you have to lose? You're not using them now."

He gave me a level stare.

"I don't do things to make you happy, boy. Why do you care, anyway? What do you get out of it if I let him use the fine tools?"

"I don't like to see a good man go to waste," I said.

He was silent, skeptical.

"Maybe I can work with him."

"Ha!" he said, triumphantly.

He walked around, boiling off excess energy. I felt sure he was going to throw me out, and keep the rainbow disc, too. Before I knew it, he'd grabbed the scruff of my tunic. He put his face close to mine, and spoke in a low voice.

"You're *really* going to work with him? You, The Brat of the Little Forum?"

"Yes!" I shouted. "I want to see where *that* comes from. Besides he's weird and interesting."

"Well, then, I'll hold you to it," he said, pushing me away as he let go of my tunic.

To my surprise, he held out the disc for me to take.

"I've got Metellus and Arnicus as my apprentices. I can't spare either of them to help Tenobius. If you want him to have a chance, he's your project. If you don't work for him, it's off."

"How long do I have to do this?"

"How long do you think it will take to prove him? If he burns his hands and doesn't know what to do, he'll be back to pumping the bellows tomorrow. I'll give him two weeks to accomplish something."

"Like what?"

"I've got a *fibula* someone wants repaired. I haven't got the time, and I know my two boys wouldn't know how to start. Let's see what Tenobius can do. And you. Do you agree?"

"Yeah. Yes, I do."

"Swear by Castor you'll work."

"What, am I a girl? I swear by Mercury I'll do as you say."

"All right, then. Let's get Tenobius out of the back."

~ * ~

Tenobius had the bewildered look of a cow brought in from the field before the end of day. His not being able to speak proper Latin was going to make this difficult. I would have to do it all in pantomime. He looked from me to Marcus, then back again.

Marcus motioned for us to follow him to a table in the back. He took the workpieces off the table, then broke off a branch with leaves from the tree outside and brushed the table off. He brought out a box, placed it on the table, and swung the lid up. He looked at Tenobius.

The Stranger shyly came over and peered into the box. He reached in and pulled out a pair of brass pliers. They were tarnished, dirty, and bent. They were also smaller and finer than the crude iron tongs hanging in the shop.

Tenobius' face lit up with delight. He knew precisely what these were and what they were for. You got the sense he couldn't wait to use them. He worked them open and closed. He put his finger between the jaws, closed them down carefully, and pulled his finger away, judging the force it took. Even Marcus could see he'd used these before. Tenobius carefully placed the pliers down on the table and reached into the box again.

This time he removed a small saw. He ran a finger along the edge and sighted down the length of blade, holding it up to his eye. After examining it, he placed it on the table, next to and parallel to the pliers.

He kept taking things out, examining them, and putting them down.

I could identify a hammer, a file, some clamps. There were other things I couldn't identify, but Tenobius evidently could. He emptied the box, and seemed disappointed there wasn't more. I think he was hoping for some tools he used, but weren't there.

"Very well, "said Marcus. "You know what these are. I can see that. You, use these there to fix this." He used sweeping gestures to illustrate what he said, and held up the two pieces of the *fibula*, one in each hand. He mimed putting them together, then pointed to Tenobius and to the tools.

Comprehension dawned in his face, and he inhaled suddenly. Overcome by the thought of the task, maybe. He grabbed for the sleeve of Marcus' tunic, then turned and held up one of the tools I couldn't identify, and said something I couldn't understand. Tenobius mimed using it to do something to the *fibula*, making sounds with his mouth.

I had no idea what he was trying to say, but Marcus did. He nodded. He stepped across the shop and returned with what looked to me like a blob of metal. It certainly wasn't any kind of tool. Tenobius was puzzled, too, for a moment, but his face lit up. He nodded rapidly. He got that confused look again, and spoke in a worried tone. This time I understood the words.

"The running!" he said "The running!" He closed his eyes tightly in concentration. "It flows! Flows!"

Marcus seemed to figure it out, because he went across the shop and returned with a dirty little pot of something. Tenobius crooked the mouth toward himself so he could get a look inside, then carefully sniffed it. He looked at Marcus and nodded, slowly this time.

"Good," said Marcus. "You and you, Argus, have one week to do something with that." He illustrated this with pointing at both of us, and at the Fibula, and held up seven fingers to indicate the week. Witthout saying anything more he turned and left.

Tenobius looked at me. I returned the look, and repeated the gestures.

"You and me," I said. "Fix that. In one week. Seven days. You understand?"

He nodded once, emphatically, the pulled up two stools to the table, indicating I should take one. Immediately, he sat down and started to study the *fibula*.

~ * ~

It didn't take us a week to repair the piece. It only took us hours, but they were very long hours. Much of it was me trying to get things for Tenobius. This was difficult because it was hard to make out what he wanted, between his lack of language and my not knowing my way around a smithy. Part of it was because I had no idea where anything was in the shop. I tried to ask Matellus and Arnicus, but they were wrapped up in trying to make a dozen spikes before Marcus got back, and they were making a botch of the job. They really didn't want to help me, anyway.

"Apprenticed to the Wild Man, are you, Argus?" asked Metellus.

"Keep it up, and you'll be a really good madman yourself, one of these days," answered Arnicus.

They both laughed like it was the funniest thing in the world.

Tenobius started by turning the pieces over and seeing how they fit together. I'd never seen a fibula in use before. It's a kind of pin used by ladies to held their clothing together, usually a cloak. After you stuck it through both pieces of cloth you locked the needle part against the decorative front, so it wouldn't come apart. In this case the part holding it in place came off. Tenobius looked at how it had been attached and shook his head. He explained things to me in barbarian talk, and I nodded my head as if I understood. We seemed to be getting along fine. From watching his hands, I got the sense. *This shelf is too small where it was attached. That's why the pressure of the pin broke it off. If I just put it back on, it'll break off again. I have to change the way it's attached.*

Tenobius took the small hammer and a tool like a chisel, and had me find a small anvil. He re-hammered the piece and re-formed it, giving it a broad base. He took one of the tools I couldn't identify and the small piece and put them in the charcoal fire. Finally, he had me pump the bellows until the fire was hot. He pulled out the piece with the pliers and used a stick to apply some of the stuff from the pot, then pressed the blob of metal to it. Some of it melted from the heat and stayed there. Tenobius put that down and used the hot tool from the fire to do the same thing to the back of the *fibula,* cleaning off a patch with the pot stuff, but when he tried to melt some of the metal onto it, it wouldn't work.

He ran through several tries without success. *It's not getting hot enough*, he eventually made me understand.

He ended up putting the entire pin among the charcoals and had me heat it. With the entire pin heating up, Tenobius was able to melt metal onto it. He took the small bit he'd worked on and heated it in the fire along with the pin, then stuck them together were the melted metal was. He had me pump up the fire again. He held the piece in place with his pliers and had me stop. He held it for a while until it cooled. When it set, he carefully pulled it out and let it finish cooling on the bench.

The piece was firmly attached, and across a broader face than before, but some of the grey metal had run down out from between the two pieces, leaving a trail that ended in a blob of gray metal. Tenobius wasn't happy about that, but I could see it was on the back of the pin, where it wouldn't show. More of a problem was that the pin had been in the fire, and was crusty with ashes and discoloration.

After it cooled, he tested the link, and decided he was happy with it. He set about carefully cleaning off the *fibula* with water. I found him some soap, which he gratefully took. The surface looked cleaner, but still had discolorations on it. Tenobius had me fetch some wood ashes, which he mixed with water into a kind of paste, and used this, rubbing the surface of the pin with his fingers. The surface gradually cleared, but it took a very long time. Tenobius certainly had patience. I was falling asleep just watching him.

After Marcus got back from wherever he'd gone, and finished yelling at his idiot apprentices for ruining a lot of his rod stock, with only some pitiful excuses for spikes to show for it, he came over to see what progress we had made. His mood wasn't the best. His face brightened when he saw the *fibula*, now cleaner and shinier than it had been. The corners of his mouth dropped when he saw the back, with the re-fashioned stop and the blob of metal on it, but he was better after Tenobius showed him how the refashioned stop was not only stronger, but also protected the wearer from the point of the pin. I'd never seen anything like that before. He was even willing to accept that unsightly blob on the back. He gave Tenobius a handful of coins, and one to me.

~ * ~

I figured after our completing the *fibula* repair in only a day I was home free, and done with any obligation I had to Marcus. Marcus saw it differently. His idea was that he had me for at least two weeks of helping Tenobius get going, being his runner, all-around helper, and interpreter. In fact, he kept hinting he had me for even longer than that.

If I was the kind to take a stand on principle, I would have then. I didn't, for a lot of reasons. As I said before, adults feel contracts with *liberi* don't really count, and figure we don't have any principles. I wanted to stay and see what Tenobius would come up with next. I wanted to see what I could learn from him. In particular, I wanted to know how to make a rainbow disc. So, I stuck with him.

After Tenobius proved he could fix a decorative fastener, and improve it at the same time, Marcus decided to give him a backlog of repair pieces that were building up. Marcus hadn't had the time to fix them. I suspect he didn't have the skill, either, Marcus has huge, glove-like hands, and maneuvering small and delicate parts wasn't for him. Tenobius had fine and delicate hands, perfectly made for fitting tiny things together. He obviously did this sort of work before. He let me do a few pieces by myself.

One thing quickly became clear to me. Tenobius was a craftsman, but he was no artist. He could bring together parts and stick them together with the *solder,* that, I learned from him, was the term, but he couldn't arrange them into a pleasing shape or pattern. They were functional, but not... I don't have the right words. They weren't *pretty*.

Marcus didn't care. He was getting paid, and so we got paid.

~ * ~

One day Tenobius found something while rummaging through the shop, and he got all excited about it. He forgot the work he was doing completely, and wanted to use the thing he'd found. It was some kind of wooden frame with a stone set in it. A perfectly round hole had been made through the stone. I learned later from Tenobius that it had probably been done with a *pump drill*. At that time I'd never heard of such a thing, and couldn't have imagined it. It looked like a completely useless piece of equipment, and I couldn't see what it was good for. But Tenobius was going crazy over it.

He took a piece of gold from what we were working on and hammered it completely out of shape. He made it into a sort of root shape, tapering to a point, which he tried to push into the hole. It wouldn't go, so he kept hammering it into a longer and longer taper. I tried to get his attention, to see what he was trying to do, and to see if I could help. I was also trying to get him to stop, or at least slow down, because I was afraid his frantic hammering would attract Marcus' attention.

It did. Marcus came back to see what the commotion was, and got angry at Tenobius for making a turnip out of his gold. There was a lot of yelling and protesting as Tenobius tried to explain what he was trying to do. Marcus, not interested, just wanted him to stop. Suddenly, though, Marcus stopped, and started to pantomime with his hands. Tenobius eagerly nodded. This made Marcus stop altogether and take a long, quiet look at Tenobius, his hand rubbing his chin.

He held up a finger, then got a piece of metal made very thin. I later learned this was *foil*, and learned how it was made by Tenobius. It was so thin he could put it down on the table and cut it with a sharp knife, which is what he did. He cut a long thin strip from one edge. It started to curl up after he separated it from the rest of the sheet.

Marcus took his thick fingers and twisted the end into a tight little taper, easily smaller and thinner than what Tenobius had been trying to hammer the lump of gold into. He took the point and pushed it into the hole in the stone, checking first to be sure he was putting it into the correct side. He took the pliers and grasped the protruding point. He indicated Tenobius should hold the wooden frame tight. Marcus grabbed the pliers with both hands, squeezing them tight on the metal point, and *pulled*. Nothing happened at first, but as I looked closer, I could see that the point was being pulled out of the hole. The rest of the metal strip was slowly following. It was no longer a flat strip of metal, it was now emerging as a round thin rod of metal, shiny and perfectly round. I looked at where it was going into the other side and could see the strip curling up at the edges as it was being pulled into the hole.

Marcus continued pulling, and the strip continued to disappear into the hole, emerging as a round wire on the other side. It was clearly difficult thing to do, but Marcus had muscles of iron, strengthened by years of hammering at the forge. The pulling continued until the last of the strip emerged from the hole. I could see Marcus slowing down as the end approached so it emerged slowly and smoothly. The metal was now not only formed into round wire, it was also stiff and straight, despite its thinness. I reached over to touch it. Marcus tried to push my hand away, but I was too fast for him.

It was hot! That cool metal strip was now as hot as if it just came from the fire. It burned my fingers and I cried out, sticking the fingers in my mouth, where they tasted of metal. Marcus just grunted at me, as if to say *Well, I tried to warn you. Now you know better*.

He turned to Tenobius and handed him the pliers, which still gripped the end of the wire. Marcus spread his hands out. *There. That's how you do it.* I mentally added what I could now see those looks meant. *I thought you knew how to do this.* He walked back to whatever he was doing at the front of the shop.

Tenobius, uncharacteristically, didn't thank Marcus. In fact, he acted as if Marcus and I didn't exist. He slumped down onto his stool, laid the wire down on the benchtop, next to the rest of the metal sheet, and simply stared at it. I'm not sure of everything he was thinking, but I'm pretty sure of one part of it. *I wish I had the strength of Marcus' arms,* is one of the things he was thinking.

~ * ~

At the end of the day, Tenobius was still sitting there at the bench, staring at the wire, or maybe at nothing. He needed to get away from there, so I pulled at his arm until he got off of the stool. He walked stiff and lifeless as a slave out of the backroom. I guided him easily out of the shop, because he didn't really care where he was going. There was a *taberna* a couple of blocks away at the corner, and I steered him there.

I hadn't seen Tenobius drink before. I hadn't seen him eat, for that matter, but I assumed he must do both. Did he even know about wine? When we got to the *taberna* I weaseled our way in and pinched a seat for Tenobius. I could stand. I put down a coin and when I got the keeper's attention, I indicated Tenobius. In a moment the keeper returned with a broad flat pottery *calix* full of red wine, which he placed in front of Tenobius on the counter. Tenobius still didn't notice it until I flicked the bowl with my finger, making a dull ring. I pointed at it and indicated he should drink it.

Tenobius grabbed the sides of the *calix* uncertainly, as if he'd never held one before. He raised it to his lips using both hands and gingerly took a sip. He held it away from his mouth while he tried to decide if he liked it. He made a face, but took another, longer drink.

I managed to get another, shorter stool and pushed it in close to Tenobius. He was still dazed, so I hit the arm he was leaning on until he noticed.

"Are you feeling alright?" I asked. "Why are you so quiet?"

"I think I know how to make that. You know? But no. Had to be shown. It's more work than I think. Need more strong."

"I know," I said." I could see you knew what that thing was. You really wanted to use it. Unfortunately, it was more complicated than you thought. I guess you've only seen it used before, huh? You never did it yourself?"

"Yes."

"Yes. You're starting to talk, but I think you can say more. I think you're afraid to talk, because people will think you're dumb, or stupid. Don't worry about that. Just talk, and who cares what it sounds like. The only way you'll get better at talking is to talk. Say something."

"Wish I had arms as Marcus does."

"I'll bet you do. Why? What's it good for?"

"Make wire. Put pebbles, put *beads* on wire. Better than string."

"Yeah, I could see that. It wouldn't break as easy, like it did when you grabbed my beads. Why do you want to do that?"

"Make things."

"You can speak better than that."

"I want to make things."

"Why? Why do you want to make things?"

Tenobius picked up the *calix*, in one hand this time, and raised it to his lips. He was thinking, I knew. Of his answer maybe, or maybe just how to say it.

Tenobius took a bigger gulp than before. I thought he was going to cough it out, but he controlled himself and swallowed it. He exhaled. Not looking at me, he spoke.

"I want to go to house. My house. Where I live."

"You want to go home."

"Yes. I want to go home."

"Where *is* your home, Tenobius? Where do you come from?"

He smiled and gave a small chuckle.

"How to answer? How can I tell you? How can you understand? I come from far away. Very far."

"Which way?"

"Which way? I could say East, West, North...uhhh?"

"South?"

"East, West, North, South. All of those. None of those. I come from some other place."

"Everybody comes from some place."

He thought a moment.

"I come from the...from the other side of the rainbow."

"Ha! You know that word! They say if you go under the rainbow your wishes will be granted. Is that what you mean?"

"Not under. Over."

Over. Have it your way. Tell me when you're ready to say. I don't care if you're a slave or if you're a crook. I know lots of slaves and crooks."

"Crook?"

"Bad guy. Man, who commits crimes. Guy who steals, cheats, does wrong things. I don't even care if you're an actor."

"Actor?"

"I don't want to sit here teaching you words. It's easier to show you. Finish your cup and I'll take you."

~ * ~

There was usually a show after work hours at the makeshift theater in the ruined temple. The Temple company liked it because it was big enough for a crowd, but small enough they could make sure everyone paid. Since nobody owned it, it didn't cost them anything. They didn't put on fancy plays, like the tragedies or the high comedies of Plautus and Terentius. That suited me fine, I didn't like their brand of talky plays. Like most of the carters and laborers, I didn't want anything I had to think about too much. Tenobius wasn't ready for clever wordplay yet, anyway. Comedies where the actors spent most of their time slapping each other should be just about right for him.

The show was already in progress when we got there, but that didn't matter, people drifted in and out all during the show. Nobody cared about the plot, anyway. One of the actors was waiting at the entry, his face painted in weird colors so we knew who he was. He held out a bag of coins and shook it so the coins jingled. Tenobius paid, this time. He held up a couple of coins in front of the actor, who himself held up three fingers in reply. Tenobius dug another out of his belt and threw them in. Saisfied with the payment the Painted Man let us go in.

The stage was the floor of the temple, illuminated with daylight coming in from where the roofing stones fell in. The audience skulked among the columns along the side or sat on the steps.

There were three actors in the light. They didn't wear masks, all they had were painted faces. One had his tunic stuffed so that he looked grotesquely fat. Another was bald, and a third had great tufts of hair that stuck out. They seemed to be playing burglars who were trying to break into a house and steal something, but they were very bad at it. Bald kept dropping things, and when it seemed as if he'd picked them all up, he would drop them again in picking up the last one. Tufts had trouble opening the door, and slammed it on his fingers. Fats seemed to be the leader and was getting exasperated at the doings of his clumsy companions.

Tufts was able to find something in a chest. It was, perhaps, a bar of silver, or some carefully made candlestick. When he pulled it out, he revealed it to be only an ordinary set of iron tongs, which he held triumphantly as if he'd found something valuable. Fats took it, looked at it, shook his head, and turned to the audience as if to say "Look at what I have to put up with."

He suddenly took the tongs and used them to grasp Tufts' nose with them. Tufts struggled, crying out to be let go, only his voice sounded funny, because his nose was pinched. Bald came over to help, but Fats took care of him with his other hand, slapping Bald. Bald finally managed to dodge out of the way of a slap. Fats feinted at him and moved in an unexpected way, slapping Bald from the other side, all the while pulling on Tufts' nose.

The audience was laughing hysterically, with some people laughing so hard they had to catch their breaths. Suddenly, I realized some of the laughter was coming from Tenobius. It was the first time I'd heard him full-out laugh. He'd chuckled before, but not given a full belly laugh. Maybe the wine loosened him up. He was laughing harder than everyone else, I saw. Maybe he needed to laugh. Or maybe he saw something that I did not.

"Pretty Funny, eh?" I yelled at him over the noise.

Tenobius just laughed harder, then struggled to inhale a breath of air. Once he caught his breath he laughed it out again. He raised his hand and pointed at each of the funny actors in turn, and pronounced names.

"Lari!" he said, pointing to Tufts. "Kurli!" pointing to the Bald one. "Mo," said Tenobius, pointing to the leader.

I didn't think those were their names, and I turned to Tenobius to tell him so. That was when I could see his face and wide-open mouth in the light, and I noticed something I hadn't before.

Tenobius had metal teeth.

Not all of them were metal. Some were normal. Some were only partly metal. Some of his molars, well in the back, were completely metal. They shone and glinted as only metal can.

A chill went down my back, and it felt as if the hairs at the back of my neck were standing up. I've seen mouths full of rotten teeth, and mouths with only gums. Mouths with the open gaps where teeth should have been. It was just Life, and it never bothered me before. There was something unnatural about that mouth full of teeth, with many of them completely or partly made of metal. Who did that? How could they do that? Were his people such perfect jewelers they could make perfect teeth in metal? Did Tenobius maybe really come from the other side of the rainbow?

I ran out, not wanting to be near him until I figured this out.

~ * ~

I didn't go back to Marcus' smithy the next day, or the one after that. Instead I sat in Tullius' tree, looking down at the square and thinking. Tullius, seeing my mood, hadn't even demanded anything in return. After the first morning, he came up there, too. Even Publius ventured up there, daringly, on his own. They could see something was wrong. Finally, I swore them to blood oaths of silence, and told them all about Tenobius and what he'd done the last few days. Afterward I told them about his teeth. Tullius was unimpressed, and made a noise. The Runt was aghast, and stared at me.

"Are you sure they were metal, Argus?" he asked. "In the temple the light..."

"I'm sure. I took a good look. I've been looking at a lot of metal lately."

"Maybe it was something from the cup of wine," suggested Tullius. "I've seen how well they clean the cups at Catella's."

"It wasn't dregs of wine. Nobody can have grains of metal in his mouth and not know it. He has metal teeth."

"Garolus down at the Water Market makes false teeth," suggested Publius.

"He makes them out of the teeth from corpses and from animals," countered Tullius.

"So, would *you* want that in your mouth?" countered Publius.

I hadn't expected a counterattack from him. He was learning.

"Have you ever sucked on a piece of metal," Tullius shot back. "No matter how long you leave it in your mouth, it still tastes like metal. I wouldn't want it in my mouth."

"Maybe he had no choice," I said. "Maybe you get used to it."

"You thinking about going back?" asked Tullius.

"I probably will. When I first saw those teeth, I was scared. It's like seeing a ghost. The more I think about it, the less scary it seems. I mean, it's just Tenobius, right? He's still the same strange guy, even if he does have metal teeth. I don't think I'm not ready to go back yet."

"Why not?"

"I still have to get used to the idea."

"Can we come by and see his teeth?" asked The Runt.

"Yeah, I guess so. Just don't be obvious about it. Don't go saying 'Show us your teeth'."

~ * ~

It took me more than a day to find my courage and return. Marcus yelled at me for being away. I told him I was sick. Wasn't I back now, anyway?

Tenobius was excited to see me. He couldn't wait to show me something. He'd been busy while I was gone.

There was a strip of wood attached to the long edge of the bench. It had deep notches chiseled out of it at regular intervals. Clamped to one of the short ends of the bench was the thing Marcus had used. I saw immediately that, with the block clamped in place, Tenobius didn't need anyone to help him make the wire. Where would he find the muscles to pull on the metal strip?

Tenobius took a strip of metal foil and twisted it into a point, then stuck it through the hole. He produced a set of pliers, but they were attached to something. There were hooks at the ends of the handles, and these were tied to a hole in a long stick. He placed this on the table and grasped the protruding foil with the pliers. He stuck one end of the stick into a notch in the strip of wood on the bench. He got on the other side, grabbed the end of the stick, and pulled. The pliers grabbed the metal strip. The more Tenobius pulled on the stick, the tighter it gripped. Something else was happening. As he pulled on that stick with both hands, it pivoted around the end stuck in the notch, and it pulled at the pliers. I didn't realize it, but when you use a stick like that, it makes your pull much stronger. Tenobius explained it to me later. He called it a *lever*, and said people in shops use them all the time to give their effort more force. I'd seen men using rods to lever rocks out of the ground, of course, but I just thought it was just a way to redirect your effort. I didn't realize using it in this way let Tenobius' weak arms do the same work that Marcus did, with all his effort. I didn't realize it until I tried it for myself, later, but it works. With less effort than Marcus used, Tenobius was able to pull the strip through the hole, turning it into a round wire. Whenever it seemed he'd run out of space with his pulling, he just shifted the lever to another notch in the bench. As I watched the pliers pulling on the strip, I realized it was like Fats pulling on Tufts hair with the tongs. That must be where he got the idea.

Tenobius signed that there was more. He was so excited he wasn't even trying to put it into words. He'd made another frame, drilling a hole in another piece of stone. Only this one was smaller. He reached into a box and pulled out another piece of wire. It was thinner than the one he'd just made. I had a feeling it wasn't just the smaller hole. Looking at the way Marcus strained, I suspect he couldn't have made the wire any thinner. This took more effort, more than Marcus could give, but Tenobius could, with his lever.

Tenobius looked at the thin wire, then at me. He smiled. "Beads," he said.

Of course. He wanted to thread the beads onto metal wire, and now he could. This would, he thought, help him get home. Maybe he hoped to make money selling necklaces of beads strung on wire, and would buy passage on a boat with the money. A pretty necklace like that might be prized enough to bring him money.

He pulled out a piece of wire, strung with beads, and that shattered that idea. He'd taken beads from the sack I brought him from Publius, but they were mismatched, strung crazily on the wire. It looked like a misshaped mess. No one would want to buy that, even if it was strung on wire. It was a disaster.

Tenobius didn't seem to realize it looked like a mess. He was grinning like an idiot, proud of his accomplishment. Was it true, he could be such a master craftsman and such a hopeless artist? What could I possibly say to him about this?

For a time, I even forgot completely about his metal teeth.

~ * ~

Marcus was excited about the wire maker Tenobius made. He had Tenobius show him how to do it over and over again. He couldn't believe how easy it made the job of making wire. He showed us how you could use gold wire to dress up any piece of jewelry by wrapping it around things, making it look fancy and detailed. It was the kind of work even Marcus' thick fingers could handle. He explained how fine wire could be wound around and around in loops to give a decorative feel to a brooch or ring. Encouraged, he and Tenobius set out to drill even smaller holes in stones so they could make the wire even smaller. They set me to doing the drilling, which is how I learned about the pump drill.

It all turned out to be more complicated than I thought. You used the smaller holes to make smaller wire not from strips of foil, but by using the wire you'd already made. To do this, you had to prepare it first by heating it in the fire. There were other tricks, too. If you pulled too hard or too fast the wire would break, and you had to work to get the wire out of the hole, or else make an entire new stone. Tenobius knew how to solve some problems, but others they had to play with until they solved the problems.

It was late at night when Tenobius was standing over the bench, ringed with oil lamps, and drawing on the surface with charcoal. He and Marcus were designing a better way to make the wire. I stayed there with them, drilling holes, cleaning out the *dies*, as they called them, and doing little chores. It was late, and I was tired. I got up to leave, but Tenobius caught my eye, unseen by Marcus, and held up the smallest wire they'd made. He held it up and smiled. Somehow, I knew what he was thinking. *This is what I wanted. I got all of you to help me.*

What was he going to do? Make a hundred necklaces, all of them ugly? It was too much to think about this late at night.

~ * ~

They spent the next couple of weeks working on their new toys. They made wire and sold it to other smiths and jewelers, then bought more metal to make more wire. They tried different metals, making gold and silver wire, they made copper wire and bronze wire. They made tin wire.

Some things just snapped off, but others were very pretty. Soon other workers were bringing the metal to them.

They built a new machine for pulling that used a big wheel. At first, they had me work it, but in time they turned it over to Metellus and Arnicus. They sent me out running to find customers and deliver wire. They started out just sending loops of wire, but then started winding it around sticks, and eventually on the spools they use for thread.

It started to seem too much like work, and it wasn't interesting anymore. I figured Marcus got what he needed out of me, so I took the money he gave me and some samples of wire, and went off to sit in Tully's tree and watch the world go by. Tullius was fascinated by the wire, and kept playing with a piece. He ended up cutting himself with it. That was something I didn't realize you could do. I congratulated Tullius on figuring out a new way to hurt himself. He threw a stone at me. Where did he get a stone from, up in a tree...? Even so he kept the wire.

~ * ~

"Argus?"

It took me a moment to recognize the voice. It was either Metellus or Arncus, one of Marcus' goons. By the time I realized that, he had one of those big hands on my shoulder. I thought about running, but I was hemmed in, and he was too close. I turned and saw that it was Arnicus.

"He wants you," said the apprentice.

"I don't care. Marcus has no call on me. He paid me off, and I'm no 'prentice."

"Not him. The Crazy Guy wants you. Tenobius."

"Oh. What for?"

"How would I know? He's crazy. You can ask him yourself."

"Oh, no. He's a good guy, but he's got no call on me, either."

"Well, Tenobius says he wants you, and Marcus says to go find you. If I come back without you, Marcus'll take it out of my hide, so you're coming with me."

Arnicus' tone left no room for haggling. He exerted pressure with his hand to turn me around, and we started walking back to the smithy. I tried making a break for it once, but he was prepared for that.

That's what I get for being too concentrated on my goals, and not keeping my eyes open to what was around me. I had been watching the moneychanger, and I could tell he was getting sloppy in his job. He wasn't paying attention to the silver on his table, and the pile was starting to build up and was about to fall. A swift and clever fellow could...but it was at that point that I felt Arnicus' hand on me.

He propelled me into the backroom, where I saw there were several new things set up -- the thing with the large wheel for pulling wire, and another thing that looked like a table with a vertical rod above it. Tenobius was working on this when we came in.

"Here," said Arnicus, pushed me in, and left.

"Argus!" said Tenobius, looking up.

His face brightened, and broke into a big smile.

"Hi, Tenobius," I said, then couldn't figure out what else to say. "You've been busy."

"Where have you been? I need your help."

"You're talking better, too. How long has it been?"

"I need your help."

"I helped you already. It looks like you're doing well."

"You don't. Let's go for a walk. I'll buy you a bowl of stew."

I was shaken by his getting straight to the point. I hadn't eaten yet, so his offer made my belly agree, even if the rest of me didn't. We went.

~ * ~

Tenobius knew his way around by now. He took us straight to Madame Nux's stand and bought two small pots of stuff. It had real meat in it, and I hadn't had any in days. I ate it all down as Tenobius watched. We'd taken a spot under the shade tree, and no one was trying to push us out of the way. We could talk.

"I've been working with the apprentices," he said. "They're good if you tell them what to do, but they don't want to think. I have to tell them every step. I didn't have to do that with you."

"Is that what you want? You want me to come back because they're too stupid?"

"It's not just that. You know how to find things. I need to find a lot more things so I can get home."

"Are you still planning to get home by selling beads? Because that string you made looked terrible."

"Oh, I'm getting better," he said.

He reached into his tunic and took out another string. This set was beautiful, at least compared to the first set he showed me. It was made of the Egyptian glass beads, all strung on the finer wire that Tenobius made. They were all uniform beads this time, and the necklace looked much more professional. He put it back, away out of sight.

"I'm not selling them. I need them for myself."

I was going to ask him why, but he went on again.

"There are others things I need to find. I don't know my way around, but you do."

"Are you going to steal them?"

"I have enough money from our wire to buy things now. I do know the money will not last. You can only sell so much wire, even in Rome. I'd like you to help me. There's something we need to talk about first."

"Yeah? What?"

"That. Your attitude. You act differently. I'm not sure why. I think maybe you're afraid of me. Is that it?"

How do you answer someone who asks you that? I finished my stew.

"You're a strange guy."

"Yes, I know I must seem that way"

"You're very strange. Nobody's like you. You didn't speak right, but now you're speaking well, in a very short time. You know all these strange things that nobody else does, but you don't know your way around the city. Did you fall off a boat? Are you an escaped slave? Where did you come from?"

"Far away."

"If you want me to come back, I want to know more than that. I want to know why your eyes are so strange. I want to know why you have metal teeth."

"Metal teeth? What do you...? When did you see my teeth?"

"When you open your mouth wide. You put your hand over your mouth when you yawn, but you didn't when you were laughing in the Temple theater."

"Metal teeth. I don't.... Oh, by the gods. I don't have metal teeth."

"I've seen them. I know the look of metal. I worked in the smithy, by the gods. Do people have metal teeth in your country?"

Tenobius looked at me for a long time, then away, up into the branches of the tree. Finally he looked back at me. He sighed.

"Yes. They do. In a way. Look, you must have seen people with rotten teeth. Missing teeth."

"Yeah. Old people, mostly."

"Well, we have special doctors who drill out the rot in a tooth and repair it with things. Sometimes they repair it with metal."

"They don't."

"They do."

"How do they get it to fill in. How do they get the right shape? They'd have to have the hands of jewelers, and do it in your mouth."

"Look, I'm not one of them, but I do know they study for a long time. Do you know about Liquidsilver?"

"Liquidsilver?"

"Yes. It's called Live Silver, too. Water Silver. Quicksilver. It's bright and shiny metal that's a liquid."

I had seen it. Publius had a little jar with a couple of drops in it that he showed me once. The Live Silver stayed in little balls and rolled around without getting the inside of the jar wet.

"Yes."

"Well, they have a special way to mix it with other metal, and the mixture is like putty. They push it into the place they drilled and let it harden, then they carve it into the right shape with their drills."

"Like the pump drill? I don't see..."

"They have special drills on handles with pulleys. The first ones had foot pumps, but they have better ways to do it now."

"Like they have an apprentice pumping it?"

"Sort of."

"If you told me this as a story, I'd say you were lying. But I've seen your mouth."

"Would you rather have me tell you that a magician turned my teeth into metal?"

"I'm not stupid. They really have machines that clever where you're from?"

"A lot of them."

"Why did you leave a place like that?"

"That would take a long time to tell. Just say I didn't plan to move out. I wanted to see other places. I wanted to see your Roma."

"And now you can't go home."

"I hope I can. It won't be easy. I need your help."

We were silent for a time.

"Why do your eyes look like that?" I asked. It sounded strange and rude, but I had to know.

"Like what?"

"Your eyes don't look like everyone else's. They're strange in the corners. I thought they were tilted at first, but they're not. Were you born with eyes that are different? Does everyone have eyes like that in your country? Do they hurt?"

He looked puzzled at first, then he started to laugh. He didn't try to cover his mouth. In fact, I think he was deliberately showing me his metal teeth.

"I hadn't thought about that," he said. "My eyes must look strange to the Romans, but I never thought of it. You may not believe me, but it's true. When I walk down the street, people stare at me, and I wondered why that was. I thought they all knew I was a barbarian, but I didn't know why. I thought it was my clothes, or the way I walked. I never thought about my eyes.

"No, they don't hurt. Do your eyes hurt? This is just the way they are. Some people would be insulted by the question. I'm sure you've never seen eyes like mine. You're innocent. Is that the right word, 'innocent'? So, I forgive you.

"The place where I come from has people from many places, so not everyone looks like me. There are places far to the East where everyone does look like me. I'm surprised that there aren't any others here in Roma. This is the biggest city in the world, isn't it? Everything is drawn here, sooner or later. "

"So, are you from the East, then?"

"The father of my father of my father, on and on like that, he was from the East. I'm from somewhere else."

"If you don't want to tell me..."

"I would like to tell you, but I can't. I've told you what I can, and I've tried to be honest. I'm sorry if it doesn't sound like it makes sense. Some time I'm going to ask you to tell me where you come from."

"Me?"

"Most of the boys your age I see are apprentices or else they're rich. You're not either of those. You're smart, you're clever, and you're inquisitive. You may not have metal teeth or strange eyes, but you're as strange in your way as I am. Well, I'm not asking right now. I've told you about me. Now can I have your help? You should like this. It's like a hunt for a treasure that has been hidden."

"What do you want me to find?"

"A lot of things. The first thing I need is scraps of leather and hooves of cows. There must be a leatherworker around who has small castoff pieces of leather he can't use."

It was my turn to laugh.

"What's so funny?" asked Tenobius.

"You are. I thought you were going to ask for something hard. My friend Tullius' father has a hide shop. He should have lots of pieces. We'll ask Tullius about it. You must know, he'll want something in return."

"What?"

"Probably another rainbow disc. I showed him mine, and he wanted his own. I could see it in his eyes. You should probably show him your teeth, too."

~ * ~

"Let me see your teeth," said Tullius.

We were up in his tree. It was the first time I've ever seen a grown-up in the tree. It was always just us *liberi* before. Of course, Tenobius was different. I guess because he was something different, he wasn't like other adults, and we decided he could come up into the tree. He was also the only adult I ever saw who was interested and willing to climb into the branches. Most adults would think it was beneath their dignity, but he just didn't care. He swung up as if it was the natural thing to do. Now he was reclining against the minor trunk with no fear of falling off.

"I hear that I shouldn't just show you my teeth. I ought to get something for it."

"Who told you that? This slug?" He indicated me. "You are getting something, you're in my tree."

"Well, then, I should use the time wisely. I want to get scraps of leather. The things that are left over after you've cut out what you want from a skin, and you've got little thin pieces left that aren't good for anything."

"When my Dad cuts things out of a hide, there's almost nothing left. He cuts patterns out so close they say you can hear the cow moo."

"They do, huh? Even a master like that will still have shreds left over. You can't help it. Little threads where it gets trimmed. Triangles of hide where three patterns came close together. Things like that."

"I know what you mean. Rubbish. We sell them to the beggars for a few *sestertii* for a handful."

"I'll give you twice that."

"In coin? No promises."

"I'll give you coin in the hand. You can tell your father you sold the scraps to the beggars, give him the usual fee and keep the rest."

"I'll want something else."

"What?"

"One of those rainbow things, like you gave him."

"If I give it to you, it's a one time only gift, you understand? I can't give you another the next time I need hide scraps. I'll want hooves, too, if you have them."

"We've got a few. How much?"

"A *denarius.*"

"Two."

"Two *denarii* for three."

"Done. How much hide do you need?"

"As much as you can give me. What do the beggars do with the scraps?"

"They boil them to make soup."

"I'm not going to be starving them, am I?"

"You're worried about the beggars? They'll just go to Andrus the Sicilian if they don't get scraps from me."

"Good, then. As a token of my good faith, you can have this."

Tenobius held out his hand, and in it was something that flashed color like a rainbow. It didn't look like the one he gave me. It was smaller, and rectangular, but it had the same bright colors in the sunlight that streamed in through the leaves. Tullius took it.

"It doesn't look like the one you gave him."

"Does that mean that you don't want it?"

"No, no. It's good. I was just saying." He studied it carefully, playing with it by rotating it so that different colors lit up his face.

"How do you make it?"

"That's a secret. One that's worth a lot more than hide and hooves."

"Good. It's your secret. I want something else."

"What?"

"You still haven't shown me your teeth."

~ * ~

We collected the leather scraps and three hooves in an old cloth bag. Tullius and Tenobius argued about how much there was in scraps, and what Tenobius owed, but they finally came to an agreement, which included paying for the sack. As we walked off together, I told Tenobius he'd been robbed.

"Why, Argus?" he asked

"Because you shouldn't have had to pay for the bag.," I replied.

"It took his mind off what I paid for the rest. Now that he thinks he's cheated me, he'll be happier. I'll want to come back and buy more leather. Besides, I need the sack. Speaking of which, where can I get more?"

"More sacks?"

"Any kind of cloth. It doesn't have to be new. Old cloth, worn cloth, the more worn the better."

"I don't know. There must be rag dealers down at the little forum on Market Day. Just be careful."

"So, I won't be cheated?"

"No. I hear a lot of the clothes are from people who died of disease. I wouldn't want them."

"That's all right. I'm going to wash them after I get them anyway."

"Wash? Who washes rags?"

"I will."

"You are as strange as a three-headed goat, Tenobius."

"I'm just getting started. I have a shopping list. Where can I get...uh...I need the word. Sand from wood."

"Sand from wood?"

"The stuff you get when you saw wood."

"Oh, sawdust. We've got some in the shop."

"Not enough. I need sackfulls of it."

"For what?"

"For my soup. I can't just live on leather scraps."

I looked at him in exasperation. It wasn't a good joke. "Very well, don't tell me what it's for."

"Where can I get it? Are there shipbuilders nearby?"

"For ships you'd want to go down to the harbor at Ostia. There are probably shipyards there."

"Is that far?"

"I think so. I've never been there."

"What's closer? Are there carpenter's shops?"

"There might be, on the East side. That's where the rich people shop."

"Good. That gets me rags and sawdust. I also need pots."

"Pots?"

"What am I going to make my soup in? I don't want to spend a lot. I need used pots."

"I never had to buy kitchen stuff. There's Rufius the Tinkerer. His shop is full of junk."

"Is it far?"

We detoured to Rufius' shop. It was a cluttered room, open on one side, and full of mostly broken things that Rufius was trying to sell to someone else. Some of the things were fascinating, but others were disgusting. Rufius never bothered to clean any of his things out.

Tenobius loved it. He kept holding up things he found, asking what they were. You'd think he'd never seen a *strigil*, a *dodecahedron*, or doctor's instruments. He seemed fascinated by things. He was looking at them, alternatively gazing away, as if trying to figure out what he could do with them.

He finally just bought four iron pots. One was a tripod pot with two of the legs broken off., so that if you tried to stand it up it would just fall over. Tenobius didn't care. Two were small pots with stuff caked into them. The third was cracked at the bottom, with a big hole you could see through. He should have gotten it for free, but Rufius saw that Tenobius was interested in this useless item, so he had to haggle for a price. I think he was robbed again, but Tenobius walked off happy. I ended up carrying the pots back to the shop.

~ * ~

The next day Tenobius had a large jar of water he'd brought from the spring. His plan was to put some into a large pot and boil the dirty smaller pots in it to clean off the scum on them. As he went over to the forge to get some coals to light his fire, I stopped him.

"You're not going to use fire from the *shop*, are you?"

He looked at me, amazed.

"Why not? It's as good as any other fire."

"Isn't this for your project? The thing you're doing that you say will help you get home?"

"Well, yes. I hope so."

"Are you're going to use ordinary fire for it? This is the fire from Marcus's shop. It's got Metellus's and Arnicus's mistakes all over it!"

"What? Fire is fire, Argus."

"Is that what they taught you where you came from? If you want luck from your fire, you have to get it fresh."

Tenobius looked at me with an odd look on his face, even for him. I think he was surprised, then he was amused. He started to chuckle.

"All right," he said. "Where do we go to get a fresh, lucky fire?"

"Where everyone goes for new fire. We go to the Temple. We have to take an ember box."

"A what?"

"A fire pouch. Something to carry the coals in."

"Oh. Yeah. Well, one of the pots I was going to clean will do, I guess."

"You have to line it with some wood chips or something."

"If you say so."

"Haven't you done this before?"

"Well, no. I never brought fire from someplace else."

"You know how to strike a spark from metal and stone?"

"I can strike a light in a different way. I'll show you sometime. But show me what I have to do next"

"That's all. If you had a lid for the pot, you'd put it on, but it's not necessary," I told him.

I took him to the Temple of the Skinny Venus in the Little Forum. It was quiet there this time of day. You'd think that Tenobius had never been to a temple, the way he looked around at everything as we went up the steps. He hesitated at the top, because the sanctuary was dark compared to the outside. I told him to go inside, and his eyes would get used to the dark.

I hadn't been inside in a long time, not since I came with my mother to get fire for the family hearth. When I tried to come in by myself the priests yelled at me to go away, and if I didn't, they tried to hit me with their sticks. One reason I wanted Tenobius to get his fire here was so that I'd have an excuse to come back, and would be with a grown-up, so they wouldn't try to make me go away.

Tenobius was still looking around, seeing things at last as his eyes got over the light and adjusted to the dark.

"What's that?" he whispered, pointing to the statue.

"It's Venus. Venus Fortuna, the priests call her. Everybody else calls her the Skinny Venus."

Tenobius tried to keep his chuckling to himself.

"Where's the fire?" He asked.

"We have to summon a priest."

"How do we do that?"

"One usually shows up to chase me away by now. If they don't come, you're supposed to hit the bell with the stick."

"What bell? Oh, this thing."

Tenobius picked up the stick, it was more like a wooden hammer, and struck the metal gong with it. The noise was surprisingly loud. He must have struck it harder than anyone I knew ever did. The sound hurt my head as it echoed off the walls. We heard the slapping on sandals on the stone floor and saw the silhouette of a robed priest at the door.

"Yes?" a voice called, a little uncertain.

Tenobius looked at me, not knowing what to say. Maybe he never *had* been in a temple before.

"Praise to the goddess," I said, remembering the words from when I was a kid. "We come to ask for her fire."

The priest looked at me closely. Maybe he remembered me from all those years ago. "Hm!" he said, and turned to Tenobius.

"I have not seen you here before," said the priest.

"I am a Traveler," said Tenobius. "I have not been in the city for very long."

"Where are you from?"

"Far away. I have been through Britannia."

"So. Do you know the Daughter of the Sea?"

"I know her as the one who rules love and generation, the mistress of the home."

"You must come here for worship. I will be expecting you. Now there must be silver to beget fire."

Tenobius looked at the priest, not knowing what to do. He glanced at me, and I rubbed my thumb and forefinger together, a sign that even a barbarian must understand. Tenobius did, too, although it took him a moment. He undid his purse and reached inside, putting two coins into the priest's hand.

The priest looked up at him, and Tenobius put more coins in his hand, but it still didn't satisfy the priest. Tenobius put a third set of coins in the priest's hand, and finally he must have decided that it was the right amount, or else he was weary of waiting for Tenobius to figure it out. He turned and signed for us to follow.

Around the corner was a room with a marble brazier, in which a low fire burned. The priest took a pair of brass tings from the wall and motioned for us to take out our ember box and bring it close to the brazier. He used the tongs to catch up some coals and transferred them to the box. He leaned close and blew on them to bring life to them. In the semidarkness the embers glowed brighter orange with each breath. He motioned us away.

He put the coins into a metal collection box through a slot in the top, and the coins clanked noisily. The priest opened another box on the floor and used the tongs to take out some charcoal, which he arranged among the coals in the fire, replacing the ones he gave us.

"Go," he told us. "Use them to light the heart of your home."

He walked us to the front, making sure we were out of the temple before he turned and went back inside.

Back in the sunlight, Tenobius looked at me with a lopsided grin.

"You didn't tell me it was going to cost me money," he said, accusingly.

"I thought you knew," I replied. "It always costs you something to go to the Temple. Doesn't it do that where you're from?"

"Usually. I don't think they'd charge me for fire, though."

"What else are temples for, besides fires and sacrifice?"

"That's a deep question. We'll talk about it later. I'll get you back for this."

He sounded angry, but I could tell he wasn't. He found the whole ritual amusing, I think. He didn't really *act* angry, anyway.

"Come on," he said. Let's get these back to the shop, before I have to pay for more fire. I hope it's worth the money."

~ * ~

Tenobius had a strange way of doing things. That should be pretty clear by now, but he kept surprising me with it. Just when you thought you had him figured out, he would go and do something else odd.

He did it again when he started building a fire in the fire pit behind the smithy. Any normal person would have simply put down some light stuff, kindling, and wood, then just dumped the embers in the center of it and blow to make the embers flare up and catch.

Tenobius went about it very carefully. He arranged the tinder in a little cone, then set his kindling in a larger cone atop that, and made a little structure out of the wood, first the thin branches and then the larger ones, before carefully inserting the embers in the middle of all of this with the tongs from the shop. It was a lot like the way the priests built up the ceremonial fire at the big festivals, so after Tenobius got the fire going, and the whole construction started to fall in on itself, I had to ask him if this was some kind of devotion to his gods. I had to explain what I meant to him a couple of times before he understood what I meant.

No, he said, it wasn't some ceremony. It was just the only way he knew how to build a fire. That seemed crazy. He'd been working in the shop all these months. Of course, they almost never let the fire go out in Marcus' shop. This was the first time I ever saw him build a fire from nothing. Maybe it was the first time he'd done it here. I asked him what he did where he came from if he needed to cook something or heat water, like he was doing now. He said that there was always a fire where he lived. The only time he needed to build one was when he slept out in the woods.

I asked him why he slept in the woods if he already had a home, and he laughed. He said he did it for fun.

~ * ~

He suspended the big pot from the shop over the fire and filled it with water a little more than halfway. While we waited for the fire to heat the water, he took out the things he'd bought. We laid out the small pots and things in a neat row, and piled the cloth in a stack. Tenobius went into the shop and came back with a couple of hammers and other tools and a block of something.

"What's that?" I asked.

"Soap," he said.

It was the ugliest block of soap I'd ever seen. It was even worse than the stuff they have in the public latrines. It looked more like a hard block of old cheese, and I told him so.

"I know," he said with a sigh. "It was cheap, and I think the *lye* in it might help scrub out the *crud* in these pots."

I had to ask him what those barbarian words meant.

"What are the hammers for?"

"*Pre-treating*," he said,

"What?"

"We're going to do some cleaning before we put these in the hot water. We're going to take the hammers and hit the *crud* that's stuck on the pots. Only the metal ones, though. I have a feeling we can just break a lot of this off. The less we have to scrub off with this cheesy soap, the better."

He grabbed the pot with the hole in the bottom with one hand and the blacksmith's hammer with the other. He positioned the pot open end up, and aimed the hammer at the solid black mass inside. After three blows with the hammer the black stuff broke apart, and pieces fell out through the hole.

It looked like it would be pretty easy, so I took another pot and hammer. I started hammering away at it. Tenobius laughed.

"Don't just go *bashing* away at it," he said. "Aim your hammer so you hit the stuff stuck on the side and break it off. Only hit it in the center like I did if it's a big mass and you're trying to break it up. Do it like this."

He demonstrated. Once you got the idea, it wasn't difficult.

After we went through the pots Tenobius put them one at a time into the heating water and shaved most of the soap in with a knife. He used his knife to scrape what he could from the clay pots and put them in. He flapped the pieces of cloth to shake off what dirt he could and put them in, as well.

"Now we wait while the soap and hot water go to work cleaning it all off." He sat down and shook his hands off. "It's like making soup."

"I wouldn't want to try eating it, though."

"Neither would I. Jupiter alone knows what was in the dirt we broke off those things."

"Do you have Jupiter in your country? And Venus?"

"My people don't worship the gods of the Romans. They have their own."

"That's what The Runt says."

"That's your friend Publius, right? His father's some kind of government official?"

"Yes. He's a Senator, he says."

"What about your father, Argus?"

"I don't want to talk about my father."

I should have run out then, but Tenobius asked something again.

"Argus, listen to me. I want to know something. Where do you live?"

"What?"

"You heard me. The Runt's father is in the government. Tullius lives with his father the leather worker. Metellus and Arnicus are apprenticed here and sleep above the shop. I know where they're from and why they're where they are. What I don't know is anything about you. Other boys are apprenticed, working on the farm, or their families are rich enough to have them schooled and tutored. You're none of those, as far as I can see. You come and go as you like, you're not working for anybody, except for Marcus when you feel like it. You're not rich. So, what are you, and what does your family do?"

"What do you care?"

"You helped me out when I needed help. You care what happens to The Runt. You're intelligent and you have a sense of honor. You're basically a good kid and I'd like to help you, but I don't know what you are."

"What did you call me? A little goat?"

"We call *liberi* that name all the time, where I'm from. It's not an insult."

"Don't call Tully that. He'll pop you."

"You see, you care enough to warn me about trouble. Let me help you."

"How?"

"Tell me about your family. Leave your father out, if you want. You must have a mother."

"Yeah. I have a mother. She has plenty of little 'goats' at home. I don't know how many now."

"You have brothers and sisters?"

"Too many. Too many for the rooms we live in. Too many to feed."

Tenobius didn't say anything. You could hear the pot bubbling.

"So, you left. You're living on the street."

"What do you mean, 'living on the street'? Nobody lives on the street. Even the beggars have their hideaways. I find my own bed. I get my own food. I know my way around."

"What about your mother?"

"She doesn't miss me. She has enough trouble with the ones at home."

Tenobius' brow was knitted up. He had a worried look on his face.

"How does she live? How does she feed them?"

"Look, she does. She works. She sews clothes. She boils laundry in a pot like that. When my dad gets his leave, he comes home and gives her money from his pay, if he remembers."

"Your father's alive?"

"Of course. He's in Caesar's fortieth legion. SPQR, the Golden Eagle and all. If he catches me at home, he hits me. He thinks I should be in the legion, like my brothers. I'm never going there. Not if they're all like *them*."

The water bubbled more as the pot came closer to boiling. Tenobius looked away. He got up and stirred the pot with a long stick. He reached in with the tongs and re-arranged the pots inside. He came back and sat down.

"So, you live on the street, getting by however you can."

"'Live on the street'? What is this 'Live on the street'? You say it as if it means something. I told you, nobody lives on the street. Anyone can find a bed if he tries."

"It's an expression we have. A *word making*. It means doing what you're doing. You take small jobs when you can and use the money to buy food. You stay with friends when you can. You bribe Tullius to let you sleep in the stables, or in the tree."

"I never slept..." I started, but he didn't let me finish.

"You stay in the places you can. I'll bet you've stayed in that Temple used as a theater. You don't stay at the Venus Temple, because they watch there. Sometimes, when you're hungry, you might even take things."

"I pay them back."

"Argus, you can live like that for a time. You can do it when you're *liberi*, when you're a kid. People don't like to see a kid starve. Unfortunaely, you can't do it forever. If you don't find a place, a real job, you'll end up like the beggars, living in a hole someplace and eating boiled leather scraps. You're smarter than that. Why not become an apprentice?"

"You think it's easy? You have to be a relative, or your father has to be friends with someone. Some of the masters make you pay if you even want them to look at you. The only reason Marcus lets me stay is because he thinks it helps you to work. He won't take me on. He's got Arnicus and Metellus, and their families paid him so they could work here. He knows my father, and he knows my father won't pay an *as liberalis* to let me work."

Tenobius was quiet. I think he didn't know what to say. He just sat there, scratching his arm.

"Argus, one of my cousins lived...well, say he lived as you do. He was older, and he ran away from home. We found out that he was living in the city, without a home. Without a job. He couldn't be an apprentice, either. He didn't eat well, and the weather was hard on him. And... Well, I think worse things could happen to him there than could here in Rome. I saw him before he died. He was in his twenties, but looked thirty years older. He was starved and pale and sick. Living...living on the street just wore him out, broke him down. He died not long after that. I don't want to see that happen to anyone else, ever. I want to help you."

"You do? How? What could you do for me? You need help yourself."

"Yes, but I don't let it stop me from trying to help others. I can try to get Marcus to take you on for real as an apprentice, or see if someone else can. I can teach you to read."

"You? A few weeks ago, you couldn't even speak!"

"Yes, but I could read. I studied the language of Rome in my own country."

"What?"

"We have teachers who, well, let's say they came here to learn, and took the knowledge back home. I learned to write Latin, but not to speak it. I can teach you to do it, too. Besides working in the shop, I'll show you how to do things no one else in the city can do. I'll teach you to read and write. I'll show you how to add up numbers and keep track of money better than the way Marcus does."

"Why would you do all that? Why would I agree?"

"I told you why. Nobody should end up like my cousin. You're too clever to deserve to. Besides, I expect to get more help out of you. I have too many projects I have to work on, once I get these pots and cloths clean. So very much to do."

~ * ~

We didn't get any work done immediately. The next day Marcus came to Tenobius early in the morning and yelled at him about being a lazy foreigner who hadn't done any useful work in a week, and when was he gong to start fixing the backlog of pieces brought in, and he had to start earning his keep. Tenobius judged that this was not a good time to talk to him about making me a formal and permanent part of the deal, so after Marcus left Tenobius told me to come back in a couple of days while he soldered some jewelry back together.

I went to see Publius The Runt, knocking at his back window with a stick so his family wouldn't know. When he came around the back, we went off down the street to talk. I told him about Tenobius' offer. He seemed to think my learning to read and write was a wonderful idea. We could exchange messages, instead of having to rap on the back window. He said he would let me use his *wordbook*, if I was careful with it and would return it. I wasn't that keen on getting something I couldn't read yet, but I figured it would probably make Tenobius happy, so I agreed.

He wasn't surprised there was some Elder in Tenobius' country able to read and write Latin. According to his father, there were a lot of educated barbarians. Every chief wanted to have one to read the messages from Rome, and to write replies. He was curious about how good Tenobius' education was. His father was particular about which master was teaching Publius, because there were bad masters out there whose Latin wasn't very good.

That took me by surprise. I thought if you knew how to read and write Latin, that was it, and any teacher would be as good as any other. Publius said that, no, there were different types of teachers, and there were different types of Latin.

Look, he said, there was the language of the senators, that you can hardly understand, and the language of the priests. There as the language of the Forum, used in dealing, with its careful insults, and there was the language of the ditch-diggers, full of foul curses. The senators don't go around using the curses of the diggers, he said. At least not in public. They don't string their words together as carelessly, either. A good teacher could make you sound like a senator. A typical one would make you sound like a merchant in the Forum, and a bad one would make you sound like a ditch digger.

"So, what would Tenobius make me sound like?" I asked.

"Well, you already speak like a beggar, Argus, but with him teaching you, you'll write like a barbarian. At least it's better than writing like a ditch digger."

Ditch diggers don't write, of course, but that was the joke. I was beginning to see that there might be words and language I wasn't aware of, because I didn't live with people who spoke it.

"Tell me what he teaches you, after he starts," said Publius. "I'll tell you what's Barbarian-speak and what's good Latin."

~ * ~

Publius smuggled his *wordbook* out of the house the next day, and I looked through it. It meant nothing to me, but it was interesting to look at the shapes of the words. They were written in two columns on each she af of the scroll, and I could see how the beginnings of the words in one column were almost the same, but differed at the end. It looked kind of pretty, but meaningless. Some slave who knew writing must have spent hours carefully copying this in a neat hand on the vellum, I knew. In its way, this was more work than hammering out a *pilum* on the anvil was.

~ * ~

I went back in the evening one day after I thought Tenobius would have had enough time to satisfy Marcus. I approached the back of the smithy through the trees, staying in the boughs so I couldn't be seen, and saw Tenobius working where we had boiled the pots to clean them. He had one of the cleaned pots now, filled with water over the fire, and it seemed to be boiling, too. Instead of going over to him, I sat and watched. I wanted to see what he would do. I noticed I wasn't the only one watching him. There was a face looking out of the window in the house behind him looking down at what he was doing.

Tenobius didn't notice he was being watched. He continued to tend the fire and examine the boiling water. He went inside and brought back a sack. He put his down near the fire and reached into it, bringing out a large handful of something, like coarse powder. He dumped this into the boiling water then added another, and another. He got a large pestle and began stirring it. From the way he as acting, the powder wouldn't sink, but floated on top of the water. He kept trying to push it under with the pestle, but it kept floating back to the top. Nevertheless, he kept mixing it up and trying to push it down into the water.

I had an idea from the way it looked and behaved what the powder must be, and confirmed it later by looking in the sack. It was sawdust. Tenobius had gone to a carpenter's shop like he'd said and had gotten a bag of sawdust, and now he was trying to boil it. But sawdust floats, and it wouldn't stay down. Why would anyone want to boil sawdust?

Tenobius was getting agitated with not getting able to keep the sawdust down. He went back into the shop and emerged with a metal disc, which he lowered into the pot with tongs. I knew what he was doing. He was using the piece of metal to weight some of the sawdust down. It wasn't enough, I guess. He threw more sawdust in and stirred it again. Of course, it still wouldn't stay down, so he got more bits of metal from the shop and started alternately putting in sawdust and a metal holder for it. Tenobius had the pot full, with some metal sticking up above the surface, and with water running over the sides of the pot. There wasn't any point in trying to stir it, so he just kept adding water to replace what boiled over.

The person in the window was leaning out now and looking down to get a better view, and I could see she couldn't believe what she was seeing. I had a hard time myself, and I was already familiar with the odd things Tenobius could do. To her he must have seemed like a madman. She pulled herself inside and must have come downstairs, because there she was, walking around the corner. She shouted to Tenobius. I was too far away to hear their words, but I could see their gestures and imagine what they were saying to each other.

"What are you doing? Why are you cooking sawdust?"

"I'm making something."

"From boiled sawdust? Who does that? I've never seen anyone cooking wood."

"You can make a lot of things by boiling wood..."

He was probably telling her how you could make something for jewelry, or some kind of ointment, or soup, for all I knew. *I* don't know what you can make out of boiled sawdust, but Tenobius was going on with his explanation. He clearly didn't see her exasperation. Tenobius isn't as good with people as he is with making things.

"I've never seen anybody doing this, and I've lived in this house for here years. They heat up metal and hammer it into shapes. They don't do crazy things like cooking wood."

"Well, I'm different."

"I'll say you're different. You're crazy!"

"Well, it may look crazy, but you'll see."

"I'm not staying. You're crazy."

She walked off. I saw her again, later, looking down at him from the same window as he worked. He never noticed her.

After he had let the sawdust cook for what I guess he thought was the right time he used the tongs to pull out the metal weights. He scooped the sawdust, which seemed to be right at the surface, so I guess it just floated back up again after he took out the weights, out with a big scoop onto a piece of cloth and let the water run out. I guess he wasn't making some kind of soup, because he didn't try to save the water. He examined the sawdust, taking some in the palm of his hand after it was cool and stirring it with a finger, then rubbing some between his thumb and forefinger. He didn't seem happy.

Tenobius brought out a small anvil and placed it on a cloth, then piled the boiled sawdust on top. With a large forge hammer he began beating the sawdust, as if it was a 'pig' of heated iron he was forging into shape. The pile of wet sawdust just flattened at the first blow, a lot of it scattering off the anvil onto the cloth. He kept beating what remained on the anvil over and over again. He'd stop and gather dust from where it fell back onto the cloth and piled it back on the anvil. He repeated this, examining the dust every now and then. He was clearly not happy with the result, and shouted things I couldn't hear. Up in her window, the woman continued to watch.

Finally, Tenobius took the boiled and battered sawdust and put it into a pan, added water, and threw in something light and fluffy from a container he had. He mixed it with the iron spoon over and over. Then he brought out something couldn't quite make out, like a small drum. I later learned this was a lithe branch he'd plaited into a circle, like the wreaths the Priests of Venus make for the Festival, but with one of the cleaned pieces of cloth stretched over it, like the skin of a drum. He placed carefully this in the pan with both hands, holding it horizontally beneath the surface and then bring it gently upwards, letting some of the stuff in the pan settle on the cloth. He put the stuff-covered cloth on the grass and got out another such drum-like wreath, and did the same thing. He repeated this until he had five such drums set out on the grass, evidently to dry. He picked up the first one and looked at it carefully, frowning.

He wasn't happy, but he'd been at it a long time, and decided to stop. He put out the fire, drowned the ashes, and put away his tools. The drums he put up on the table to continue drying. Then he went inside.

I was going to leave, as well, but I saw something move. The woman had come down from her upper room to examine what Tenobius made. She looked around to see if was watching, but didn't see me, and she looked closely at the drying drums without picking them up. Finally, she touched one with a finger and brought he finger to her lips to taste. She made a face, then ran away. Tenobius' sawdust cakes weren't good to eat, I guess.

I decided not to see Tenobius right then. He seemed in a mood to bite nails in half, so I thought it would be better to let him calm down first. I returned the following morning to find him examining his drums, which were now dry.

He said, "Good Morning, Argus," to me when he looked up and saw me, but went right back to inspecting his work.

"What's that?" I asked, as naturally as possible, so he wouldn't know I had been spying on him.

"A failure, probably," he said, without looking up.

He took a knife and used it to cut near the edge of the cloth stretched over the wreath, being careful not to cut the cloth. He tried to peel off the mixture adhering to the top. Holding the drum up at eye level, he tried to slide the knife under the edge. It started to lift up a little, but then the crust broke and crumbled, sending particles of now-dry sawdust tumbling off. A few of the bits of sawdust were stuck together on strands of fiber, and fell together like miniature sawdust necklaces.

Impatiently, Tenobius reached up and scratched the surface with his fingernails. The sawdust cascaded down in a cloud. He threw the drum away angrily.

"*Damnate, damnate damnate! Damn Hank Morgan! Damn Martinus Padwei!* They make it look so damned *easy*."

He picked up another drum and held it upside down, so the coating was on the bottom. It clung to the cloth, but when he shook the wreath, the sawdust fell away. He sat down hard, cross-legged on the ground, and buried his face in his hands.

I wanted to ask him a question, but I didn't want to sound stupid. Obviously, the sawdust crust was supposed to stay together when he pulled it from the cloth, but it wasn't behaving itself. Tenobius looked as if he wanted to hit something. So far, he'd been the gentlest *magister* I'd ever heard of. He hadn't hit me once. But he might decide this was a good time to start.

~ * ~

Tenobius stayed that way a long time then slowly pulled himself out of it. He raised his head from his hands and blinked his eyes open. They looked pink and bloodshot. Even so, he seemed strangely calm. He looked at me for a long time.

"I must look pretty silly," he said. "Is that the right word? Silly. Stupid. Ridiculous. What's the word?"

"Strange," I suggested. "You're worried and angry about that...thing you've been working on."

"You're right. I'm angry that it didn't work, and I'm worried I won't be able to make it work. If I were like a lot of people I know, I'd get mad now and start tearing these frames apart. I'd feel good for about a minute. I'd just have to rebuild the frames. I'm too lazy to do that."

"You can do that? I'd just tear them apart."

"It's not worth it. I've relaxed now. As for being worried, I shouldn't be. I *know* there's a solution. I've seen this done before. I just have to figure out how."

"How to do what?"

"You'll see when I do it. I'd hoped to use it now, but since it isn't ready, we'll have to struggle without it. Wait here a minute."

With that, Tenobius walked into the shop and returned with a couple of things that looked like boards.

"I talked to Marcus about having you formally be apprenticed to me. The plan is that I teach you stuff that neither he nor his boys know, and you can continue to work if I should disappear."

"Are you going to disappear, like a magician?"

"Only if I work really hard. I also said I'd teach you how to read and write, which is more than his boys can do. He might be satisfied with that alone."

"Are you sure I can learn to do that?"

"Why not? You're clever, Argus. If you can read and write, you can probably get a job anywhere in the city. That's what these are for." He put down the two boards, one in front of each of us.

"These are *Tabulae Cerae*, Wax Tablets," he said, "and this is a *stylus*."

He held out a small brass rod about the length of my hand and the thickness of a twig. It came to a blunt point at one end, while the other end had been flattened with hammer blows, or by being squashed in a vise. Tenobius pressed it into my hand, and took out another for himself.

"What do I do with it?"

"You hold it in your hand like this," he said, showing me how he cribbed it between his thumb and forefinger. I tried to do the same, but couldn't get it right. He had to show me a few times.

"Now," he said, when I sort of had it held right. "We use it to write. Don't press too hard into the wax. Hard enough to make an impression, but not so hard you hit the bottom."

Each of the 'boards' was really a kind of shallow wooden tray with a raised edge. The space enclosed by the edges on all four sides had been filled up with wax. I sniffed it, it was good beeswax, not animal fat or soap. The stylus easily carved into the wax. The first time I tried, I pushed too hard and went deep into the wax, carving all the way to the bottom. Tenobius showed me how to do it. He used a lighter touch and just marked the very top of the wax.

"Here," he said, making a series of vertical lines on his tablet, "Just make ones. Just make some lines, until you get the idea."

We made vertical lines, and horizontal lines, and diagonal lines. He had me draw circles until I was able to make them look like circles. Then he showed me how to take the other end of the *stylus*, that flat paddle-like end, and use it to smooth down the wax, almost as if I hadn't written on the tablet.

We went through the alphabet, one letter at a time. He had me make each of them five times, saying their names as I did so. *Aaaaayyyy. Aaaayyyy. Aaaayyyyy Aaayyy aaayyyy,* like a set of spears braced against each other. *Beeeeee, Beeeee, Beeeee Beeee Beeee,* like two bowls next to each other, on end. *Seeeee Seeeee Seeeee Seeeee Seeeee* like a piece of a broken hoop. And so on.

By the end my hand hurt, and I had a small blister on my thumb where the stylus rubbed. Tenobius said I did a good job. He told me to keep the one he wrzote on on, so that I would have a copy of the letters. He said he'd make me another copy. I should erase my own tablet and try again, repeating the names of the letters. It turned out that the flat end didn't completely remove the marks, but I could do a better job by putting the tablet near enough to the furnace to melt the wax, but not so close that the wax ran out. He made me promise to work on this so many times that I decided I really would, at least once.

"Good, then, Argus," he said. "For doing that, I've got a treat for you."

He took out a small wooden box and opened it.

Inside were transparent and slightly brownish crystals.

"Take one," he said.

I did. It was light, and not as cool as I'd expected.

"Put it in your mouth," he said.

I looked at him crookedly. Who puts jewels in their mouth, unless they're trying to steal them, like Menelaius the Pickpocket?

"Like this," he said, and took another jewel and popped it into his mouth. "Don't swallow it, and don't bite down on it."

I did. There was a single shocking burst of flavor. It was like honey, only sweeter. I had to spit it out into my hand. I could still taste that intense sweetness.

"I'm sorry," he said. "I didn't know it would have that effect if you're not used to it. You can lick the side to get the flavor."

"What is it? Is this some barbarian food?"

"I got it right here at the marketplace. My people use it in cooking, but here it's only used as medicine. I had to buy it from Speculus the Physician. It was expensive."

"You put this in your food? How much?"

"Too much, I'm sure. If you use too much of it you have to fix the holes in your teeth with metal, like mine. It's called *saccharum*, The Greeks call it *saccharin*. Whatever you call it, it's expensive. It comes as a brownish powder or a thick liquid. If it's really pure, it's white. I purified some the best I could and grew it into crystals."

"You...made these crystals?"

"Yes. It's a nice trick, but it has no practical purpose."

"You could probably sell these."

"They don't last. They dissolve in water. In humid weather, they sort of dissolve and flow away."

"Still, I'll bet someone would be interested in it. It's...different."

"I can't. I need all I can get for myself."

"So, you can eat it and get more metal teeth?"

"No. I can use it to repair my...Well, I can use it to help get back home. I hope. need more. A lot more. I bought all that Speculus had. I need your help, or maybe your friends'. Look through the City for more *saccharin*, or for sweet brown liquid like this."

"Like honey?"

"No, it's not honey. You can taste the difference, can't you?"

I nodded my head.

"It doesn't have to be best quality. It can be thick and brown, but I need a lot of it. I'm sure if someone will have it."

~ * ~

The Runt couldn't believe it, either that Tenobius was teaching me to write, or that I was actually making the letters. He admired the Wax Tablets, and said that Tenobius must have paid a good price for them. To prove it, he showed me his tablet, a little thing the size of your hand and not very flat. It was only good for a part of a lesson. On mine, he said he could write an entire letter.

He also found some of the things strange.

"I never heard anyone give the letters the names he told you, Argus," he said. "It should be *Aahh, Beh, Keh*, not *Ay, Bee, See*. It must be some barbarian way of naming the letters. The letter he calls *Wye* should be *Greek Eye*. Or *Greek Iota*. How does he get *Wye* out of that?"

I just shrugged.

"And he adds these barbarian letters. This *Eye* with a tail that he calls *Jay*. Then he calls a *You* by the name *Vee*, and creates a new rounded letter he calls *You*. This one he calls *Dubbel You* at least looks like two *You's* put together."

"He says '*Dubbel*' means 'twice', so it makes sense."

"All I can say is that they made some changes to our language wherever he's from. If he tries to make you spell a word with any of these, you should tell him that it's not the way they do it here in Rome." Publius copied the strange letters into his own wax tablet.

"You going to show those to your Dad?"

"Uh Huh."

"If he asks you where you got them from, don't mention Tenobius."

"Why not?"

"I'm worried about what might happen if he starts talking to Tenobius. It might get him in trouble."

"I don't see how."

"Please, trust me on this. Don't say anything." I don't think Publius ever saw anyone taken away by the Guard or by the Army because they suspected them of something. Some of the adults we knew had vanished because they bothered someone, or were too strange for the tastes of the soldiers or the police. Tradesmen don't care about strange, and can live with it.

Publius helped me go through the alphabet again, telling me the right way to say their names, and fixing the way I drew them. I had to agree to bring him to talk to Tenobius again. He didn't know where to get *Saccharon*, but he knew about it, and said he'd ask around.

~ * ~

Being an apprentice meant an awful lot of cleaning up, I learned. When I was just goofing around with Marcus, getting Tenobius things for his projects, it was a lot more fun, and I didn't have to sweep up, or shovel out the ash from the furnace. Now that I was one of the staff, there seemed to be no end of chores that needed doing. And most of them involved me getting dirty. The pay didn't make up for it, and I would have quit, even if it meant I'd end up as a beggar, if it wasn't for the things Tenobius found for me to do. After I learned about the pump drill and how to use it to put fine holes through things, like through gems and pearls, to make necklaces, it was relaxing to sit with a pile of beads and just keep putting holes in them, one after another. Using Tenobius' tiny wire saw to cut thin pieces of stuff to make fine slabs for jewelry and the like was fun, too. It beat taking a turn at pumping the bellows.

As I sat at the bench, drilling another bead, Tenobius came over with what looked like a thin, dirty wheat cake, which he handed to me. I almost took a bite before I realized that this was not food, it was the same size and shape as those frames he was playing with, and I'd seen what went into that broth. He'd done something different this time, though, and it had evidently come off the frame in one piece this time, instead of flaking apart.

I looked from it up to Tenobius, who was beaming. He was very proud of his little disc.

"It stayed together, this time," I said.

I know he wanted to hear some kind of compliment, and I hoped that would do. "What is it?"

"It's a failure, Argus," he said, smiling. "Only not as bad as before."

"What's wrong with it? What's it supposed to be?"

"As for what it is, you'll have to wait. It's supposed to be nice and flat, though, without all these bits sticking out of it. And it should be lighter in color. But, look, I can bend it, without it breaking in half. I can almost fold it. I'm getting closer."

~ * ~

If Tenobius wasn't going to tell me what his wood cakes were for, I wasn't going to press him about it. I figured I should change the subject.

"I haven't been able to find your *saccharon* yet. Unfortunately, nobody I know can tell me. I do have a couple of ideas though."

Tenobius sat down and put his disc away in a pouch.

"What are they?"

"You could ask the servant girl next door about it."

"Who?"

"The woman in that house," I said, pointing. "I've seen her looking at you working out back."

I didn't want to let him know I'd been spying on him, so I left it vague like that. There were plenty of times that I'd been working out here with him when he might have been seen without him noticing it.

"That house? What's her name?"

"I don't know. I've seen her looking out of the upper window at you." A thought struck me. "Maybe she's in love with you."

Tenobius snorted at that suggestion.

"Why should I ask her then? If I ask, she might think I'm in love with *her*."

"I think she's a servant. If she is, she probably cooks for them. She'd know where to get foods, and medicines."

"Maybe." He was silent for a time. "How do I ask her? I can't just knock on the front door and ask to speak to a servant."

I hadn't thought about that. When I wanted to do something, I just did it. Adults have all these rules, though, about how hey can act and what they can do. I always thought of Tenobius as another kid. A bigger kid maybe, who was still learning to talk correctly and who had weird eyes. He clearly wasn't an adult like Publius' father and mother, with their clan of relatives all over the city, and all their obligations. He wasn't a shop owner like Marcus. He wasn't even a soldier like my far-off dad. He wasn't belonging to anyone, with no ties. He was free, like us, I figured. For some reason he didn't want to be. He was trying to get back to where his people were, he said.

Only he wasn't really free. He was still stuck in those rules adults had. If you thought about it for a moment, it made sense that he couldn't just knock on the door. The family that lived there would want to know who he was, and why he was asking for their maid, and what his connection to her was. They'd start asking about his clothes and his accent and his slanted eyes. They might even end up reporting him to the Watch, and who knows what might happen then? If he just walked around the city, he wouldn't be bothered. He was just another person in the crowd, even if he looked a little odd. As soon as he tried to talk to someone, he became a part of their lives, and how he related to them became important.

I thought about telling him to start making another batch of his Wood Soup and yelling about it. That would bring her out. I didn't want him to know I'd been watching.

"I don't know," I said finally. "You should do what you told me. Keep your eyes open and be ready for when you get an opportunity."

"I said that? I don't remember. It makes sense. What was your other idea?"

I'd forgotten I had another one. I had been thinking about how he could ask the servant girl so much that my other idea almost escaped. But I caught its tail and pulled it back.

"This liquid that makes *saccharon* that you told me about. You said it would be easier to find than the *saccharon* itself. "

"Yes."

"It's brown and thick and sweet?"

"That's right, Argus"

"It sounds like honey. Why not use honey instead?"

"Well, honey's not the same thing," he began. "It..."

He stopped right there. He didn't just stop talking after that word, he stopped moving, as well, and his eyes seemed to be looking at something very far away that only he could see. If I hadn't seen him still breathing, I would have wondered if he was still alive. As it was, I wondered if he had that illness that some people claim comes from the gods, where you fall over and have fits.

After a long while he began talking, but to himself.

"Honey *is* a *saccharon*," he said, except he didn't say *saccharon*, but some barbarian word that sounded like it. "But it's an upside-down *saccharon*." I *think* that's what he said. "That shouldn't affect the way it (barbarian words). It's worth a try. I *have* to try something."

He seemed to wake up and notice me.

"My first thought was that nobody I heard of ever used honey. Still it might work. Do you know where to get a lot of honey?"

I didn't expect that, but after all this time with Tenobius, I should have. He always wanted to know where to get something or to do something, but he didn't know where anything was in the City.

"...a LOT of honey" he repeated.

That could mean anything to him. Who ever got a lot of honey? You only got as much honey as was drizzled onto the sweetcakes. There again, I was thinking like a kid. If I wanted to help Tenobius, I had to think like a grown up. What would a grown-up do?

You could ask the servant girl, was my first thought. We'd just been talking about her, after all, and how she ought to know where to find food things. Of course, he didn't know how to ask her, so that was no help. What had I just been thinking?

"They use it to make sweetcakes. You could ask Madame Nux or one of the bakers in the little Forum. They probably have *amphorae* full of honey."

He had a thoughtful look on his face, and nodded his head.

"That would probably be true. Thank you," he said, and patted my shoulder.

~ * ~

It wasn't until a couple of days later that I finally saw the honey. In the meanwhile, there had been a lot of work at Marcus' shop. I strung several of those beads together into a necklace. I had a couple more sessions with Tenobius over the wax tablets. We had gotten past the letters and their sounds, and he was trying to teach me words. Sometimes he didn't have the right words himself to tell me, so he would try to draw on the wax tablet to explain it. Some of his drawings were hilarious. They were either very bad, or he had no idea how to express it. I found that I was trying to get him to define words that way even if I knew what they were, just to see what he would come up with.

He eventually realized this, and that put an end to the vocabulary lesson for that day.

~ * ~

When Tenobius stored the tablets away, I noticed something else in his collection of things. It looked like a short piece of a log, only too regular. It was about the length of my forearm and half as much around. I asked him what it was.

"Oh, that's the honey, Argus. I bought it from the baker."

"What IS that thing? It's not a jug or amphora."

"This? It's a *barrel*," he said, calling it by some barbarian word, as if it was the most natural thing in the world.

"What is it, though? I've never seen anything like it. Did they hollow out a log or something, then fill it up?"

"No, they take wooden staves and shape them with a sharp knife until they fit close together, then hold them tight with rope or green wood braided around it, and they put round wood discs on the ends. You really haven't seen these before?"

"No. Do they have them where you're from?"

"A few, but not this small. It's stronger than an amphora, and it won't break, so you can ship it a long way. I think this came all the way from the forests of Germania."

"How do you open it?"

"I think there's some clever way to do it, but I took one of our shop's brace and bits and just drilled a hole in the end. I did that at the bakers. I wanted to be sure I was getting a *cask* of honey and not vinegar or something else. After I tasted it, I stopped it up with a whittled wooden peg. See?"

He pulled out the peg and held it over the hole. Some honey clung to the peg, slowly gathered into a drop, and started to fall back inside. I reached out a finger and collected it, then put my finger in my mouth. It was honey, all right. Thick and sweet, but without that otherworldly sweetness of the *saccharon*.

"What are you going to do with it?" I asked.

Not make honey cakes, I was sure.

"You'll see. I'll probably want your help tomorrow. Right now, we have a stack of work to do for Marcus."

~ * ~

When I arrived the next morning Tenobius was already out back with the largest of his pots set up suspended above a fire on a tripod. It was already starting to boil, and the smell seemed odd but familiar. I climbed down from the tree and went over to Tenobius. I didn't even have to ask, I just gestured with a nod of my head.

"I'm making soup!" he said, with a grin.

Tenobius obviously wasn't making soup, so I went over to the pot and looked it.

Whatever it was, it wasn't that wood soup he'd been using to make those strange discs. There was no sawdust or anything floating on top. There was more than water in there, and the smell seemed oddly familiar, and food like. I was thinking hard, trying to remember where I'd smelled it before.

"No joking," I said to him. "What is it, really?"

"It really is soup, Argus," he said. "Of a kind. Do you remember what your friend Tullius told us? Up in his tree?"

"He's not really my friend," I said quickly. "What did he say?"

I tried to remember what we'd talked about when all three of us had been together. Suddenly I recalled.

"You mean the way the beggars would take the scraps of hide and boil them to make soup?"

Tenobius nodded.

"You're not really going to EAT that, are you?"

I'd seen the way Tullius' father treated his spare hides and scraps, and what was mixed up with them.

"I wouldn't dream of it," he said. "Though, you know, some people in my country boil down the hooves and hides to make something they do eat. They use it as *dessert*."

"What's *dessert*?"

"They call it 'second table' here. It's something sweet at the end of a meal. I think a lot of the time here it's just fruit of some kind, but back where I come from, they usually make sweet cakes. Well, some people take the stuff from hides, refine it, sweeten it, and add fruit juice to it. For Second Table."

"That sounds like a lot of work."

"Well, most people just buy it from someone else who makes it."

"So, is that what you're going to do? Make Cow Hide Soup and add honey to sweeten it?"

It was a joke, of course. If this was the same hide material that Tullius dragged in from the garbage pile and the dung heap, the idea of putting honey in it was like putting face powder on a pig to pretty it up. To my surprise, Tenobius got a big grin on his face.

"Yes!" he said. "That's *exactly* what I'm going to do!"

~ * ~

It took a long time. We boiled the scraps of hide until they mostly fell apart, and skimmed off the crud and pulled out the fibers, and boiled off much of the water. At one point, Tenobius had us transfer the liquid to another pot, carefully pouring it out so that the solid stuff got left behind. Then we boiled it down some more.

Eventually it started to thicken. We transferred it to a smaller pot, and the liquid went from almost clear to a transparent brown, and began to get sticky. When he judged it had gotten sticky enough, he started adding honey, a bit at a time. *Adding sticky stuff to sticky stuff would make something REALLY sticky,* I thought, but it began to get more solid. Then Tenobius added a handful of some white powder.

"What's that?" I asked him.

"*Tempering,*" he answered, which left me as confused as before he answered, so I didn't ask anything else.

Tenobius got a rope and threw it over the lowest of the branches in the tree overhead, then got the pot with the crack in it and placed it near the fire to warm. He went into the shop and brought out a coil of wire on a cloth, and handed me another cloth.

"What's this for?"

"I'll tell you in a minute. I have to get something else."

He went back into the shop and brought out a container and a soft brush.

"That?" I asked, indicating the container.

I hoped he wasn't going to just say some unfamiliar word again, but he didn't.

"Powdered chalk," he said, removing the lid. "I was surprised to find it so easily, but you use it for the same things we do, marking things, and snapping down chalk lines."

"So, what are we going to do with it? Pour it in there?"

"Only if I have to. Here's the plan."

He took hold of one end of the rope and tied a string onto it, then took hold of the end of the wire. He stopped, and gestured with the string and the wire.

"I take this wire and put it on the cloth on the ground, like this, to keep the sand and dirt off of it. You have that other cloth, which you will use to wipe off the wire before it disappears into the pot, just to get any last-minute dirt or grease off of it. "

"What do you mean?" Before I could finish, he held up a hand.

"I take the wire and feed it into the crack in the bottom of this pot, then pull the end through, and twist it into a loop. I put the pot on this tripod, and then I tie the string on the end of the rope to the loop in the end of the wire. Understand?"

"I know what you're saying. I can't say I understand it."

"That's all right. Now comes the tricky part. I take our mixture from the other pot and pour it into the cracked pot. If I've done it right, it's so stiff that it doesn't pour out through the crack. We let it settle into place around the wire. If we leave it there too long, it will eventually settle right through the crack. We're not going to give it time to do that."

"No? What are we going to do?"

"Well, I am going to grab the other end of the rope, the part that went over the branch, and I'm going to S-L-O-W-L-Y pull on it. The wire is going to be pulled into the pot through the crack in the bottom, but not before you wipe it off. Wipe it right now. Good, but don't pull back on it. Just press around it enough to get any clinging sand or dirt off. I don't want the wire to drag dirt into the pot.

"And," he continued, "As I pull, the wire comes up out of the mixture in the pot, coated with a thin layer of it. If I pull slowly enough, and the mix is just sticky enough, it forms a complete and unbroken coating."

He inspected the wire as it came out, and continued to pull slowly.

"That's good," he said, "but we can't stop. We should keep pulling at a constant speed. The only problem remaining is that the coating is still sticky, so we can't let it touch anything. I have a way to prevent it from sticking even if it does touch something else."

He dipped the brush into the finely powdered chalk and rapidly and lightly brushed the coated wire all around.

"There. The chalk will stick to the coating and keep it from sticking to anything else. So, we just keep doing the same thing. I just keep pulling on this rope, and you feed in the wire, wiping it clean, while I inspect the wire, and finally give it a coating of chalk."

He talked in a rhythm like singing, matching his speech to our actions, and we tried to keep the wire moving smoothly along.

"Why are you doing this?" I asked.

"The coating isolates the wire from the rest of the world. We call it *insula* (something barbarian). Do you know what an *insula* is?"

"Yes, I answered, wiping down the wire as I fed it in. It's one of the blocks of the City."

"What?" asked Temobius, surprised. He almost broke his rhythm. "What do YOU mean?"

"One of the blocks of houses, like the collection my mom lives it. It's called an *insula*. Don't you know that?"

"No, I didn't, to tell the truth. They always taught me that *insula* means an island. Doesn't it?"

"Well, I guess. I haven't seen any islands except the little ones like the Island of Rabbits in the Tiber. I thought they named them after the city blocks. I always pictured a mom rabbit with her kits living packed in, like a Roman street."

"Huh. I never knew that. I think it goes the other way. The city blocks are called *insula* because they're like islands, but surrounded by the city streets, rather than by water. Don't you know about Sicilia, or Sardinia, or other islands like that?"

"I've *heard* of them. Tullius' older brother went to Sicilia on business. But I didn't know it was an island. It's just someplace far away."

"Well, you could see them on a map."

"I know what a map is, but I don't think I've ever seen one."

"Huh, again, Argus. I'll have to draw one for you. Sardinia is so far away from Italia that you can't see from one to the other. All you see around it is ocean. A lot of islands are like that. They're just pieces of land out in the ocean."

"How do you get to them?"

"Take a boat."

"I'd be afraid it would go off without me, and leave me stranded,"

I said. "Or sink. I'd rather stay here."

Tenobius started to tell me a story from his land, about how a boat with seven people on it got caught in a storm, and was stranded on an island with no one else on it. They were the captain and his sailor, and a rich man and his wife, and a girl from a farm, and a philosopher, and an actress. I had to have him explain that last word. All the ladies I've seen on stage were played by men dressed up as women. I've heard there were some women in the fancy theaters, but not at the temple performances I've been to. Tenobius said it was perfectly normal for women to be on stage in his country, even in the cheap theaters.

What were they all doing on the boat, I asked? It seemed like a strange collection of people. If it had been a ferry crossing a river I could understand, but in a boat, you would think that the rich man would have it all to his wife and himself, unless the farm girl was a servant, or something. Tenobius said there really wasn't a good reason. It was just an excuse for the story, which was a funny one, like the one I had taken him to in the temple. He said some of the people in this story hit each other all the time, just like the ones in the Temple.

I asked why a philosopher was there, and he said the philosopher was also an artisan and mechanic. He made all the things that the rest of the group needed, since there was no one else to turn to. He said they made a lot of things out of something called *coconuts*. This led to a long discussion about what *coconuts* were, and about exotic trees and fruits from faraway places.

"You're like that philosopher," I told Tenobius. "You're making coated wire out of things you found. And honey comes from plants."

"I guess I am. I'm a *Professor*," he said, lapsing into barbarian words again. "I just hope you aren't my *Gilligan*, Argus. That was the sailor. He used to do things like dropping *coconuts* on the captain."

We finished coating the entire length of wire. Tenobius tied another piece of string to the end, attached it to another rope, and drew it up so that it all hung from one branch to another without touching anything.

"We'll let it set overnight, and see how it looks in the morning," he said. He continued to stare up at it for a long time.

I thought I ought to say something. It was a long piece of wire coated with dirty brown stuff that was a little lumpy in places, all coated with a layer of chalk. If I hadn't helped to make it, I would have thought it was another weedy vine hanging from the trees, and an ugly one at that. What I said was, "It looks pretty good."

Tenobius took it as the truth, and as something obvious.

"Yes. Yes, it is. For the first time since I came here, I feel like I've accomplished something."

I left him to look at his wire, and glory over it. I don't even think he noticed as I walked away.

~ * ~

The next day Tenobius took down his coated wire and carefully examined it. The coating was still flexible, he said, and a little sticky still. He dusted it with chalk again, then coiled it up with cloth between each coil. He said he was afraid that if he let the coated parts touch, they might stick. Then he put it in a wooden box with a latch on it.

It was just in time, it turned out. Marcus ran in and told everyone there was a big rush order. We had to turn out a run of hooks, billets, and spear tips. An army company was pulling out soon, and they needed supplies. All the furnaces had to be running. There were people in the shop I'd never seen before. Marcus used them sometimes, or borrowed them from other shops.

Since I wasn't a smith, that meant I mostly had to shovel charcoal, work the bellows, or sweep up. Marcus, Arnicus, and Metellus were heating up the rod stock. Soon they were hammering, bending, and cutting away. Tenobius and Corticus, he was one of the ones I hadn't seen before, were doing finishing work. It was continuous work, with another job begun as soon as the previous one was finished.

The parts weren't of the highest quality. There just had to be a lot of them, and they had to mostly match. The army was used to getting unfinished stuff and finishing it themselves. As it was, we weren't mounting or hafting any of the pieces we turned out, that was up to the soldiers themselves, or their quartermasters. We simply collected them into baskets and boxes with the right count.

We worked through the day and into the night. Marcus had people bring in bread, soup, and other things to eat. We drank a lot of water, because it was hot in the shop with all furnaces going, and you'd sweat continuously. I had a few breaks when they sent me with Corticus to go get more charcoal, or more boxes and baskets.

The shops around us closed, but we kept hammering away. As the night progressed Marcus had me take over for Arnicus, who slumped in a corner and fell asleep. I was tired, too, but this was the first time he was letting me work on actual pieces in the shop. I learned how to bend a proper hook, after only three tries, then he let me go on my own. Later on, I was cutting and pointing the tips for the *pilum*.

After I had done that for a while Marcus came over, inspected the parts I was making, and decided he didn't like them anymore. I went back to pumping the bellows, for Metellus this time. Tenobius was at the table, filing spear points to a better edge than hammering got them.

It was well after midnight when we finished, and Marcus saw to it every one of us got a loaf of bread and a drink of wine before we finished the last piece, which Marcus heated up and then quenched in a bucket of wine. He said it was an offering to Vulcan, but I don't know how serious he was. All I knew was that I was tired and my arms ached. We limped off into the back, where I'd planned on collapsing on a pile of baskets and cloth. But as I passed the box with the wire, I thought I saw it *move*, and heard a scratching noise from within.

I lost my sleepiness in a hurry. This was the box with the wire, all right, and it was still sealed. Did it come alive at night? Or turn into something? I lifted the lid and looked inside.

My first thought was that a snake got into the box, a big, furry snake. That couldn't be right. It took a moment for my sleepy brain to realize what I was looking at.

"Mice!" I shouted. "Mice are eating the island!"

Later I realized how silly that sounded, but it roused Tenobius, who came running over, and seemed to know immediately what I was saying. He looked into the box and screamed. He picked up the box and dropped it on the ground. The mice, which had been nibbling the coating on the coil of wire, scattered in all directions. Tenobius reached for the cloth separating the coils and pulled it up, disgorging another company of mice that burrowed down into the cloth and been trapped. Tenobius took the wire by the end and wiggled it back and forth to free it from the cloth and the mice.

Finally, the wire was free of the little monsters. Tenobius gathered it back up and carried it over to a still-lit lantern and inspected it.

"It's gone, Argus," he said. "They stripped it almost perfectly clean. By the gods, they even ate the chalk." He drew it through his fingers, carefully looking at it from one end to the other.

"It's like we did nothing at all. At least it's clean for the next try. It's a good thing they don't eat metal, like the mice from the moon."

"There are mice that eat metal on the moon?" I asked.

"It's a story from back home. I'll tell it to you sometime. Maybe." He threw his head back and groaned.

"Why didn't I think of mice? If beggars would eat hide soup, mice would, too. I also added honey to it, as well. It's a wonder they didn't try to eat it as we were making it. How did they get into the box?"

In answer, I retrieved the box from where he'd dropped it. I looked quickly over it and pointed out a tiny hole in one corner.

"They all got in through *there*?" Tenobius asked.

"You know how mice are," I said. "They can squeeze through holes that look too small for them."

"No, I didn't know that, actually."

"What kind of place do you come from that doesn't have mice?"

"A place with better boxes. What can I do about this, so they don't get in again? Should I seal it in heavy cloth?"

"They'll gnaw through the cloth. You really *don't* know about mice, do you?"

"What about a metal box?"

"Not if there's any opening in it. They can slip through a space so small you'd have to work to get a *denarius* through."

"A tin box, then, with a tight-fitting lid. No, *damnate*, I can't put it in a box of any kind. I want to *use* this wire. I can't keep it boxed up. I need to find a way to keep the mice from eating it, or else find something else. Argus. Do you know of anything hot I can put into the coating?"

"Hot?"

We'd just spent almost an entire day in a room like a furnace. Come to think of it, we weren't bothered by mice in there, I had to agree.

"What happens after it cools down?" I asked.

"Uhh, no. Not that kind of hot. I mean...Spicy. Do we have something so spicy mice won't eat it?"

"I don't know of anything mice won't eat. Why make it tasty for them?"

"No. There is a kind of spice we have that makes your mouth burn, as if it's hot, but it's not really hot. Some people like the taste and the feel. Mice and birds hate it. Do you have anything like that?"

"I've never heard of anything like that. Where do you get it?"

Tenobius pointed his hand in the direction where the horizon was starting to get lighter already.

"About five thousand *mille passus* that way. Unfortunately, we'd have to swim most of the way."

"They sell poison in some of the places in the forum. I think they get it from mushrooms."

"No, I don't want poison. I'm not trying to punish the mice I just want them to stop eating my...islands. If I mix poison into the stuff, then what happens? The mice eat the coating, go off to their holes in the wall, then they die. When they do, my wire is left without a coating, just as if they lived. I want to put something into it that will make the mice take a nibble, spit it out and stop eating, so that I keep my coating. I need something that tastes awful to mice."

"I don't know of anything like that."

"Well, we can start with something simple. I want to find something that tastes awful to people. Maybe the mice will hate it, too. Keep your eyes and your ears open."

He walked over to the pot with the crack in it he used to coat the wire.

"I should still have some left in here that I can mix something into..." He stopped suddenly.

I looked at him, wondering why he stopped. In answer, he turned the pot over. Three mice fell out and scampered away.

~ * ~

The next day, everyone was too exhausted to do anything. The last of the workpieces had been hauled away, and Marcus was paid. For once, he paid everyone off right away, before the money was gone, and closed the shop for the day. The fires were fueled and banked up so they'd stay lit until everyone returned to work.

Tenobius and I went to the soft nests we'd made during that long session and collapsed onto them, right in the back of the shop. When I got up, I noticed Tenobius was already gone. Probably in search of his hot spices, whatever those were. He returned around noon with several small containers, then set about boiling more hide fragments. It was easy work for a lazy day. He sat there watching the pot boil, skimming it and doing what he did before. He didn't ask me for help, and I wasn't very interested in watching him do this again. I think I knew him well enough so I could see what he was doing, and I didn't have to hang around to see that. I decided to go out and walk around. I wanted to get as far away from the shop as I could on this day.

I spent the day walking through the shops, seeing what was going on along the river, checking in on the friends I hadn't seen in days.

When I got back later that day, Tenobius finished preparing his mixture again, and I could see him dividing it into separate pots and mixing the stuff he'd bought into them. Each pot contained just one of the things he'd bought.

"Are you going to leave pieces of those out overnight, to see if the mice eat it?"

"Yes."

"What have you got?"

"I'm not sure. I don't know all the words for plants, but I wrote them down. I think this is made from mushrooms, and this is from some kind of rock. I have no idea where the others come from, except that they assure me they taste very bad."

Tenobius hadn't even looked up. He just continued to mix.

~ * ~

The next day I came back to the back yard of the forge where Tenobius mixed his pots of stuff. He'd slept there overnight, apparently, and was now looking at the pots, all arrayed in front of him. He looked up and saw me, and before I could ask, he picked up one of the pots and upended it. Nothing came out. He did the same with the next pot, with the same result. He continued doing this until he got to the last pot, which he held out to me.

I took it and looked inside. There was the inert tiny furry body of a mouse.

"Is it...?" I asked.

In answer, Tenobius grabbed the pot while it was still in my hand. He turned it upside down, as well. The furry body dropped out and bounced on the ground. But an instant later it got up and scurried away. There was none of the stuff in the pot.

"I think they like the taste, Argus" he said. "I'm a gourmet chef to the rodents."

"You should definitely talk to *her*," I said, indicating the house.

"I will. I have nothing to lose." Tenobius sighed. "We have casting work today. Have you ever cast anything in metal before?"

"No."

"Well, then. A new adventure awaits. Mice don't like iron, so they won't eat it."

He got up and walked into the shop. He was smiling and joking, but I could see the string of failures was beginning to affect him. I had already seen how when he was feeling sad, he buried himself in his work. That meant I was going to get buried in it, too, and learn this 'casting', whatever that was.

It was the end of a long sweaty day when we finished up. I had some burns here and there from getting careless with the molds, but at least I now knew what casting was. It all looked simple, until Tenobius explained there was a lot to it, knowing the right mix of metals, knowing how to prevent impurities from ruining the casting, designing the mold so it could fill completely. I decided I'd never know enough to have anything to do with running a shop. Tenobius told me Marcus had probably started out like me, and if he could do it, I could too. The last straw was when he suggested Metellus and Arnicus might end up running this very shop. That made my anger hot enough to melt bronze.

Just getting away from the shop, it felt like a cool day in autumn, and it was good just to trudge away up the street and let our sweat dry off. Tenobius offered to buy us each a cake and something to drink.

I was so tired I almost missed her, but suddenly I noticed that the maid from next door had just passed us. I spun around and tugged on Tenobius' tunic.

"It's her!" I said.

Tenobius turned around, only a little interested.

"Who?" he asked wearily.

"The maid. She's going that way." Tenobius didn't move. "Go talk to her!"

He started uncertainly after her, so I gave him a push, which earned me a nasty look.

She was retreating up the street toward her house, carrying a basket She'd obviously been to the market picking up things for the house. She was going so fast I was sure Tenobius, going as slowly as he was, was not going to catch up to her before she went back into the house.

That was when something happened. She stopped and tugged at the basket. A man going the other way either got snagged on it, or was trying to steal it. She didn't let go, and started yelling at the man.

Suddenly, he yanked it away from her and held it up. I recognized him. It was the one they called *Petrus*, the Rock. He was a porter in the little forum, using his size to haul around loads for pay. He was also known as a petty thief, a bully, and was proving it now. The Maid reached for the basket and he easily pushed her away. He started looking through the basket. Pulling out a bunch of grapes, he began to eat them while looking back at her.

He was so intent on his taunting he didn't notice when someone suddenly ripped the basket out of his grip and tossed it to the Maid. He turned around in surprise to think anyone would do that to him. I was surprised, too, because the one who did it was Tenobius.

Tenobius shouted something at Petrus in barbarian, but nobody understood it. Tenobius must have realized what he did, because he shouted again in Latin.

"Leave her alone!" he roared.

Petrus' surprise turned to a sly grin. He was looking forward to a scrap with someone who didn't know who he was. He turned away from the maid and faced Tenobius. He said something, but I was too far away to catch it. Instead, I was running toward them as fast as I could. I didn't know what I was going to do, but I was sure Tenobius was going to get hurt. Petrus had a name as a brawler, and he had ten *librae* at least on Tenobius. He was a laborer, and Tenobius was a craftsman and a scholar. He was going to get killed.

My father taught all of us how to fight. He started us all out with it, when he still didn't know how we'd turn out. Before it was clear my older brothers would be the real soldiers in the family, and I was just a nothing, he gave us our start. He showed us all how to spar, how to block a punch, how to throw one with the drive of our bodies behind it. He taught us how to kick and gouge. He'd attack us at unexpected times and see how we'd defend ourselves, holding back a little on account of our ages. We still got bruises and bloody noses, and one of my brothers got his nose broken that way. He was tough and unforgiving, my father. I think it helped me survive on my own in Rome.

I say all this to show that I know how to brawl and defend myself. I can judge a street fight, and Tenobius looked as if he was going to last just one punch from Petrus before he crumpled. He was standing all wrong, and his guard wasn't properly up. He looked as if he was *inviting* Petrus to hit him.

Petrus drew back a beefy fist and launched it at Tenobius, clearly intending to take care of him with that one punch. What happened next happened very quickly, and I'm not even sure I saw it all. I've gone over it in my mind since, and what it looked like was this.

Temobius moved quickly to one side, much more rapidly than I thought he could move. At the same time, he threw up his arm to the side in a peculiar way, so that it caught Petrus' arm and diverted his punch away from Tenobius. At the same time, he drew his other arm in the opposite direction. He then drove this right into Petrus' now unprotected jaw. I was shocked to see there has no windup, and he didn't follow through with the force of his torso the way my dad taught me to do it. Instead, he kept his body upright and withdrew his fist, but at the same time propelled the one he'd blocked with right at Petrus, hitting him again. The way my dad taught me, that should have made both punches weak and ineffective, but Petrus reacted as if Tenobius threw his whole body into it,

Tenobius wasn't finished. He threw a third of those barely-moving punches at Petrus. It all happened in the space of a couple of seconds, Tenobius' arms moving together like the arms of a balance, one advancing while the other retreated, and his upper body not participating at all.

Before Petrus had a chance to respond with another blow, Tenobius did something else. He kicked Petrus. It was a kick like I'd never seen before. It was no smooth arc up from the ground, aimed at the soft target of Petrus' balls. Instead, Tenobius turned partly sideways and drew one leg straight up, bending his leg at the knee until his foot was at the level of his own groin. He pushed it straight out, not toward Petrus' unprotected groin, but above that, aiming at his stomach. He didn't use his toe. Tenobius turned his foot so it was the edge that struck Petrus in the pit of his stomach, hard.

Petrus had been coming forward, both from the force of his original punch and with an effort to approach Tenobius, so the kick hit with more force than if Petrus had been standing still. It knocked the air out of him completely and pushed him over backward. Petrus collapsed on his butt.

I thought he would climb right back up, but he didn't. He couldn't. Petrus was not only taken by surprise, he was hurt. He convulsed like a man trying to throw up, falling forward onto his arms, making retching movements but only giving dry heaves. He wheezed in a breath.

Tenobius walked over to him, and I thought he was going to hit him again. Instead he simply growled at him. "Leave her alone!" With those words he turned and stiffly walked away. I ran after him, but everyone else seemed rooted in place. Except for the maid. She disappeared a long time ago.

Tenobius and I rounded a corner, and it wasn't until we were out of sight of Petrus and the crowd that he started limping, favoring the foot he'd kicked with. He made our way in a roundabout fashion back to the shop so no one saw where we went.

As soon as we were safely in the back, I wanted to tell Tenobius what a brave thing he'd done, and to ask him how he did that. Before I could, he reacted, shouting a string of curses in Latin interspersed with barbarian.

"*My God* that was a stupid thing to do! Stupid! Stupid! Stupid! *Idiot! Stupid Idiot!* We could have gotten hurt or killed. There are no *hospitals* here. No *antiseptics*. I don't even know if their damned doctors can set a fracture! The *police* might have picked me up! Stupid!"

"You did the right thing!" I told him. "We all wanted to, but nobody wanted to fight Petrus. They all wanted someone to beat him up. That's why no one stopped you."

He acted as if he hadn't heard.

"Idiot! Idiot! Idiot! What did you do that for? You don't even have a Brown *Cincture*! You didn't even get a chance to talk to her! What was the point? Idiot!"

He kept on like that for quite a while, and I didn't know how to stop him. I tried to go over and put my hand on his shoulder, but he just shook it off. Usually Tenobius is annoyingly cheerful, or at least calm and rational. I hated to see him acting like this.

I was trying to figure out what to do to break him out of it, when I noticed something. I think it was the change in my manner and my voice that finally did get him to notice me.

"Tenobius. Look," I pointed past him. He stopped doing what he was doing and slowly turned to see what I was pointing at.

There on one of the boxes behind us was a round cooking pan. It was filled with something that looked like a cross between a meat pie and a stew. It was hot, and we could smell it was freshly made. Both of us suddenly realized we were very hungry.

It was from her, of course. Her house abutted the shop at the back. Neither of us saw her come, but we had no doubt that she was the one who left the food. I ran into the shop and got some wooden plates and utensils.

After we finished eating the backdoor of the house next door opened with a loud creak, and a procession came out. I expected to see the maid, but instead, I saw the oldest-looking man I ever saw, hobbling along while leaning on a staff. Clinging to him was the oldest woman. Following behind them was the maid.

Their progress was so painfully slow that we got up and went over to them. They stopped and looked at us, then the old man turned haltingly around to look back at the maid, and pointed a shaking finger at Tenobius.

"Is this one him?" he asked in a voice as shaky as the rest of him.

"Yes," she answered, simply.

He turned back to Tenobius.

"Lillia has told me what you did for her. I want to thank you. Do you understand?"

Tenobius nodded, then said "Yes."

"Lillia is my niece. She helps out with the shopping, cooking, and cleaning, and we give her a place to stay. I am M. Rufus Placidus, and this is my wife, Alena."

Alena peered closely at Tenobius, as if really seeing him for the first time. She opened her eyes wide, then whispered to her husband.

"My wife wants to know if there is something wrong with your eyes."

"My eyes?"

"Yes, your eyes. They look...strange."

"I got hurt while picking rice," said Tenobius.

"Eh?"

"It's nothing. Everyone has eyes like this where I'm from,"

"You are a barbari...a foreigner?"

"Yes. I've come to see Rome, but I hope to go back home someday."

"You work in the shop now?" He indicated our smithy.

"Yes."

"Are they teaching you well?"

"He is teaching Marcus a thing or two," I said.

"Ah," he said, as if that explained everything. "We must go back inside. I am certain Lillia will want to talk with you. Goodbye."

With that they turned and slowly made their way back. Lillia did not help, but remained where she was and watched them return. When they passed through the door, she turned to Tenobius.

"So. Did you like the *minutal*?"

"Is that what you call the food? I have not heard of it before. Thank you."

"You are a very strange man. You do not know words. You boil sawdust. You have an odd face. Still, you could beat up Petrus, and for that I thank you. Why did you do it?"

"You needed help. I know what that's like."

"I have given you food. Is there anything else I can do?"

"There is. Do you know how to get rid of mice?"

~ * ~

I think Lillia was as surprised by that as by Tenobius' fighting Petrus for her. It turned out she *did* know about keeping away mice, and a lot about housekeeping. She and Tenobius talked for a very long time about little things like housekeeping and food. After a while I left them alone and wandered the streets, looking in the stalls.

When I got back, she was gone, and Tenobius was working, sawing up some lengths of brass. I went over to help him, and we talked.

"She's clever, Argus," Tenobius said. "She knows a lot of things, and she's not really shy. She can speak her mind when she gets roused. Do you think she's really their niece?

"I don't know. You don't think so?"

"She doesn't look much like them."

"I know plenty of cousins who don't look at all alike. She might not be related. It's possible she might be some more distant cousin. She might be a girl come to the city, and they took her in and started calling her 'niece'. They might even believe it now. Who knows? Who cares? Why do you even want to know?"

"Well, it's just that with what you've told me about your family, and with what I see about them, well, it just seems like you Romans are awfully casual about family."

"People do what they have to. If an old couple takes in a girl to help them out, who cares if she's really a relative or not? She gets a place to stay, and they get someone to take care of them. It all works out, everybody profits, right?"

"I guess."

"Are you in love with her?"

Tenobius looked shocked, then laughed.

"I can talk with a woman without falling in love with her."

"You like her, though."

"I guess so, yeah. Do you know what I really like about her?"

"What?"

"She knows what I can use to keep mice away."

He opened a squat pot on the table. It was full of some gray powder.

"I'm going to try it out tonight," he said.

~ * ~

The next morning, I found Tenobius happily looking into a container. When he showed it to me, I could see there was a blob of his mixture in it, although colored kind of gray from the powder. He grinned from ear to ear.

"I left it out overnight with the lid off. I wanted to give the little beasts a good shot at it. I even put one out in the open" He pointed to a piece of the stuff sitting out on one of the tables.

"We're supposed to be making some boxes today, but I want to try my wire again with this new stuff. Are you with me?"

I said I was.

Remarkably, Marcus never came by that day to yell at us for not doing what we were supposed to be doing. Tenobius went through his now-familiar routine of boiling the bits of hide, adding honey, then working in the gray powder. He set up the rig for coating his wire, and we ran through it all again. At the end he had a long piece of wire, coated with his mixture, now grayish, and powdered all over with chalk, hanging from the tree like some weird kind of fruit.

When it was done, he shouted and thrust his fist into the air, shouting something in barbarian. He sat down on the dirt under it and continued to look up at it happily.

"You know, Argus, for the first time I think that I might really be able to go home."

"I'll happy for you. Can you tell me how that piece of coated wire is going to get you home?"

"No, I don't think I can," he said. "I'd like to. I don't think I can give you an explanation you'd understand, or believe. You'd think I was crazy."

"I already think you're crazy. It's a different crazy than Rusticus the Screamer has. He just shouts at the top of his lungs at everybody who looks him in the eyes. You build weird things, and you have to get them *just right*. I have no idea what you're doing, or how it can help."

"Well, if somebody had to get home by ship, and spent a lot of time learning how to twist fibers into rope, you'd understand that, right? Say he lost all his rope. It burned, rotted, or something. The only way he could work his ship was with new rope he had to make himself. The probem is he never made rope before, so he had to figure it out. That's what I've been doing."

"This Island Wire is the rope for your ship?"

"It's an example. What we call an *analogy*. I'm not saying that this is my rope. It's a part of my ship. My Dreamship, I call it. My Rainbow Ship. Even so, it's only one of the parts I have to build."

"Tenobius, what happened to the other sailors on your...Dreamship?"

"There weren't any others. Just me."

"You could work your Dreamship all by yourself?"

"Uh-huh."

Now I knew he was crazy. I decided to push further.

"Did your friends have their own Dreamships?"

"Well, I wouldn't say friends. The people I worked with had other ones, yes."

"So why haven't any of them come for you? They know you're missing, right?"

"They do. A better question is why I don't use another Dreamship to come and get me."

"I don't understand. If you're here, you can't use a ship from your country to come and get you. How could you come for yourself, anyway? It doesn't make sense."

"I know it doesn't. Anyway, that's how it works. Even if they know I'm in trouble, the others won't come to get me. Unless I can get back, they can't come and get me."

"You're making even less sense. *Why* won't anyone come to rescue you?"

Tenobius was silent for a long time. I was going to ask him again when he spoke.

"*Temporal discipline,*" was all he said.

"What does *that* mean?"

"It's a set of laws we all pledged to. Like a soldier's oath. We can't depart from it."

"Who would know if you did?"

"It's not that kind of rule. It's not like getting whipped or getting extra guard duty if you break the rules. It's more like the rule about not sticking your hand in the fire. The punishment is that you lose your hand, and it's enforced by the fire."

"So, no one is going to come for you because they'll be punished by...What? The fire?"

"No." He thought again.

"They'll be punished by the *Paradox.*" He laughed. "It's a fearsome monster, worse than the *Jabberwock.* Or the *Bandersnatch.*" He laughed again. I wondered if maybe he wasn't almost as crazy as Rusticus.

"I joke about it," he said, his voice in earnest. "But it's a real danger. Nobody is coming for me. If I can't pull myself out, I'll never see home again."

~ * ~

The next day, after the morning's work, Tenobius went to the backdoor of the Placidus house and talked with Lillia. I was amazed. After all his getting worked up about it and worrying, here he was simply going over and knocking on her door. His saving her from Petrus changed things, of course, but I was still surprised. When he finished, I asked him what they talked about.

"Rags," he replied.

"Rags!" I shouted.

Here I thought he was arranging to get together with her, perhaps go to the tavern or the Little Forum. I'd hoped that some sort of romance was starting, but it was just Tenobius being practical Tenobius.

"Why rags?"

"Well, I need them, and I thought she would know where to get them."

I wasn't going to ask him why he needed them. He'd either make a joke, or tell me some wild but true reason he wanted them. The worst part was I couldn't tell the difference between the two. But I could still push him about it.

"Don't you have enough rags here?" I asked, pointing to his piles of them scattered about the yard.

"Not the right kind of rags. I'm looking for fine stuff. Linen, if I can find it. I thought Lillia would know.

"She's going to bring me some linen rags, she said. She also told me to try the Temple of Isis. Where is it?"

"Isis? I don't know. That's one of those strange foreign gods, I think. I don't know anybody who goes there."

"I think it's in the center of the City, near the Forum. The main Forum. I still haven't been there yet."

I wasn't happy about the idea of Tenobius going to the City Center by himself. Even though he was a grown up, he was so unaware of things I felt letting him go alone was like letting a toddler go there alone.

"I'll go with you," I said.

I hadn't been to the Old Forum in a long time. I'm more comfortable where I grew up, and where I know all the people and the places. When I leave the neighborhood, it's like a completely different world. I may know the streets, but I don't know the people, and I don't know which gangs control what. It's always interesting to see new things, but I'm never comfortable until I'm back home.

Tenobius, though, seemed happy as a puppy. He was smiling and looking around. He didn't notice the times that people stared at him, hard, and didn't know they clearly didn't like him being there. One time we passed a slave chain, with the slaves bound in a line by their waists with a rope. It may as well have been a chain, because they made no moves to run away. The drivers looked at Tenobius and instantly took in his clothes and his face, with those non-Roman eyes. I could see they were sizing him up, so I yanked him away and told him not to look back at them. That only made him want to look even more. I told him to trust me, and hurried him out.

I figured we were safe once we got to the Forum. That place was filled with all kinds of people, from all over the world. Tenobius didn't stand out so much there. He was just another Strange Human Beast. There were men with red hair there, and dark skin, men covered in tattoos. Tenobius' face was just another part of the show.

Most of the other non-Romans were merchants or performers. Since Tenobius had no goods to sell, I'll bet most people were waiting for him to start juggling, or something. We just shouldered our way through the crowd, and I asked likely people the way to the Temple of Isis.

It was big. Much bigger than the one for the Skinny Venus in the small Forum, and it was much cleaner and in better shape. Even the bottom steps were clean and square, and not engraved with names and gameboards. Across the way was another temple, to some other Eastern god. The paint on the front of the Temple was fresh and clean. There were fittings of brass, gone all green, but there were highlights of gold, and that was polished and bright. This was the Temple Important People went to. I suddenly felt rough and shabby.

If Tenobius did, he didn't show it. He started right up the steps without a second thought. I had to run up after him. He didn't get to the top, though. A priest saw him coming, and started down the steps. They met near the top. I was just in time to hear the opening words.

"Stop." said the bearded priest, holding up his right hand as his left held his staff.

He stood one step up from Tenobius, which made him seem taller. "You are about to enter the awful presence of The Goddess. Are you known to her?"

He studied both of us, and I coul tell he thought we looked out of place. "I am a stranger," said Tenobius, "and do not want to offend. I want to ask something of the priests of Isis."

"We do not speak Her name, but if you truly are a stranger, I forgive you that. Are you a slave? Are you in need? The Mother is Mother to all."

"I am no slave, but a smith and an artisan. The boy is my apprentice. My name is Tenobius."

"What are you here for, Smith and Artisan Tenobius? Do you seek the Mother's Love? I have not seen you here before. If you are here for worship, it is the wrong day, and the wrong time, and you wear the wrong clothes."

"My apologies, Priest of the Mother. I am not here to show reverence to the Goddess, but for business,"

"What business? Are you looking for work? We have no need for repairs."

"No, Holy One. I am looking to buy old shirts and garments for my business."

The priest looked surprised.

"Do smiths forge linen, then?"

"No, but I make other things besides metal."

"Indeed? You are well-spoken, and no beggar. You should come to Initiate's services next Market Day. As for old garments, you should know we already have an arrangement for them. We sell them to one of the used clothes dealers down there in the Forum."

"May I ask, holiness, which one?"

The priest looked annoyed at first, then amused.

"I know even that. Celinus is his name. We feel that even priest's garments can be used by the poor as clothing. The Mother is compassionate. Come and visit us. Perhaps you will learn, or be called if we need to repair something."

The priest took his staff and made some sort of gesture with it. Tenobius later told me it was probably a blessing. With that, he turned and walked back up the steps.

"So...you're too late," I said to Tenobius. "They already have a buyer."

"No. This means that we go see Celinus and buy *his* old things."

With that he was down the steps.

~ * ~

Tenobius figured Celinus would probably have a stall in the Forum market, which made sense. We couldn't find it, though. Nobody had ever heard of Celinus. It wasn't until Tenobius described the kind of business he was looking for to a used-garment seller that we learned that everyone called him 'Baldy'. Nobody seemed to know his real name. Except, I guess, the priest. But it turned out that everyone knew Baldy. He bought linen and fine cloth from everyone, not just the Priests of Isis.

Baldy was easy to find. He really was as bald as an egg. I don't think he even had eyebrows. When he found out that Tenobius wanted to buy old cloth, he treated him like a lost cousin and showed him the shop. He gave me a fig from a dish of fruit he kept near the door.

I followed them around, listening in. Baldy washed everything he brought in. He was his own fuller, using urine from the public toilets to clean out the dirt and rinsing them thoroughly. He took the cleaned robes and cut them down to tunics, if they were in good shape. The excess he made up into small bolts he sold to seamstresses. He had others make him underclothing and children's clothes. The pieces that were too small he sold to others who made napkins and toys. He had an entire room set aside for rectangles he sold 'for the monthlies'. I looked up from my fig and asked what 'monthlies' were. Tenobius said he'd tell me later. Baldy laughed at that.

Finally, Baldy asked Tenobius what sizes he wanted to buy. Tenobius surprised him by saying he wanted something he hadn't mentioned. He wanted smaller than small. He wanted little bits left over after patterns had been cut from cloth even in the cleverest way. He wanted bits of fluff and individual threads, he had to ask me to give him the words for 'fluff' and 'thread'. He wanted the leftover waste that was too small for anyone else to use.

Baldy scratched his head at that. I don't think anyone ever asked for that before. He took Tenobius into the back, where there was a big box built into the wall, filled with such little bits of cloth.

"Is this what you want to buy? We throw this out, or we burn it."

"I'll take all that you have there for fifteen denarii," Tenobius said. Baldy looked at him.

"It's against my principles to take the first offer, but I can't see a good reason not to. It would cost me more than that to get this hauled away by Peregrinus. You really want all of it?"

"Yes, and I might want more in the future."

"What for?"

"I'm going to try to make something out of it."

"What?"

"I don't think you have a word for it. I'm not sure it will work."

"Describe it, then."

"It's sort of a very thin, very cheap leather."

"Out of *that*? Good luck to you. I'll sell you all you want."

Baldy found a big, dirty sack and shoveled as much in as he could. Tenobius paid him half the money, saying he'd give him the rest when he came back for the remainder of the linen bits. He twisted the opening up, tied it in a knot, and hauled the filled bag over one shoulder. I tried to carry the back of it so it wouldn't drag on the ground.

It took a lot of dodging to get it through the crowd in the Forum and into a less-crowded side street leading back toward the Forge. When we did so I spoke to Tenobius.

"What's a monthly?" I said.

"What?"

"You and Celinus were talking about using small squares of linen for 'monthlies'. When I asked what they were, you said you'd tell me later, and Baldy laughed. It's later now. Why did he laugh?"

"Um," said Tenobius.

He seemed to be thinking.

"What?"

"How much do you know about men and women? You know, the differences between them?"

"I'm no child. I've seen the women without clothes in the baths."

"I'm afraid to ask how."

"It's not difficult. My mother used to take us into the women's baths when we were little. Boys or girls, it didn't matter to her."

"I guess that makes sense. Like the *Japanese*."

"The who?"

"Another barbarian tribe. Although they'd kill me if they knew I called them that. Their men and women sometimes bathe together, or at least within sight of one another."

"Uh huh."

"So how much do you know?"

"Women don't have a *pipinna*. A Snake. The thing in front."

"Eloquently put. Even so, they do have a structure there. Do you know about that? Did your father tell you? Did any of your friends?"

My father didn't tell me much of anything. I didn't trust my friends especially not the other boys to know or tell the truth. I'd heard talk.

"Women have a *fossa*, I've heard," I told him, so he wouldn't think I was a complete idiot or baby.

"*Fossa*, huh?" he replied, thoughtfully. "That's a new one to me. I was expecting something more obscene. You have educated friends, Argus. Did Publius tell you that?"

I had to think it over. Where *had* I picked up that word?

"I don't remember."

"It doesn't matter. I'll bet it was him, though. Tullius would have found out the most obscene word he could, I think, just because."

Tenobius then gave me a description of the way of women's bodies. I had never heard anything like it before, and would have thought he was making it up to fool me, except that Tenobius never did anything like that. I noticed something. The way he described it was the way he described machines. To Tenobius, the body was just like a complicated machine, each part of which did something when it was pushed by some other part. I don't think anybody else would have described it that way, and told him so. Tenobius just gave me other examples, the way my muscles worked to move my arms and legs. The way that we ate food and it got pushed through our bodies. Everything seemed to work by something pushing something else. Could it be right? Were we just some kind of machine?

"Why didn't my little sister need these linen cloths?" I asked.

"How old was she?"

"She's less than eight," I told him.

"She's not old enough yet."

"How about my mother?"

"She probably uses them, or something like them."

"I've never seen her use it."

"There are probably a lot of things she does in privacy. Don't you?"

I thought about it. Even though we lived in the same cramped space, we all had our own lives. I'd never seen her put on all her clothes, or making herself up, or using the public latrines. I don't know why, but it made me think of her differently, as a person, and not just Mother.

"Why don't men have to do something every month, then?"

"Because men and women are different. If you're going to ask me why men and women are different, let me tell you right now that I'm not going to get into that. I refuse to be drawn into a discussion of *metaphysics*."

"What's *metaphysics*?"

"Deep stuff. Takes forever to explain, and there's no definite answer. Some people are touchy about their explanation being the right one. Right now, I have enough problems that have definite solutions I have to answer. Like how to use all this linen scrap."

"Baldy, he was laughing because I didn't know what he was talking about."

"Yes."

"I'm not a stupid kid."

"No, you're not. There's nothing wrong with not knowing things. We all have to learn."

When we got back, Tenobius emptied the linen scraps into a box so that he could take the bag back for more. He didn't go back right away. He set up the big cauldron, filled it with water, and started a fire underneath. He wanted to start making whatever it was right away.

"I can go back tomorrow for the rest," he said.

As he waited for the water to heat, he undid his purse from his belt and counted out his money.

"I've got enough to pay for the rest," he said. "but I'm going to need more money soon. I'm getting some from my work here at the shop, but

I'm going to need a lot more."

"Make more wire," I suggested.

"I could, but there's no market for it. We've filled all the orders that have come in. If I make it, nobody will buy it. I have to find something new to make. Do you have any ideas?"

"Why don't you make more of those color discs like the one you gave me. You know how to make those, right?"

"I know how, but I don't have the tools. I don't think I can make them with what I've got here. It's like trying to make a *tricorder* with stone knives and bearskins."

"What's a tricorder? Why would you use a knife made out of stone, or bearskins?"

Tenobius laughed.

"It's a saying among the people we call the *Trekkies*," he said, and laughed again.

"I've never heard of a people called the *Trecci*," I said.

"No doubt. They're only in my country."

A sudden thought struck me.

"You know their sayings. Are *you* of the *Trecci*?"

He spluttered and looked surprised, then laughed.

"Those are indeed fighting words," he said, solemnly.

He sounded stern, but I could see the smile under it.

"Some of my friends would hit you for suggesting something that vile."

I had to keep up this talk. I might learn something from it.

"What do they do that's so awful?"

"They dwell too much on the past. Which, oddly, is in the future. The future as it was." He thought a bit, the smile draining from his face. "By that definition, maybe I *am* a *Trecci*. I should start greeting people like this" He held up a hand with his fingers spread in two bunches.

"Do they really do that?"

"It's their *Signum Specialis*."

"Well, it can be ours, then, since there aren't any of them here in Rome," I said.

I tried to get my hand to make the sign, but my fingers stubbornly refused to spread the right way.

"Keep practicing," Tenobius said. "You'll get it eventually."

When the water started to boil, he put in a lot of the linen scraps, along with a lot of the beaten reeds he kept in a jar, then let it all cook together.

~ * ~

It was a couple of days later, after we'd spent much of the day repairing metal items and forging nails that Tenobius showed me his results from boiling the linen and reeds.

He held up a round disc. It was very light in color and it was smooth, with no pieces of reed or fibers sticking out. He gave it to me and I took it carefully. I looked at both sides and ran my fingertip across it. It was very even and regular. Not like 'very thin leather', really. Not like anything else I'd ever seen or felt. It was kind of beautiful.

"I think it's the best one you've made yet. Is it? Is this the way it's supposed to be?"

"Almost. It's called *paper*. It's like the *papyrus* you sometimes see, but better. It has no holes or grain in it, and it won't fall apart. Like papyrus, you can write on it. Unlike the wax tablets, it's permanent. He took a piece of charcoal from the edge of the fire in the forge and drew a careful straight streak across the disc.

"You wouldn't be able to see it so well on my old paper," he said. "It was too dark and irregular. I also dipped this into hide soup, that's to help it keep its shape and not blot up ink. Hide glue is better than clay for that. To make it look good, I used the press on it."

"So, what's it all for. After all that work, is this just for writing things on?"

"You could use it for that. I think I'll use some of it for that. You can write out your lessons on it. I have some other uses in mind for it. Here's one."

He took his knife and cut away the outside, leaving a perfect square. He then folded it in half, corner to corner, then opened it out and did it the other way. I lost track of what he did, exactly, but at the end he had folded it into a tight package. He stuck one corner in his mouth and blew into it, using his hands to pull it into shape. When he was finished, he had a perfect cube, which he carefully placed on the table.

"I wasn't sure it would stand up to that. I've wanted to do that for a long time."

I picked it up, carefully. It was very delicate and weighed almost nothing.

"What is it?"

"Some people call it a *balloon*. It's also a Water Bomb. You can fill it with water and throw it at your friends."

"Why?"

"So, they get wet. When they do, they throw their Water Bombs back at you."

"This is the real reason you spent all this time making your *paper*, isn't it? You wanted to have a fight with these water things."

"Well, fixing the Dreamship is important, but you have to have priorities."

~ * ~

Tenobius was busy the next couple of days, and I had time to myself. I visited with Publius and showed him the thing Tenobius made. I wanted to know if he'd ever seen anything like it before, either the *paper* or the folded thing it became.

He was fascinated by it. He said the *paper* was like papyrus without grain. He got a piece from his father's *cubiculum* and showed how they differed. You couldn't fold the papyrus the same way you folded the *paper*, because the fibers in it kept wanting to push the papyrus only in certain directions.

As for the folding, that was something new to him, too. He said he'd seen parchment pleated into folds, but never anything as different as the *balloon* Tenobius made.

I remembered what Tenobius said about needing money, and asked him if he thought we could sell these *balloons*. Who'd buy them? Publius asked, and for what? We tossed ideas back and forth. Unfortunately, we didn't come up with anything. If you were going to charge a lot for them, nobody would want to just fill them with water and throw them at each other, like Tenobius said. We decided it was just an interesting thing to look at, and to hold.

Publius wanted to take it and show it to his father, but I snatched it back. I didn't want to draw too much official attention to Tenobius. What if The Runt's dad wanted to talk to Tenobius about where he got his ideas or why he looked the way he did? I had visions of him being tossed into the Tullianum before being examined by a judge, just because he was suspicious.

After I left Publius, I visited Tullius to buy more bits of hide for Tenobius, he had given me money for this. I was also supposed to ask about getting some small squares of soft tanned leather, the size of my palm, for something Tenobius wanted to try. I was able to get three pieces like this, and a fourth that could be cut up into two or three more, but it cost all the money Tenobius gave me.

~ * ~

Tenobius was delighted when I showed him the soft leather pieces, I got him, even more than with the leather scraps he used for his *island* stuff and making his paper. He said he had plans for them, but wouldn't say anything more right then.

In addition to piecework at the shop, he'd found time to make more of his *paper*, now in the shape of big rectangles, all clean and white and smooth. I asked what it was for, and he said for the same thing as the leather pieces, but also, he wanted to give me a piece to write on. He also pulled out a *stylus*, a metal rod like the one I used on the wax tablet, only this was some different metal, and Tenobius had jacketed it in wood, so it was easier to grip. He showed me how he could write on the *paper* with it, but I shouldn't push too hard. Also, once the mark was there, it wasn't possible to get it off, so I should be careful in how much *paper* I used to write.

He said he was going to teach me numbers, I'd learned enough of words by now. There was a way to use the same letters to mean different numbers. One, two, and three were easy, just up and down strokes with the *pencil*, as Tenobius called the jacketed *stylus*. I ripped the paper a couple of times before I learned not to press so hard. This was the same way we used to keep score with games on the Little Forum. The number *four*, instead of being four lines, was a down stroke and a *V*, which didn't make any sense. Tenobius showed me that *five* was a *V*, and that putting the *I* in front meant that it was subtracted from the five. I said it looked stupid and didn't make any sense, why not use four strokes for *four*, like we did when keeping score? Tenobius agree that it was more logical, and that some people *did* use *IIII* instead of *IV* for *four*, but that the *IV* was considered proper.

He showed me how you added strokes to make *VI, VII,* and *VIII* for *six, seven,* and *eight*, but that *nine* was weird again. It was *IX*. Tenobius explained that *X* was *ten*, and using the *I* in front meant that it was subtracted again.

I got frustrated by this, and asked why not use *IIX* for *eight* or *IIV* for *three*. Tenobius said that it was the way custom made it, but he said that I was pretty clever for coming up with those other ways of writing the numbers. He said that he thought somebody came up with *IV* instead of *IIII* and *IX* instead of *VIIII* in order to save space on paper, so you wouldn't use as much of it.

He had me write out the first hundred numbers in order, and I could see there was a pattern, and the pattern was kind of pretty, but it still didn't make a lot of sense. They seemed to be made up because someone just felt like it. Tenobius said, yes, it did seem that way. He said it was *arbitrary*, which meant the same thing, only it was more grown up way to say it. He asked me how I'd change it. I told him the first I'd do is get rid of that stupid 'putting it in front of other bigger number means subtract it' rule. He said that would make some numbers really long.

Well, I said, after thinking about it, why not use a different symbol for each number. That way they each take up the same amount of space. His eyes got all wide at that, and he didn't talk for a long time. Finally, he asked me what made me say that.

I told him it made sense. If too many figures took up too much space, just use one for each number. You just had to remember an awful lot of them. He told me that it was a very clever idea, and not everyone would think of it. I felt good about that. It was like I had something nobody else did. Tenobius said you didn't need a different symbol for each number, just a few different ones, and you could use them in combinations to make up all the numbers. And you could do it without the 'subtract in front' stuff. But he said he couldn't say more than that, or else the *Temporal Discipline* people would get mad at him.

~ * ~

"I should be working..." objected Tenobius.

He was carrying a basket and trying to keep up with us.

'Us' were Lillia and me. We were walking fast, and Tenobius had to walk fast to keep up, carrying the basket and all.

"We both need to rest. You work too much," I shouted back at him.

"Slow down, because I'm working too much keeping up with you," he objected.

"Not now," shouted Lillia, "We're almost there."

Staying ahead of Tenobius was her idea. It kept him from thinking too much about what was going on.

"You're always saying we're almost there. Stop lying to me."

"This time it's true," she said. "Right under that tree."

Tenobius sped up his pace and dropped the basket under the tree. It was on a gentle slope going down to the river, and it was a nice-looking spot. I was surprised there was a place like this inside the city.

So was Tenobius, apparently. He stood up and looked carefully around, breathing heavily.

"What is this place?" he asked.

I wanted to know, too. Lilia was the one who found it.

"It's the Field of the Dioscouri. Every year they have the ceremony down by the water, so they can't build here. The rest of the year it's just empty. People bring their goats to graze."

We sat down in the shade of the small tree and unpacked the things. There were nuts and figs, some small loaves and a two-handled jar with some kind of paste in it. Another jug held light wine. Everyone helped themselves. I didn't touch the stuff in the jar.

"How do you know about this spot, Lillia?" asked Tenobius. "Are you a worshipper of the Twins?"

"Me? Phhht!" said Lillia, without looking up. "I haven't been to a ceremony of any god since I started wearing adult clothes. I do know a good spot when I see it."

"So how do you know that it's the Field of the Dioscouri?"

"How? I ask. If I see a field in the City not being used, I know it belongs to someone with pull, so I want to know who."

"The gods won't mind if we eat here, then?"

"Neither the gods nor their priests. Everyone comes here."

"Well, it's a nice spot," agreed Tenobius.

I tried to ignore a dead animal carcass that was floating by, and didn't want to draw attention to it. I think Tenobius saw it, too, but if he did, he didn't show it.

"And you," said Lillia, talking to Tenobius, "what gods do you pray to, where you come from?"

"There are many different groups where I lived," he said. "Most of them worship the same god, or so they say. From what I see they do it in different ways. We have some of the same groups that Rome does. If you look hard you can find people who worship the Twins, Zeus, and Isis. There are not many of them. We have Jews, and Christians, like you do. I'm not religious myself.

"We have open land like this, too, but not because it's used by a cult. They just decided it would be a good idea to have some land with trees and no buildings inside the city, where people could go and eat like this."

We ate quietly for a while. I wanted to get them talking, but not about religion. I pulled out something I got from the shop.

"Lillia, do you want to know what he's boiling up in the back of the Shop? He's making this."

I held up a piece of Tenobius' *paper*. This one had scribblings of his all over it. I couldn't tell what they were. Some were letters, but there were other marks. I couldn't read any of it.

"What is this?" she asked, taking hold of the *paper*. She was more interested in the stuff itself than in what was on it.

"Where did you get that?" asked Tenobius at the same time. "Those are my calculations. I need those."

"What *is* it?" Lillia asked again.

"He calls it *paper*," I told her. "He boils up crushed reeds and old linen pulled to pieces and some other stuff and puts it on a screen to dry, and this is what it comes out like."

She rubbed it between her fingers.

"It feels like a seed pod, or locust wings."

"Yes, well, it's good for a lot of things. Argus shouldn't have taken it without asking. I need those scribblings."

"Tenobius is teaching me to write," I told Lillia, proudly.

"You can *read*?" she asked Tenobius, surprised. "How is that possible if you're from a barbarian land, like you say?"

"Well, yes," said Tenobius. "That's no excuse." He said it as if he expected us to laugh.

"What does this say?" she asked, pointing to an odd marking on the sheet. I looked over, but it was something I'd never seen before.

"It says...." Tenobius hesitated, then decided he might as well read it aloud. "It says *tau equals Are See*."

Lillia still looked puzzled, and looked at me. I just shook my head.

"Anyway, it isn't important right now. It's one way I use to figure out how big to make things, or what the proportions are. I hear that they found design work like that on the stones of temples, only they're hidden away where you can't see them. "

"Tenobius," I said, "I've never seen you do that before. I've seen you make lots of things. I never see Marcus do it."

"Eh? Well, most small things you don't need to do it. If the proportions are important, or if you're making something really big, it helps to figure things out. You wouldn't want to put up the columns for a temple and not find out you made them too short until they were standing up, right? I think I'm boring our hostess. Look, I've already done the calculations. All I need to save is this corner here." He carefully folded the corner over back and forth, then tore it along that fold. He put the torn-off piece into his purse.

"Did Argus tell you I can do something else with *paper*?" he asked Lillia. She shook her head.

"Well watch, then."

He carefully folded the paper to make a square, then tore it along those folds. I thought he was going to make another *balloon*, but he started doing something different with the sheet. When he was finished, he had a completely different thing in his hand, which seemed to be all points and corners.

"See?" He said, "It's a bird, a crane. This is its head and beak over here, and its tail at the other end. These are its wings. If I hold it by its body and move the tail, I can make the wings flap."

He did so, and suddenly I could see how it was a bird. He handed it to Lillia, who tried to make it flap, but she did it wrong. He had to show her how to do it. I couldn't believe she couldn't remember something so simple, or that it took Tenobius so long to get her to do it right.

"What are you making now?" I asked.

"It's lots of things," said Tenobius. "You can put it down like this on the points, and it's a *salt cellar*, a container for salt that you put on the table. Otherwise, you could do what my sister and her friends used to, and put your fingers into it and move it back and forth like this." He alternately opened and closed it first one way, and then the other.

"They wrote different things on it, so after you chose one panel or another, you opened it up and it told you your fortune. I can't do that, I don't have a *pencil* with me, and the *paper's* all covered with calculations, anyhow. There's another thing you can use it for. You open the thing up like a bird's beak, and you can use it...to grab noses!"

He went to grab mine, but at the last moment he swerved and got Lillia's. She was surprised, and screamed a little, then laughed. She made as if to hit Tenobius. He got up, much faster than I thought he would, and ran toward the river, Lillia followed him, laughing.

They came back, eventually. I worked out the next two numbers that had square roots by then. They were still laughing, and out of breath.

"So why do you make this, this *paper*, Tenobius?" Lillia asked. "To make nose catchers and flapping birds?"

"He's fixing his Dreamship," I answered.

"So. Does this go with the other things you're boiling in pots?"

"Yes. I have a lot of work to do for this. That reminds me, do you have any more of that gray powder to keep the mice away?"

"Gray powder," Lillia said dismissively. "What you need is a cat. Do you know about cats? Do they have them in your country?"

"Yes. We have cats."

"I'll get you one. I know a woman who has one about to give kittens."

"That's all right. I don't need a cat."

"That's alright, I'll get one for our house, and it can keep mice away from yours, too. Don't you like cats?"

"I don't love them. More important is cats don't like me."

"It will love your mice. You'll see."

"Argus got me the soft leather squares I need for my next steps. With *luck*, I'll be able to get my next parts made soon."

"*Luck?*"

"Yes, you know, *Fortuna*. Maybe I should hang a horse shoe over the shop to bring me Good Luck."

We both looked at him in surprise.

"What?" we both said.

A Shoe for Horses? I tried to imagine a sandal for a horse, the thong passing over the hoof. No, that would be better for an ox, with its cloven hoof.

"You know, a horse shoe," Tenobius said, pronouncing the two words distinctly and tracing a shape in the air with his finger. "You put them on their hooves to protect them."

"What are you talking about?" Lillia asked.

I could see Tenobius go from confused, to knowing, then to that glint he gets when a crazy idea has taken him over. He looked at us, then off far into the distance. He slowly got up.

"You don't know what a *horseshoe* is. A *horseshoe*." He ran off toward the nearest road and looked up and down until he saw a horse. He looked at its feet, and watched as it lifted its legs in walking. He looked at another, and another. He ran back to us, laughing. It was a different laugh than when he was using the nose grabber. That was a having a fun laugh. This was his planning something laughable.

"Nobody here has *horse shoes*. Argus, we're going to make a

MILLION sesterces!" he said, and laughed again. "Come on, let's go!"

"Go? Go where?" asked Lillia.

"Back to the shop! We're going to make us some *horseshoes*!!"

~ * ~

Of course, it was a LOT more complicated than that. Lillia got sore at Tenobius for cutting the meal short, but I knew there was no stopping him once he got himself wound up.

He got a rough idea of the size of a hoof from a hoof imprint in mud and marked it on his *paper*. When we got to the shop, he got some rough iron rod stock and had me pumping the bellows on the charcoal fire. He worked and he worked on the rod stock, heating it until it glowed yellow-orange, then taking it to the anvil to hammer it into shape until it cooled down too much, then back into the coals for more heat.

First, he bent the end of the rod into a crude letter 'U'. He wasn't happy with the shape, so he reheated and rebent it until it matched his paper. He reheated it and hammered it flat. He used the pointed tool to drive holes through it, then he shaped the edges of the holes in an odd way. He called it *countersinking*. Finally, he liked the shape, so he cut off the finished piece and let it drop to the floor to cool.

He was making the second of the nails for it, with its odd-shaped head, when Marcus came in and demanded to know what he was doing. I don't think he'd ever seen Tenobius using the forge before when he didn't have too. Tenobius preferred the finer work, and the use of brass and fine metals. Having him hammering rough iron with a pounding hammer instead of carefully sawing and soldering brass was on the paper. Markus didn't get it at first, and Tenobius had to go over it more than once.

Why would anyone want to do this? Because it would protect the hooves from wear and tear.

Have you seen anything like this? Yes. They did it in his country all the time.

Doesn't it hurt the horse? Not if you do it right. The nails that hold the shoe on aren't long enough to reach the 'quick', the living flesh under the hoof.

If it's such a good idea, why wasn't somebody doing it already? Probably nobody thought of it here before.

Who would *want* to have this done? Why would they pay money for it? Anyone who used their horses a lot. The army might want it to protect the horses' feet during long marches. If they could interest the army, it would be a contract bigger than the one for the *pilums*.

Marcus scratched the short hair on top of his head while he tried to decide. "All right," he said, finally. "Make your set of shoes. Then see if you can get a horse to stand still while you hammer nails into its hoof. If you can do that, then we'll see."

Encouraged, Tenobius started on the second shoe. He went at it with gusto, even though I could see he was tiring. Tenobius had put on muscle since he started at the forge, but he still wasn't up to what Marcus could do, or even Metellus or Arnicus, the apprentices. Once he got started, as I say, his mind drove him on.

It took him a while to get the second one made to the same size as the first. He had to unbend and rebend it twice until he was happy with it. He did the third and fourth mechanically, hammering in a daze and getting it done, it seemed, without thinking about it.

Finally, he was finished with the set of shoes. He looked at the forge, thinking he had to make three more sets of nails, but knowing he wasn't up to it.

"I'll finish tomorrow," he said, before going his sleeping space and collapsing onto the bed.

The next day Tenobius couldn't even get up. His arms were so sore he couldn't raise them. Metellus and Arnicus picked up his horse shoes and brought them over, asking Tenobius about them. They were not convinced, but interested. Metellus rubbed Tenobius' arm briskly. He cried out, but didn't complain.

How were these supposed to be put on? Tenobius explained how the hoof had to be prepared, cleaned and filed, then the shoe was fitted to the hoof, and reworked, if necessary. Finally, it had to be nailed in so the heads of the nails were below the level of the shoe, fitting completely within the countersinks.

Arnicus asked how you got the horse to stand still for all this. As far as he knew, horses were skittish animals, but strong ones. They wouldn't stand still for harsh treatment. He knew of one horse that knocked a soldier's brains out with a kick. In his opinion, the easiest way to make sure you could get the shoes on would be if the horse were dead.

Tenobius said horse owners had to clean out their hooves, in any case. A properly trained horse would be used to a person lifting its hoof and doing things to it. They needed to find a good subject. A well-trained and tolerant horse. Both Arnicus and Metellus told Tenobius he was welcome to try, then walked away.

~ * ~

"Is that really true?" I asked, after they left.

"What? That horses will kick? Will they tolerate handling? Both of those are true. It's also true that if you handle a horse carelessly, you'll be in big trouble."

"So, how many times have you done this before?"

"Never."

"Not even once?"

"Nope."

"You might not want to tell them that."

"Can you do this for me, Argus?" Tenobius suddenly asked. "Find me a docile horse and an owner that we can use for a test. We'll tell him there's no charge for the shoes, and they'll protect the horse's hooves. If we have to, we'll pay him for the privilege. Don't tell him that, except as a last resort."

"I'll see what I can find. What are you going to do?"

"Well, I *was* going to try some lighter hammer work on some gold, but I don't think I can even raise a light hammer right now."

"I'll tell Lillia you're lying here and can't move."

"NO!" he shouted.

I was already running for the Little Forum to find a horse owner.

I didn't find a horse owner who was interested in something new-fangled for his horse's hooves, and Tenobius still wasn't feeling up to heavy smithing the next day.

"This should be a lesson for me," he said. "I have to learn to take it easy." He rubbed his upper right arm.

"You won't, though," I said. "The next time you get excited you'll just go running off and plunging in."

"Well, if I do, you have to stop me. Whisper *Norbury* in my ear."

"Why? What does *that* mean?"

"Sorry. It's a joke. Just remind me of how my arms hurt. I'm going to try something less strenuous."

I watched him, wondering what he would try this time. He got out one of the brass hammers, some metal shears, and the squares of soft leather I'd wrangled from Tullius' dad. He went to his box of things and pulled out some things wrapped in *paper*. They looked like small irregularly-shaped flat pieces of metal. Tenobius noticed my interest.

"These are gold plates, Argus. It's leftover from some of our jewelry jobs. I bought them from Marcus at a discount, so it's not as if I'm stealing it. I cast them and rolled them flat like this, but the edges are all crazy."

"What are you going to do with them?"

"I'm going to cut the edges into round curves, then I'm going to polish them to get rid of the dirt and stuff. After that, we'll see."

"What's the hammer for?"

"Your head, if you keep asking questions."

"You wouldn't do that. I don't think you can even lift the hammer right now."

"You're right about that. Since you're my apprentice, I'll have to tell you to hit yourself."

He stopped taking, took some of the shears, and cut around the edges of the plates. He filed the edges smooth with the finest file we had, then pulled out a piece of shark skin he kept for very fine sanding and smoothed it off more completely.

He got me to fill one of the little water pots for him, then got some of his scrap cloth and a container of rouge. He mixed up a paste and used it to polish the face of the gold plate, working in circles at first, then varying his stroke in different ways. He explained that he was trying to *randomize* the polishing, so it went equally in all directions. That way, the streaks were all evened out.

It looked like something that would take a long time, and I wasn't doing anything. I asked him if he wanted me to do one of the other plates, but he said he'd rather do it himself. He told me that there wasn't anything he needed me for, so I could take off.

~ * ~

When I returned, he was still polishing, but the plates looked different. Instead of being brownish-yellow, like old brass, they were now ovals of shining gold, and their surfaces were smooth, like mirrors.

"I can see myself in them," I said.

"Yes," he said. "Gold makes the best mirrors, in some ways. Once you polish it, it won't rust or tarnish. If you don't ruin the surface, it will stay looking good forever. The only problem is that everything looks yellow."

"Maybe we could sell these as mirrors," I suggested.

"Oh, no, a piece big enough to make a good mirror would be too expensive. Even if people could afford it, they'd be worried about somebody stealing it. There are cheaper ways to make permanent mirrors, Argus."

"How?"

"Well, you could coat the back of a piece of glass with silver. The part against the glass wouldn't tarnish. It would be a whole project to make big, flat sheets of glass without bubbles or dirt in it. Another to remember how to make the silver flow onto the back of it. Then I'd have to convince people to buy my mirrors, when they could just use the bronze mirrors they sell in the Little Forum for a handful of money. As long as they keep it polished, it will work fine. No, thanks. My horseshoe project is already threatening to eat up all my time."

"So, what did you make these for?"

"You'll see. Watch."

"What? What are you doing?"

"I'm putting the plates down on a big piece of *paper* and tracing the outlines."

"For what?"

"Comparison. Now I put that sheet away, and take out another. I cut four pieces and put a plate of gold between two of them, like the layers in what they call a 'placenta' cake. I do the same with another plate and two sheets of *paper*. Now I make my 'placenta' stack. I put down a soft leather square, I place the gold plate between paper, add another leather square, and the other gold plate between paper. Finally, just a gold plate, a piece of leather, my last plate, and a piece of leather on top."

It made a pretty tall stack. Tenobius worked the edges until it was all nice and even, the gold plates centered in the structure.

As he was doing this, and re-arranging the pile until he was satisfied, Lillia came over. She was carrying a gray kitten in her arms. Tenobius didn't notice until I went over to see. The kitten looked up at me and made a tiny "mew" sound. Tenobius noticed then.

"You see, I said I would do so," said Lillia. "The cat of a lady I know had babies, so I asked for one."

I hadn't actually seen a kitten up close, so I reached out. It swung at my finger with its tiny paws and started to bite, but not hard.

"That's kind of you," said Tenobius. "Even though I didn't ask for a cat."

"No, but you need one. Perhaps a ferret, or some people keep a snake."

"A snake?" I asked. "What for?"

"To eat the mice," she said. "But snakes aren't loyal. They might leave, and ferrets stink. Cats are clean, and friendly, if you're friendly to them."

"Cats don't like me," said Tenobius.

"No?" said Lillia. "Let's see if this one likes you."

She brought it over to Tenobius. He moved between it and his stack of leather and gold. Afraid, I guess, that the kitten would knock it down. He held up a hand to block it, which the kitten sniffed.

"Well, if you don't want it, I will keep it at our house. It can hunt for mice in your yard. I will call him Nexmuris."

"That would be fine," said Tenobius, and turned back to his work.

"What is that?" asked Lillia, noticing the pile for the first time.

"It's a pile of leather squares," said Tenobius, then brought down his light hammer on the center of the stack. He rotated it a quarter turn, and struck it again, then repeated the action.

"I like that you are insane," said Lillia. "You boil sawdust and you hammer leather. Is this going to make something new, like your *paper*?"

"With luck, yes," said Tenobius.

He went on, turning and hammering.

"When you finish, I will make you some Insane Man food."

~ * ~

He was at it a long time. I could tell he wanted to stop and look at it, several times. Instead, he kept talking himself out of it. Finally, he stopped.

"My arm is killing me," he said. "It's still too soon after I hammered the horse shoes. Let's see what we've got."

I came over to have a look as he slowly and carefully undid the stack of leather squares. I would've just taken it apart and looked right at the sheets, but he took the tower down one layer at a time. After he peeled off the first layer of leather, he used a little spatula of wood to slip under the gold and ran it from side to side before using it to lift the gold. He put it carefully down on the sheet of *paper* that he'd traced around the outside. It was now much bigger than it had been. I could see that right off, without Tenobius pointing it out to me.

"Is that why you did it, to make it bigger?"

"Yes and no. I did it to make it thinner. It was too thick before. I wanted it more uniform than normal hammering or rolling would make it. I also wanted it to be bigger. This way I get both things. There are very talented gold workers who can use this method to make the gold so thin that a breath of air will make it float away. They can make a little cube of gold into such a thin sheet that they could cover an entire statue with it. They have to handle the gold very carefully when it gets that thin with special tools, and put it in place with soft rushes. I'm not that skilled. I don't need it that thin, either."

He carefully removed the next layer of leather, slowly peeling it off the underlying leather and the gold sheet between them. The gold stuck to the leather in one spot, though, and the sheet tore as he lifted the leather away.

"That's not good," he said in a flat voice, but I could tell he was disappointed. "I'll have to clean the leather better, next time." This sheet is bigger after being pounded, too, as I could see when he laid the two torn pieces together on the *paper*.

After he removed the next piece of leather, I could see the two pieces of *paper* with the gold sheet between. The *paper* didn't stick to the leather, so he was able to remove the sheets cleanly, but he had to separate the gold from the *paper*. He tried to do this by bending the *paper* nearly double and slowly peeling it from the gold, but it didn't want to come easily. By pulling slowly and evenly he was eventually able to get the two apart.

He looked carefully at the surface of the gold. Unlike the gold that was between leather alone, this had a pattern on it, and I realized it was the pattern of the surface of the *paper* itself. Tenobius ran his fingernail across the surface, feeling the bumps.

"This might have worked better," he said, "If my *paper* was flatter. As it is, I'm not sure I can get this gold off the *paper*."

He used his spatula to try to separate them. Unlike before, he couldn't hold onto the gold and peel it, it was too thin, and would tear. He used he spatula to push up some of the gold into a thick crumple, then grabbed that with a pair of tongs and carefully peeled. The gold came off, but immediately curled up into a tube. He put it on the *paper* with the tracings. The last sheet, also between two pieces of *paper*, had to be treated the same way.

"Well," he said. "I won't be trying it *that* way again. I think I have enough here to work with."

"What are you going to do with it?" I asked.

"Nothing, right now. I want to rest before I try anything else, but you'll see, Argus."

"You'll see.' 'You'll see'. You always say 'You'll see'," I complained. "Why don't you just tell me what you're going to do?"

Tenobius had to think that over.

"Did you ever see a magician? A conjuror?"

"Yeah, lots of times. There's a man in the Little Forum who makes eggs disappear, and colored cloth appear."

"Does he tell you what he's going to do?"

"Well, no. He doesn't speak at all."

"It doesn't matter. Even if he spoke, he probably wouldn't tell you."

"Why not?"

"Lots of reasons. That way he can misdirect you, so you don't see how the trick is done. But it also means you don't know when he's failed."

"So...what? You don't want me to see how you do things?"

"Oh, no. I definitely want you to see that. I just don't want you to notice when I fail."

Tenobius left after that. When I asked where he was going, he said to see Lillia. He wanted to find out what her idea of 'Insane Man Food' was.

~ * ~

The next day Tenobius was starting to get back to using the regular smithing tools, making up nails for the shoes, when Marcus came in, bringing an old man with him. His name was Fulvius, and he had a horse he was willing to have the shoes put on. Furthermore, he had his horse as well trained as a dog, so it would probably let Tenobius put the shoes on without killing him.

Tenobius was ecstatic. He wanted to see the horse at once. That was no problem. It was waiting in the street outside.

Fulvius' horse looked about as old as Fulvius himself. I could see why he didn't bother to tie the horse up. Who would want it? It looked dazed and lost, with glazed-over eyes. When Fulvius whistled in a strange way, making a sound I'd never heard before, the horse was instantly alert. The glaze was gone from its eyes, and it looked over at Fulvius. He whistled again, differently, and the horse trotted over. He touched it, and it turned around, giving us all a look at its body. The horse was old, but in good condition. At least, I thought so. But I don't know anything about horses. It was clearly healthy.

Fulvius had the horse face away from us all, and he got behind it and lifted its left rear foot, holding it between his knees as he crouched.

"This is how I clean out the hoof," he explained, showing how he could work his fingers into the hollow space inside the hoof, and the bottom of the hoof itself.

I could see the hoof was worn. It didn't look right. "Imperator is getting old, and his feet are getting worn, you see. Marcus tells me that you have some device you can put on the bottom that will protect it."

Tenobius ran inside and returned with two of the shoes and a handful of nails. He handed one to Fulvius, who looked at it as if he'd seen it before. He instantly knew what to do with it. He placed it over the hoof to see how it fit.

"This is good," he said. "I thought you might have the kind of hoof-wrapping I've seen on some horses. I don't like them. Water gets trapped in there and the hoof rots. These just go on the bottom and lie between the hoof and the road, and it will drain. How do you hold it on?"

Tenobius showed him the nails and demonstrated that they were shorter than the hoof itself. Fulvius was skeptical.

"You can still prick the quick of his foot. It doesn't end where the edge of the hoof sits. Do you know horses, boy?"

Tenobius had to admit he did not. He'd seen these shoes made and used, but he was not a horseman himself.

"I've grown up with horses. I've slept with them. They're people to me. I won't let anyone hurt them, whether they intend to or not. I don't want Imperator hurt through a novice's clumsiness, you understand?"

He looked hard at Tenobius for a long time, eye to eye. Finally, he looked at Marcus the same way.

"Imperator is getting along now in years, and if this keeps up, he won't be able to walk soon. I thought I would have to give him the Last Drink, you know? I'd never let the leather butchers cut his throat. If these can help him walk a few years longer, it will be worth it. You'll put them on under my care, no matter what you think you know. Is that clear?"

Tenobius indicated that it was.

"Very well. You'll have to shape these better, so they fit around the edge exactly."

So Fulvius and Tenobius went to work adjusting the shoes. Tenobius told Fulvius they could mark each shoe and the corresponding hoof with a dot of color to keep them straight, but that just made Fulvius angrily ask if he didn't know enough to tell four of his own horse shoes apart.

It took them hours to get all four shoes adjusted to Fulvius' satisfaction. Early on, Tenobius told him they'd have to file Imperator's hooves flat before adjusting the shoes, but Fulvius took the suggestion as an insult. He got a flat board and placed it against the hoof, demonstrating he kept the hoof in perfect shape every day.

A few times I thought Tenobius and Fulvius were going to start fighting. I didn't want to see that, but part of me did. Fulvius was old but wiry and unbending, while Tenobius had that strange way of fighting. It would have been interesting to see what would happen. Except that if they fought, it would have ended everything, and neither of them would have been happy. They always stopped before it got too hot.

When they did get them finished, they decided it was too late in the day to try attaching them, so Fulvius agreed to come back the next day. He insisted that Tenobius check the lengths of each nail, and make certain they were sharp and straight. He whistled for his horse, who popped his head up in attention, then placed his hand on the mane as they walked away.

I had never seen anything like that in all the years that my father's companions brought their horses around the house. They all seemed exhausted beasts, foaming at the mouth and being ill-tempered. If I tried bending their leg up between my knees the way Fulvius did, they'd have kicked me into the ground.

I found Tenobius in the back, setting up four individual trays, each with one horseshoe in it and the six nails needed, which he had already checked for length. He showed me a secret mark he put on each tray showing which hoof it was for. If it had been me, I'd simply have put all four shoes on the bench and all the nails in a heap, but Tenobius always took too much care organizing things. He grabbed a quick meal he'd had warming in a pot near the forge, and offered me some.

After all that, you'd think that he would be finished for the day, but he put on a pot for the leather bits and began boiling more fragments to make his *island* stuff.

"Why?" I asked him. "Can't you simply take a rest?"

"There's too much to do, Argus," he said. "Every hour that I delay, I can feel it. It's another hour I could have been working on it."

~ * ~

Fulvius returned the next day with Imperator, and it was a Big Event. Marcus was there, along with the apprentices Arnicus and Metellus, and Tenobius and me. Corticus was there part of the time, and we attracted the attention of many passers-by, who wanted to know what we were doing to the old horse.

It took some time to work up to the putting on of the shoes. First Fulvius wanted to look over everything again. He again suggested that Tenobius must have trouble keeping his own work straight, because he so carefully put everything in its own tray, but I think he was really impressed. He carefully put everything back in its own trays, anyway. He inspected the nails and the hammer.

He lectured us all about the parts of a horse's leg, and especially the hoof. I have to admit, I always thought the hoof was just a single piece of stuff, like one of the ingots of metal Marcus had in his shop. Instead I learned it's made up of parts. Fulvius had a name for every part, and he showed us what to look for, and how to tell a healthy hoof from a rotting or diseased one. He showed how Tenobius' shoe fit exactly over the rim of the hoof, and how the nails would go in. You'd think that he came up with the idea, and not Tenobius.

Finally, we got ready to put the first one on. Fulvius faced away, looking along the direction of the horse's body, but facing rearward. He spoke softly to Imperator, and took up the hoof between his knees. He gave the hoof a cleaning with a brush he brought, and went over it with a file. He held out his hand for the shoe, and Tenobius pressed it into his hand. He moved it around until it satisfied him, then held out his hand again for the nails. He kept most of them in the curl of his hand, but carefully positioned the sharpened end of one in the groove in the shoe. Ready to begin, he tentatively hammered it in place enough so that it stuck.

I was waiting for Imperator to react, maybe throw Fulvius, or even kick him. Instead he did nothing. Fulvius hammered another nail partway in. When he had the shoe suspended by the two, he hammered them down more completely and more forcefully, still with no reaction from Imperator. After that, the rest of the nails went in easily. We all examined the hoof with its new shoe as closely as we dared. It looked as if Imperator had been born with it there, it fit so well.

Fulvius slowly let it down to the ground, rather than simply letting it drop. Imperator let it gingerly touch the ground, then raised it, let it slowly down, then raised it again, as if not willing to put his weight on it. He put it down and dragged it, as if trying to wipe the unfamiliar weight from his foot. Fulvius went to reassure him, and he slowly stopped.

We repeated the procedure for all four feet. Imperator went through the same passive allowing of the shoeing, followed by trying to scrape it off, before giving in and accepting it. With all four in place he stood, occasionally lifting one foot and placing it back down. Fulvius led him out to the street, and as soon as he got to where there were paving stones his newly-shod hooves made a strange and unexpected noise—a CLOP! CLOP—as the metal things struck the stone. Imperator seemed a little startled at first, but so did everyone else who turned to see what was making the noise in the street. Most of them couldn't figure it out. Fulvius led Imperator home, to get used to the new shoes. He said he'd be back the next day.

I couldn't just let Fulvius and his horse go, so I followed them, not letting myself be seen. Everywhere he went, people turned to see where that strange sound was coming from. Fulvius didn't take pay it any mind.

When I got back to the shop, I found Tenobius explaining to Marcus, Arminius, and Metellus how to rough out the shape of the shoe. Actually, it was mostly to the apprentices, because Marcus picked it up pretty quickly. Marcus liked the idea of Tenobius drawing things on paper, and he'd already tacked up Tenobius' full-size drawing of the shoe on the wall so they could see what was to be made. Tenobius was now trying to draw a set of pictures that showed how to make the things, step by step. There was no point in trying to write it out, neither of them could read even at my level, but they could understand pictures. Tenobius was going over the steps with them more than once. Finally, he seemed satisfied, and his pictures went up on the wall, too, next to the image of the shoe.

I told him what I saw as Fluvius went back home, and Tenobius smiled at that. He was happy. I guess he was relieved it was over, and went well. He went back to the place he usually slept in the back of the shop, and was asleep in no time at all.

It didn't last.

~ * ~

Fulvius was back, early the next morning, and brought Imperator with him. Even if you didn't know horses, you could see that something was wrong. Imperator had a limp. Something had gone wrong with one of the shoes.

Fulvius could tell exactly which shoe. Marcus, Tenobius, and I gathered around while he showed how Imperator was favoring the one foot. The shoe would have to come off.

Tenobius said that he designed the shoe so you could take it off. Horse shoes, he said, were supposed to be changed every so often. The idea was to grab the head of the nail with narrow pliers and pull it out, but it wasn't working. Imperator's clopping walk had driven the nail home hard. Markus and Tenobius eventually slipped something under the shoe itself to pry it up, and after that they could pull the nails.

There wasn't anything obviously wrong, no blood or anything. They wanted to know which nail or nails had gone in wrong or too deep. It was Tenobius who hit on the idea of inserting a fine bristle into the nail holes. When he did this, you could see that one had gone in toward the center. They decided to just leave out that nail, since another one, inserted at the same place, would be guided by the hole in the same direction. Tenobius suggested giving the nails a slight curve to carry them away from the center of the hoof for future shoes. For the present, they'd simply put this one back on without the bad nail. Fulvius insisted on putting down some ointment he used on his horse's hooves before Imperator was re-shod.

~ * ~

"We have been lucky, Argus," Tenobius told me later, over some food at the tavern. "There are so many things that could have gone wrong. We were lucky many times over. Lucky to find an expert like Fulvius. Lucky to find as tame a horse as that. Lucky that my shoes worked, and that nothing worse happened. Lucky that we caught this so fast."

"Is Imperator going to be all right? Will he get better.?"

"I think so. I hope so. What we need to do now is to find some army commander who we can interest in this. Once the army starts to buy these, we'll be set. I'm not sure how to do that. Maybe Fulvius knows some people."

He took a drink. Tenobius now drank confidently out of his terra cotta bowl, unlike when I first brought him here.

"It's something very different I'm doing here. There was already a market for wire in the jewelry trade. I'm not trying to sell my 'islanded' wire to anyone else, or my *paper*. We want people to buy our horseshoes, but they're something new and strange. I have to become a Seller, and I don't know if I can do that well. I have to sell horse shoes, and I have to sell putting the horse shoes on. I have to sell Marcus the idea that I should get half the money from this. That's a lot to do. It's not like coming up with a way to make wire, or figuring out how to make *paper*, or coat wire. Those are all *technical* problems." He used another barbarian word, then decided to try to explain it. "They're problems where you have to figure out how to make things, or put things together. I can do that by myself, thinking about it, or trying different things. This is different. I have to figure out how to work with people. People are unpredictable and complicated. I'd rather deal with things."

"So why don't you?"

"Because, at some point, you have to deal with people. I need the money, and this is the way to get that. I can't do it just by making things. If you want money, you have to sell it to people. It's a little like the story of Aladdin."

"Who's Aladdin?" I asked.

"I'll tell you about him and his story someday. Not now. It would take too long, and you'd have too many questions."

~ * ~

We were in the back behind the forge, and Tenobius had set up a pot on the fire to make up his *island* stuff. He gathered together the strangest collection of things, and was putting them in order. I was sitting at the bench with a sheet of his *paper*, copying out a lesson. He said I needed more practice with pen and ink and writing. This way I would be close by if he needed help.

I would write a bit, but pretty soon my hand would cramp up. Tenobius told me I was gripping the pen too hard. It wasn't a snake that would bite if I relaxed. Besides, he said, with practice I wouldn't cramp so much. Maybe. For now I couldn't stop thinking of my pen as some kind of thin snake.

It was more interesting to watch Tenobius, because he was doing something definite and precise, except I had no idea what it was, like a lot of the things he did. I used to think it meant he was crazy. He might still be, but too many of his things turned out to make sense. So, I just watched and tried to figure out what he was up to.

He'd spread out a piece of *paper*, selected one of his sheets of gold and set it down on the sheet. He took out one of our best knives, the kind that was ground to a sharp razor edge, and used a heavy leather belt to strop it sharper still. He placed a straightedge over the gold sheet, with a uniform width of gold sticking out. He used the metal straightedge as a guide to use the razor to cut off the gold strip. The metal was so thin he could do it with the razor edge alone. He repeated this three more times, until he had four thin strips of gold sheet, all pretty much the same width. I was so interested in watching that I didn't notice I'd started writing in a curve on the page. Tenobius noticed, and had me fix it.

"What are you going to do with those?" I asked.

"You'll see," he said, as he always did.

He took two of the strips and placed them one atop the other. He folded over a little piece of the strips, before folding it over again, pressed it flat, and opened it out. He now had a strip about twice as long as either of the strips. He repeated it with the other two, making another doubled strip.

He took one of the strips and laid it out in front of him, then folded a larger part of it down toward himself at one end, so it made a very wide, squared off 'L'. He flattened the folds so it looked as neat as a soldier's kit when he knows the sergeant is looking. He did the same with the other doubled strip, and placed it so the downward, facing end was at the other side.

"I see what you're doing," I told him. "You're folding the gold the same way you folded the paper. Are you going to make a gold *balloon*?"

Tenobius laughed.

"It's not a square sheet of gold. If I DID make a gold balloon, I think it would be too stiff to open. Who'd want to pay for one, anyway? This is much more practical."

He used his razor to cut pieces of paper a little longer than the gold strips, but these were longer from the start. He didn't have to fold two of them together. He looked at me watching him, and guessed what I was thinking.

"I had to put two pieces of the gold foil together because one of them isn't long enough. It's easy to make the paper long enough. Now look. I put down a strip of paper, a piece of gold strip with the fold at the right end, another strip of paper, and a piece of gold strip with the fold at the left end. Then I cover it with another strip of paper."

"And then...?" I prompted.

"I fold the whole thing over like this, being careful to keep it all together. I fold it over again, and again, and again, over and over. I roll it up flat like one of Mama Nux's honey-seed rolls until it's all rolled up and as wide as the first fold I made, and I make sure the gold strips at each end aren't touching. Then I glue it in place with a dot of hide glue and let it set. We're not finished with it yet."

Tenobius went on to do the same thing all over again, making another Mama Nux gold-and-paper roll. Once he was finished, he did it again. He made ten of them this way, some of them longer and some shorter. When they had set, he hung them up on a metal rod by the gold ends using some kind of clips he'd made out of wire.

"Now for something completely different," he announced.

He cut more strips of gold foil, but didn't put them together by twos this time. He cut paper into strips, but wider ones. He got out a small pot and showed me what was in it, cylindrical beads of the kind he used in restoring and making jewelry. He took one of the pieces of paper, and I saw that the strip was as wide as the bead was. He started rolling the paper tightly around the beads. He stopped, tore a little tear in each side, and folded the paper inwards toward the center on each side. He took a gold strip and wrapped it around the bead at the end, where the paper had been torn away, then took another piece and did the same on the other side. He then rolled the rest of the paper around the bead until it was tightly wound, and secured it with glue.

He made up another, exactly the same way. He made a dozen of these, some of different lengths, or with different lengths of paper wound around them. After these had set, he hung them, too, from a metal rod with his clips. That was when he did something strange.

He got an oil lamp and lit it at the forge. He carried it over and held it under the center of one of his rolled-up beads, with the tip of the flame touching the paper. I thought the paper would catch easily, the way I'd seen paper catch fire and burn when Tenobius put small pieces in the flame before. The tightly-wound paper didn't catch fire so easily. It turned brown and smoked, bfore it turned black, but it didn't burst into flame. He moved the flame back and forth until he had burnt all of the paper on the bead. He did the same for every one of the beads.

"So, you make them, then you destroy them?" I asked.

"I guess it looks that way. It's what's called a controlled burning. If I do this right, I'll have what I want."

"What's that? Never mind, I know, 'you'll see'. Why can't you explain it?"

"Now that," Tenobius said, concentrating on burning the last bit on the last bead "is a good question. There was a very wise man, among my people, who once claimed that if you can't explain something to a smart, clever audience, you don't really understand it yourself."

"So," I said, "explain it, or don't you think I'm Smart and Clever?"

"Oh, you're smart enough, and clever enough. There's one thing this wise man left out of what he said. It might take a very, very long time to explain. I think that by the time I finish, we both might be dead."

"Oh, that's ridiculous," I said. "Somebody explained it to *you*, and you're not dead."

"That's a good point. My point is that before I can explain part of this, I have to explain another part of it. Before I can explain that part, I'd have to explain something else. It's a long chain of suppositions and ideas I grew up constantly hearing and learning about, but you haven't. Like those letters you stopped writing."

"I think you're just being lazy," I said.

Tenobius stopped and sighed. I hadn't really meant it, Tenobius is the least lazy person I've ever seen. It was just a jab. Of course, he took it seriously, and thought about it.

"I suppose I *could* set up a training program, if we really had to teach you the basics. It would be a huge project. Bigger than the wire puller. Bigger than making the *island* stuff. Bigger than the horseshoe project has been, and will end up being. It would be an enormous investment in time and energy, and I just can't afford it now. I hope you forgive me."

"I forgive you. If it's that long a project, I don't think I'd want to spend that much time studying it. These letters are enough."

"Good," Tenobius said, sounding relieved. "Don't ever think I don't consider you as Smart and Clever."

With that he started yet another project. He got out a cylindrical bead and a piece of wire covered with *island*, and carefully wrapped the wire tight and close around the cylindrical bead. He attached it by the ends of the wire to a third metal rod with clips.

"Are you going to burn that, too? I don't think the metal will burn, but your *island* may."

"No," he replied. "These are easier to make." He started wrapping wire around another bead. He made about a dozen of these, too, all attached to the rod.

He went over to the pot on the fire and mixed in the honey, the mouse powder, and some other stuff, and stirred it until it was blended, then let it cook until finished. It was a little thinner than the *island* he used for coating his wire.

He then took the metal rod with the gold-and-paper honeyseed rolls and brought it over. I hadn't noticed, but he carefully spaced them so he could dip them, one at a time, into the pot. He did so, using a small stylus to make sure the things he made got submerged in the *island*, instead of floating on top. When all of the rolls had been dipped, he hung the rod up to let them dry.

He repeated this with the burned paper on the beads. In one case, all the ashes that remained broke off and floated on the top. He carefully scraped this layer away. The other burned paper stayed on the beads. Finally, he dipped in the wire-wound beads, which gave him no problems, and he set these aside to set as well.

I hadn't the slightest idea what these were supposed to be, but Tenobius was clearly happy with them. He was smiling as he inspected them, making sure they were completely coated, and that nothing was coming loose. This was obviously some very touchy and precise thing he did, but it was as lost on me as reading used to be before I started practicing.

~ * ~

The next day, after Tenobius stored his newly-made things in different boxes, it was back to horse shoes. We had built up a stock of them by now, and Tenobius was talking to Marcus about something new, shoes for oxen. Marcus was interested, especially when Tenobius pointed out how many more oxen there were than horses, but Marcus dug in his feet like a mule, come to think of it, I'd bet we could sell shoes for mules. There were more of them than of horses in Rome, too. He wouldn't make a single shoe more until we could sell what we had.

Tenobius went out into the city, and I went with him.

"I was afraid this would happen," he told me. "I thought it would take longer. We have to pull in business on our own. I was hoping Fulvius would be our advertisement. I thought people would see what he had and ask for the same thing, or that he'd talk them into it. That hasn't happened."

We went around to see Fulvius, and I petted Imperator on the neck. The horse was still using its new shoes, which hadn't worn much, and he wasn't limping any more. We learned when Tenobius asked him questions, he wasn't doing much to tell other people about the shoes, either. When people asked about them, he just sort of shrugged. Tenobius said he was doing the opposite of what he should. He tried to convince Fulvius to brag about how good the shoes were, to take every opportunity to talk about them and show them off, but it didn't seem to be his way.

On the way back to the forge, Tenobius stopped to look at a wall covered with graffiti.

"Look at that," he said. "You can't tell where one thing stops and another begins."

It was true. The wall was covered with a jumble of writing, in all sizes. You couldn't clearly make out anything unless you looked at it a long time. Before Tenobius started teaching me to read, I never even tried. Now I could make out a word here and there, but it was still mostly a collection of letters. I told Tenobius this.

"I have almost the same problem. Part of the reason is that there are a lot of abbreviations, and it's not clear what they're for. See, here it says *acc*, but you can't tell if that's supposed to be *accedo* or *accipio* or whatever. Over here it starts a word, but it finishes up over here, after all these things written the other way. I think these things are all up there for the sake of the writers. Most of them are too hard to figure out…Say, what would happen if we were to paint over a piece of the wall and put up something about our horseshoes? Would anyone object?"

"I don't know. I've never heard of anything like that."

"Really? Back where I come from a lot of people are very protective about their graffiti. If you wrote over their things they got offended."

"Well, I've never heard of anything like that. How would you paint over it? Won't it show though? When we whitewashed the walls of our apartment all the black lines still showed."

"There are different kinds of paint. You know how paint works? There are basically three parts…"

"Tenobius, I'm sure that you know all about paint. I really don't want to hear it."

"Really?"

"Really. I don't want to make you feel bad…"

"Oh, no, no. Don't worry about that."

"…but sometimes I just don't *care* about how to make something.

Other people aren't as interested as you."

"Oh."

"In fact, I think you might not want to explain so many things to Lillia. She'd rather talk about other things."

"I see. Well, it's just as well. The recipe I know for making covering paint involves sour milk, and it smells awful."

"I wouldn't put up graffiti about your horseshoes with smelly paint. It would drive people away."

"I suppose so. Still, I might put up a picture here, with an arrow pointing to Marcus' shop. If I can find a paint that doesn't stink."

After we walked further, Tenobius turned to me.

"Argus, I wonder if I can ask a favor of you."

"What?"

"Your father, he's a soldier, right?"

"You know he is."

"Where is he now?"

"I don't know. He's not in Rome, and that's what's important."

"He's with the army somewhere?"

"Yeah."

"Do you know any of his friends in the army, or his commanders? Can you visit where they house the soldiers? What about your brothers?"

"I've stayed away from all that. My brothers used to beat me up, you know. I don't think I could get into the barracks without official business. Why?"

"The horseshoes. If we can sell them to the Army we'll be in business. All we'd have to do is convince a few key men. As I said, I'd hoped Fulvius would do that, but he hasn't. Nobody in the Army is going to talk to me, not without an introduction. You probably know some people there. Still, if this is a bad idea, I apologize, and I withdraw it. I'll have to find some other way in."

"There might be some people. I was friends with some of them, as a kid. At least, they weren't mean to me. Let me talk with them."

~ * ~

I wouldn't be able to get into the barracks area unless I was delivering something. Besides, I didn't know anyone in there. My best bet was to locate one of my father's old comrades. Somebody who was invalided out, maybe, but who? I decided to try asking my mother.

I found her at home, sewing and letting the wash soak. She was suspicious at first, and asked what I wanted. When I told her, I was looking for some of Dad's old army buddies, she told me to stay away from them, afraid I'd enlist or something. She'd never worried about that with my brothers. I think she was afraid I was too delicate for the army. It's a little insulting, when you think about it. She wasn't thinking about it, this was her heart talking, so I ignored it.

I finally convinced her I was only trying to get a favor from one of them. She still didn't think that was a good idea, but eventually I wore her down, and she started going through names. So and so was discharged, but he had gone out to Greece. Another was in Rome, but they let him go because he wasn't right in the head, so he was no use. Another was dead.

There was only Mopsus. He was retired because of his leg. He walked with a stiff leg that wouldn't bend properly. He'd been a sergeant, and now ran a company of laborers the way he'd run his company. He was a tough old bird, but he might talk to me. She told me where to find him, then told me I shouldn't try. Even though she was afraid at first that I'd ask for something, she ended up giving me a handful of coins I hadn't asked for.

Mopsus worked out of a stall not far from the Big Forum. He wasn't there when I found it, so I waited. I had no idea when he'd be back, so I sat on a box in the pretty empty stall, pulled out some of the papers with my writing exercises on them, and looked them over while I waited. I drew pictures on the back with my stylus, even though Tenobius said I shouldn't, because the paper was scarce and he said he couldn't remove the marks. But it passed the time.

Mopsus came rapidly into the shop, barely hindered by his stiff leg, which he pivoted around in a great arc with each step. He was followed by two of his laborers, who had to run to keep up. He went directly to a shelf and got something, which he gave to one of the sweating men, and said something I couldn't catch about going somewhere and doing something.

The two men started walking off, but Mopsus shouted after them to get moving, and they switched to a brisk jog until they were out of sight.

Only then did he seem to notice me. He pulled a thing like a stick made of knotted rope from his belt and struck me across the back with it, but not too hard.

"Out! This isn't a schoolroom."

I think if he hadn't seen me reading, I might have been hit harder.

"Are you Mopsus Carolus, the sergeant of Eagle company?"

He stopped, surprised.

"I was. Do you have a message for me? I'm not going to pay you for it."

"My father served with you. My name is Argus."

"Argus?" He tried to recall if he'd heard the name. "Ah, wait. You're Dogface's brat, aren't you? Who taught you to read?"

"I'm apprenticed at the Forge of Marcus in the Little Forum."

"Are you, now? Do they teach apprentices to read and write while they're stoking the furnace?"

"My master does."

"Well, he's a strange one, then. Do you take orders for him, or something?"

"No. Not yet."

"You're still learning, then. Show me. Read what's there." He indicated the paper I had.

I read, haltingly. This felt like a test. He looked over my shoulder at the words. As I finished, he plucked the paper from my hand and looked at it, turning it over to see the back.

"What's this?"

"Drawings."

"What of?"

"Just drawings."

"Uh huh. Strange papyrus. Don't let him know you're wasting it on drawings. Why did you come to see me? Is Dogface in trouble?"

I tried to explain what I wanted, but it took a long time. He simply couldn't believe I wasn't after money, or a handout. The idea of the horse shoe was so weird that he couldn't understand it at first, either. I had to draw it out on the back of the paper, and it took me several tries until I was able to make him understand what it was. When Tenobius drew something, it always seemed to look like what he was talking about, but my drawings weren't so clear. Something else I'd have to learn from him.

I was lucky Mopsus didn't just get annoyed and drive me out with his baton. I think he was interested, too. Once he got the idea of what the shoe was, he realized I was trying to get an army officer interested in it, and he actually thought about who I could talk to.

"You can't just dance into the base office and ask for the quartermaster, you know," he said.

"I know that."

"You also can't do what you just did with me. Quartermaster's a busy man, and he won't have time for what some kid is trying to tell him. He'd even throw out your Marcus if he came to try and sell these shoes for horses."

"I know that, too."

"Well, you're stuck then, aren't you?"

"There must be some way to show new ideas to the Army."

"Why? The Army doesn't want new ideas. They know how they do things, and they don't like other people telling them. The only people who say to try new things are officers."

"Where do I find an officer?"

"You probably don't. They're even busier than quartermasters. Tell me this, why would he want your fancy new boots for horses?"

"Tenobius says that they keep the hooves from wearing down as fast."

"An officer wouldn't care about that. His quartermaster might, but he's not the one buying. Your officer only wants to know if his will help him in battle. Will it?"

"I...I don't know."

"Well, you better know!" Mopsus was very hard and severe about it.

He got up and walked with that leg-swinging gait around the room.

"I'm going to help you," he said, but it still sounded severe. "Because you're DogFace's kid, and because you need help. When I left the corps, I almost starved at first, until I learned how to turn a bunch of lazy porters and ditch diggers into a company, and how to find paying work for them. Nobody told me how. I had to learn. The first thing I learned is that I could always give an answer. So, I'll ask again. Wil these Horse Boots help win a battle?"

"I...Yes. Yes, they will."

"How?"

"They'll let his horses march further."

"That's not a commander's answer. Think again."

"They'll make his kicks more dangerous."

"What was that?"

"His horse will be able to kick with more force. The heavy iron will go through shields and helmets."

It was all I could think of. It was those stories about the horses' hooves kicking in people's heads, the way we'd talked about it while trying to figure out how to put the shoes on the horse.

"THAT'S an officer's answer," said Mopsus, satisfied.

"I don't even know if that's true."

"It doesn't matter. It will start him thinking. It will make him want to try it out. I know some officers who would love the idea of making their horses more dangerous."

~ * ~

I came back two days later, and Mopsus was there with a soldier in a sharp uniform, all polished and gleaming. His helmet was off, but he had it resting nearby. He took no notice of me, I was just a kid to him, and Mopsus didn't either. They sat there and talked and joked and drank from metal cups. After a while, Mopsus got up, his leg still stiff. "Come on, Quintus Flavinius, the boy is here to show us the way." He held out a hand to help the officer up, and Mopsus winked at me, showing that he had addressed the officer just so I'd know his name.

"Here, boy," said the officer, "Show us a quick and clean route and you'll have a *denarius* for it. I wanted to shout at him that I wasn't just a guide boy, showing the way, but one of the artisans forging the parts. I held my tongue. Mopsus seemed to be signaling me to do just that. I offered to take him to Marcus' forge, but Mopsus insisted on our seeing Fulvius and having a look at Imperator's newly shod hooves. So that's where we went.

For all I knew, Fulvius might be out. Fortunately, he was home, and Imperator was there in his stall. Quintus came over to Fulvius and introduced himself. I learned that Fulvius, too, had served, long ago. It made sense. Quintus seemed to know something about that. They all went over and looked over Imperator's new shoes. Under Fulvius' command the horse was as docile as a dog, and let them all handle his raised and inverted hoof. Quintus felt how the shoe touched the hoof, and struck it with his knuckle, as well as with his officer's *baton*.

He had Fulvius walk Imperator back and forth using different gaits, and listened to the sound of those shod hooves on the packed earth. He had Fulvius lead the horse onto a paved area, and looked closely at the way the hooves looked and moved.

Quintus asked a question of Fulvius that I couldn't hear, which frustrated me, because I could probably have answered it. Of course, he was paying no attention to me. Fulvius shook his head. They talked some more, and called Mopsus over for a conference.

"Boy," said Mopsus to me, speaking louder and more distinctly than he had to, "Take us to the forge where these were made."

"Yes, sir!" I said, playing the part, though I hated it.

We quickly went to Marcus', and I sought out Tenobius. He was in the back, making more of his things out of beads and paper, but he dropped them as soon as I told him what was going on.

Quintus looked surprised when he saw Tenobius, but he recovered himself.

"Oho!" he said. "Here's how you came up with these. You have a magician out of the East! Are you the one who made the things for this one's horse?"

Tenobius said that he was, and showed him some loose shoes and nails, and pointed to the diagram. They talked for a long time until Quintus started hinting, he wanted to buy a set. They picked it up only slowly, talking about how it was a good idea, how long it took to do, and how good it would look. Quintus asked about if it would make his horse's hooves into better weapons. Tenobius didn't lose a beat, but immediately talked about how much better it would be.

It wasn't until after they talked about all of this over and over that they got to the price. They haggled over this for a long time, and during this discussion Marcus showed up, which complicated everything again. They finally agreed on a price.

It was only after this that Tenobius pulled out something new and showed it to Quintus. It looked like one of his horse shoes cut in half, with some extra webbing inside. I hadn't seen this before. It must be something new Tenobius was working on. Quintus asked the question we all had, what was it? Shoe for oxen, Tenobius explained. I recalled he'd talked about such a thing, but hadn't seen it before. I was surprised at how it was in two pieces, until I recalled that Ox hooves were cloven. I'd been assuming he'd simply make a large shoe that fit over both hooves at the same time, but Tenobius had made it in two parts, one for each half of the hoof. So, they could move by themselves, I guess.

Quintus asked if these would make the hooves of his oxen into deadly Weapons of Destruction, as well. Tenobius explained that these would be good for the feet of the oxen in the baggage train, protecting their feet during the long marches on Roman roads and in unpaved paths in the wilderness. Tenobius offered a lower price for these, and I could see Quintus thinking it over before approving. Finally, they all clasped hands over the deal, and it was over.

"Did we really sell that captain horse shoes that he's going to use to kick his enemy's heads in?" I asked Tenobius when he came back into the shop.

"We sold him a set of horse shoes, that's what's important. Actually, what's really important is that we sold him ox shoes."

"Why?"

"Because he's going to need them more, and they're what's really going to make us our money. Those shoes are flashy and exciting, and the idea of equipping your horse like a killing machine sounds exotic, but it's not going to happen. Killing his enemies with them, that is. Having ox shoes to save the feet of the beasts pulling your baggage doesn't sound exciting, but it's what you really need. Besides it'll pay our bills."

"So, we're not making Quintus' horse into a weapon?"

"Well, he might think so. Probably he wants to believe it, and wants to show it off to the other officers. I hope he does. We could use the extra business when they all want it, too. He has to know, deep down inside, he'll probably never get to use the shoes that way. Sometimes you have to feed your customers' fancies. If nothing else, he'll be protecting his horse's hooves, so it's certainly helping."

"I'm confused," I said. "I thought we were making and selling people the things they needed. You're telling me that we're selling things they *think* they want."

"That's what we do. That's what most makers and sellers do." He picked up a brooch from the workbench that was there to have its pin resoldered, another of the many little jobs that Tenobius handled every week. "The woman who wears this does so because she thinks it makes her more beautiful. Does it? I don't know. What I do know is it makes her *feel* more beautiful, so the effect is the same. We're in the business of selling things and selling dreams."

"Is your trip back home a dream?"

"No. I hope not. I hope that's a thing."

That wasn't the end of it. Tenobius got into a big argument with Marcus over what the costs should be, and how they would divide the profits. Marcus felt that it was his shop, and Tenobius was only a worker there, even if he was one with good ideas, and he should only get his wages. Of course, he would raise those. Tenobius said there would be no extra work or profit without his coming up with the horse shoes, and he deserved half of it.

It was a huge battle. Marcus said no worker ever talked to him that way before, and threatened to fire Tenobius. Tenobius said that would be fine, he'd just take his designs and methods with him to another shop, and Marcus could try making things without him. Especially the ox shoes, which he hadn't explained to anyone else yet.

It went on for a long time. I think Marcus was afraid Matellus and Arnicus would start demanding the same thing, but I could have told him they weren't smart enough for that. Marcus offered him a third of the profit, but Tenobius wouldn't budge. Neither would Marcus. For a time, it looked as though Tenobius would have to pack up his things and leave. He offered to do extra work, a lot of maintenance stuff nobody liked to do, if he would get his half.

Marcus growled about it a long time, and still threatened to get rid of Tenobius. I think he knew Tenobius *would* do the things he said, instead of slacking off as the apprentices did, and that finally won him over.

Marcus walked off with loud curses after it was all over, and said to Tenobius he could get started right then and there.

I ran over to congratulate him, and to say I was sure he was going to be fired. He smiled, and said he thought he might be fired, too. He also said he had to stand his ground. He promised me a steady rate from that half of the money

Fulvius came over to do the fitting of Quintus' horse's shoes, and it went quickly. Quintus couldn't get over admiring them, and after they were in place, he rode his horse over the packed earth, over the paving, and over grass to hear the difference, and to feel it. I think that if a barbarian warrior had been around, he'd have wanted to try kicking him in the head. Fortunately, none were. Tenobius made him promise to send his quartermaster with the baggage oxen. Then he went into conference with Fulvius about getting someone to help him shoe the oxen. I hadn't realized until then that Tenobius still didn't know exactly how they were going to fulfill that part of the bargain. Fulvius told him of some men who cared for the hooves of the oxen who might help him.

~ * ~

A few days later I helped Tenobius making his first set of ox shoes, and he let me do one set myself. It took a lot longer than I thought it would, and afterward my arms hurt so much I had to tell him I couldn't do anything else, so he put me at a table in the back and told me to practice writing.

Arnicus was trying to make a horseshoe and managed to mess it up spectacularly. He was going to throw out the mangled loop of iron when Tenobius ran over and said that it was exactly what he wanted. He'd take the piece as it was, he said he had a use for it, so Arnicus threw it to the floor to cool off. After a while Tenobius picked it up with tongs and put it with his things.

He came over to see what I was doing. I'd gotten tired of writing words and sentences, and was writing numbers and adding them up. I liked the numbers better. They seemed to make sense.

Tenobius checked my sums. It took him some time to get used to my symbols for 'two' and 'three' and the other numbers, but now he could read them as easily as me.

"These are all correct," he said, "but they're all low. You don't go over twenty. Are you counting on your fingers and toes?"

"No, I can add higher than that. It just takes too long to write."

"Show me how you make twenty," he said.

I did. "For five and ten I still use V and X. Why make up a new symbol when a single one exists for each of those? I wrote 'XX'."

"That's the way everyone writes twenty, he said. Do you make 'XXX' for thirty?"

"Of course. The same as everyone else."

"How do you do thirty-two?"

So, I showed him, three Xs and a little spiral, which is my made-up symbol for two. It's one symbol less than the way everyone else writes it, which is XXXII.

"Yes," he said, "and you write thirty-nine as 'XXXsquiggle'?"

"Yes."

"Hmm. You're *almost* there. I can show you a way to use even fewer characters, and make everything neat and simple. I don't think I have to worry about Temporal Discipline. You've already come up with most of this yourself. You can write twenty using a single symbol. Thirty, as well."

"I've thought about that. If I make a special symbol for twenty and for thirty and for forty and so on, it's too much to remember."

"You don't have to make up new symbols. You use the ones you already have. To write 'twenty-one' you just write spiral and an 'I'." He did so, on the paper.

"Then how do you...? What would twenty-two be?"

"Spiral followed by spiral, like this."

I wasn't sure. There seemed to be something wrong with this. It seemed too easy, somehow."

"So 'twenty-three' would be spiral followed by triangle then?"

"Yes, you've got it."

"Wait, then what's triangle followed by spiral?"

"Thirty-two"

"But then...wait. That makes sense. Thirty-four is triangle followed by square, right?"

"Yes, *by George, he's got it*" he said, in barbarian.

"But...no. How do I write just 'twenty' then? If I just draw a spiral, it's the same as two."

"There's a secret," said Tenobius, lowering his voice, as if his Temporal Police could hear him. "You need a special number that the Romans do not use. Nor the Greeks. "

"What number?"

"We call it *zero*. It's *nothing*."

"How can *nothing* be a number?"

"It is. It's one of the most important numbers. If you have one *stylus*, as you do, and I take it away, he did, how many do you have left?"

"That's a dirty trick! I don't have any."

"Right. You have *none. Nothing*. It's one less than one. "

I thought about it. It seemed obvious, now that he said it, but useless. I said so.

"Well, it's not completely useless. I just showed you a use for it, it makes a difference between two and twenty. That's a good point. It doesn't really work unless you write the *zero* down to the right of your two, like this." He made a spiral for the two and a plain circle for this new *zero* of his.

"That's the *nothing*?" I asked, pointing at the circle.

"Correct. That's what we call *zero*. It's like an empty hole. So that's 'twenty,' and 'two' is just the spiral, with no *zero*. If I put a spiral followed by a *zero* and then another *zero*, it's two hundred,' the number people here write with two C's, 'CC'."

"You said your way was more efficient, but the old way only uses two symbols, and yours uses three."

"*Wise guy*," he said in barbarian. "When I write two hundred eight in this way it only needs three symbols, spiral, *zero*, and double square. The

Roman way needs six, C and C and V and three I's."

After that he showed me how to add and subtract with this new method and its *zeros*. It *was* easier, and you could do numbers much bigger than twenty. You could do as big as you wanted, with numbers so big they didn't make sense, they were bigger than anything in the world, as Tenobius told me. He cautioned me not to tell anyone that he told me about it.

"Why not?" I asked, but I knew the answer. *Temporal Discipline*, whatever that was.

"Why tell me this, if you're worried about what might happen?"

He sighed and thought before he spoke.

"I want to give you a hand up," he said. "You're learning some smithing, but a lot of boys in the city know that. A lot of them are stronger than you and started earlier. You're smarter than most of them. That might get you work in goldsmithing and silversmithing, but I don't know how you'll fare with the trade guilds. If you can add and figure better than anyone else, you might have a real advantage. Besides, you came up with most of it on your own. I think you can overcome any obstacle with those things at your back. I hope so, anyway."

With that, he walked over to his table and pulled out the badly forged horseshoe Arnicus made. Tenobius did something else to it, because now the shoe made a perfect loop, all the way around. He held it up.

"It'd work, on a house with a circular foot," he said.

"What are you going to do with it?"

"I thought maybe I'd choke a horse," he said.

The thing was so small that you could choke a horse, if you could get it over the head and around the neck. Tenobius didn't have that in mind. He opened his kit and pulled out some of his islanded wire, which he'd would onto a kind of spool. He took it and began unwinding it through the hole in the round horseshoe, over and over again, wrapping it around one side. I thought about asking him why he was doing it, but I knew I'd get the same kind of answer I got when I asked why he was wrapping the wire around cylinder beads. Tenobius might be crazy. It was possible he might be brilliant and smarter than any of us. His little pieces of work were carefully made. He was, if anything, a precise madman.

~ * ~

We shod two more officer's horses, and Fulviius helped us to find an oxmaster who helped us with the ox shoeing. He had us set up a stand to hold the ox hoof up of the kind he used for filing down the hooves. He used some stakes driven into the ground, but Tenobius designed and built a movable one. Having worked out the details of the horse shoes, Tenobius, Fulvius, and Caractacus, that was the ox-man's name, were able to refine the ox shoes.

In the evening, we worked at the tables in the back. Tenobius had me practicing my numbers, using our new system. Tenobius made more of his strange bead-wound things, and was checking them. He had a mysterious black box that had a glass-covered face, with a pointing needle behind it. When he pressed his creations to the box, the needle moved, and Tenobius said that how far the needle moved told him if the part was good or not. Some were good, and if they were, he attached a small piece of paper to it with a notation. If they weren't, sometimes he'd twist two or more of them together until the needle moved where he wanted. There were different tests for the different types of things he made, the rolled-up metal foil like honeycakes, or the burnt paper on a bead, or the wire would around a bead. He even had some kind of test for the bad horseshoe with the wire wound on it. They all used that box in one way or other.

"How does the box know if your things are good or not?" I asked him. "How does it know how far to move the needle?"

"Ah, now that would take a very long time to explain," he said. "Not that I don't think you're clever, but, as I said..."

"Sometimes it takes very long to explain things. You've told me."

"It's true. I'm sorry. It works a little like a compass."

"What's a compass?"

"It's when you take a lodestone and let it freely swing. It ends up with one end pointing north and the other south."

I told him I never heard of such a thing, and he seemed upset by this. He seemed to think everyone should know about it. He promised to help me make one. That way I, too, would have a needle that pointed somewhere.

Lillia came over, with a covered dish containing chicken and vegetables. She said Tenobius was working too hard. She also brought NexMuris, the kitten, which had grown up quite a bit since we saw it last, and who seemed more interested in the chicken than mice. We shared some with the beast while we ate, and we caught Lillia up with our work over the past several days. She wasn't impressed with the horse shoes or the ox shoes. She thought we had come up with some elaborate scheme to cheat the Roman Army out of money by putting these on their animals. She was more interested in the numbers we had come up with.

NexMuris finished the chicken, and a mouse had caught her eye. She was now stalking it with fierce intensity. That made Lillia look at the table, with Tenobius' ceramic things in neat groups. Tenobius explaining that there were all dipped in the 'island' stuff, with her anti-mouse powder mixed into it. What *were* they, she wanted to know. Tenobius was trying to think of a way to explain them, when I told her they were magic beads, and that seemed to satisfy her. Tenobius would never do that. He'd think it was lying, somehow, even though he's the one who always says that anything complicated enough looks like magic.

"Can I have this one?" Lillia asked, holding up what was two of Tenobius' creations joined together by their twisted gold foil ends.

"If you want," said Tenobius. "It's not really very good looking, and the islanding might start to melt and run if it sits directly on your skin. I can make you some proper jewelry if you would rather."

"No, I want this. This is one of your crazy things. No one else in the city will have a thing like this."

She picked up Tenobius' black box and examined it.

"What is this?"

"It's my tester. Please be careful. If you drop it and it breaks, we'll be in trouble."

"How does it test?"

"He presses the gold parts against the box and the needle inside moves," I told her.

"Show me," she said to Tenobius.

He took one of his things and pressed it against the box. The needle moved. Lillia laughed. "Does that mean it's good?"

Tenobius nodded.

"What about my jewelry?"

"I'll have to set it up differently," said Tenobius.

He put things together in an odd way, then touched the ends of Lillia's necklace to the box. The needle moved. Lillia laughed again.

"Does that mean it's good, too?"

"Not as good as the first piece," he said.

She gave him a little slap. "I should hit you for trying to give me bad jewelry," she said.

"You are the one who selected it," he said. "It's not bad, even for *two capacitors in parallel*. It's just not exactly what I want. Its *capacitance* doesn't affect its beauty as jewelry."

NexMuris jumped up on the table. She had given up on chasing mice, and was now chasing moths, with greater success. She smashed one with both paws and started to eat it.

"Great Hunter," said Tenobius.

"She's still learning," said Lillia. "Just wait until she's a few months older. She'll ignore these moths for the mice."

"Tenobius," I said, "Is what you said before true, about these things melting?"

"I'm not sure." He said. "I've protected them against mice now, and maybe NexMuris will help with that. I do know this material isn't the best to use. It will run if it gets too hot. I think it will crack if it gets too cold. It has a limited life. So, I can't take too long to..." He stopped, looking guiltily at Lillia.

"Too long for what?" she asked.

Tenobius didn't answer, so I did.

"To repair his Dreamship."

"His what?" she asked.

I started to explain about how Tenobius was hoping to travel home to where he came from in a ship I hadn't seen, using these strange things he was making as parts. Tenobius stopped me and explained it himself, as I knew he would.

She stared at him as if he said he was building a temple in his hair.

"It's all right," he said. "You can think I'm crazy if you want. I know the idea sounds crazy, and if I were you, I'd think that I was insane."

"The idea sounds crazy, but you don't. You sound like the sanest man I know, most of the time."

"Well, as I say, if I don't get this built and working soon, I think that these parts I'm making may fall apart. That would be too bad."

"Can I see it, too?" Lillia asked.

"If you want," said Tenobius, as if the idea had never occurred to him. "If you really want to, but only when it's finished."

"Can I go with you?"

That flustered him. It was his turn to stare now. He tried to say things several times, but couldn't. I think it was the last thing he expected anyone to say. I could see he didn't want to answer either *yes* or *no*.

I decided to rescue him.

"Tenobius, this ship of yours. How many people does it hold? Surely you didn't come all the way here by yourself. Where is everybody else?"

He had to stop and think about that. It was a while before he answered. NexMuris had time to catch and eat two more moths.

"There's only one person to each ship, but they sent out four of us at once. Each in our own ship. There was Ashok Joret, and Emily Sibyl Watkins, and Leonard Vincent, and me. We all went in slightly different ways, but we would end up very far apart. I don't expect to see the others. Avery was our leader, and he knew the most. Emily Sibyl was a *psychol*...well, she was an expert in how people thought, and how societies run. Leonard was our mechanical expert, a real artist. We were to all go out and see the world, then come back and tell the others what we found. Only my ship...foundered. There was a fire on board, and parts were ruined. So, I'm trying to fix them, the best I know how. As I explained to Argus here, no one will be able to help me if I can't do it myself. No one will come for me, and no one else in the city knows how to make islanded wire, or things like your jewelry. All I have is my own memory, my own wits, and a few things like this antique black box with a needle. It was my father's." He went quiet.

"Tenobius," I asked him. "You told us what the others did. What is it *you* do?"

"Oh, I put things together using these trinkets I make. If you want me to get dramatic about it, I control the lightning, and I make lodestones. How's that for crazy?"

I didn't think that was crazy. The crazy part was I believed him. I don't know what Lillia thought.

~ * ~

You could never tell with Tenobius what you would be doing next. A couple of days later we were in the backyard of the Forge. Tenobius had a high-quality bar of hard iron on the table, and was lining it up with a mark he'd made on the table after watching the stars overnight. The line, he said, was oriented by the rising and setting of the stars during the night, along with a sighting of the North Star. It ran, he said, precisely north and south.

Once he had the rod properly aligned, he took one of the big hammers and used it to strike the end of the bar several times while I held it in place. It was as if he were hammering the rod into a vertical board, only there was no board there, just empty air. I was sure this time Tenobius was doing something crazy.

Afterward, the bar started attracting small bits of iron to itself, which it hadn't done before.

Once he'd done this, Tenobius took an expensive steel needle and began stroking it on the bar, always the same end, stroked in the same direction. He did this for a LONG time. It was typical Tenobius patience. He stroked it for over an hour, then he stuck the needle in a cork, and set it in a bowl of water.

As he said it would, the needle turned that cork until it pointed in almost the same direction as the line on the table. He said it was a *compass*, and would always point to the north. He pushed it with his finger so that it pointed East, but the needle righted itself. He said it would always do that. I had to play with it myself quite a bit. I was almost ready to agree, but I picked up the hammer to take it back to the shop, and the needle pointed to the hammer head. Tenobius explained that if there was iron or steel close by, the needle would point to that, instead. I asked him why he didn't say that before, and he said it ruined the lesson. I said that it seemed to be a big part of the lesson. He said I was right, and very clever.

~ * ~

Now there was plenty of work, and not much time for lodestones or even Tenobius' 'little trinkets'. The word had been passed along the army about our shoes for horses and oxen, and enough of the army was happy with these that we were getting lots of orders. In order to meet the demand, Tenobius set up something he called an *assembly line*, a *coniungo lineam*, where each person did only one part of the work, and always the same part. He made drawings on large pieces of his paper and nailed them up on the wall, and had Marcus starting off the piece from rod stock, making it the right diameter and length and putting it in a box once it had cooled enough. Then Arnicus would bend it into shape and flatten it. Metellus would work the ridges. Tenobius would cut the nail holes, and I would finish. After we got this going, he had us switching roles, and he brought in Corticus to help out. He wanted everyone to try out every job, but he found he couldn't have Arnicus or Metellus do any fine work, although Corticus could work any position.

After a full work day, you'd think we could take a rest, but Tenobius pulled me aside after we washed up and said there was something he had to show me. To my surprise, he sat me down at the table with stylus and paper.

"Do we have to do this *now*?" I asked.

"Yes," he replied. "There's a reason for it."

What Tenobius had to show me was something new I could do with my number symbols. He no longer even seemed to care whether I had an idea like it or not. Once I got over being tired, it was interesting.

If you wanted to add the same number to itself, it's pretty easy to do it with the symbols, easier than with ordinary numerals. This is even more the case if you want to add the same number to itself more than once. It was much easier to do this, over and over, using my number signs that the usual XIX plus VII symbols. Tenobius showed me an even faster way of doing this by *multiplication*. It's the same process he told me about a long time back, only in this case the two numbers don't have to be the same. There's a way to use the symbols to arrive at the correct result without using addition, and it works for numbers of any size. He showed me how he could add the same number together three times, or he could multiply the number by three, and he got the exactly same result both ways. He had me do it with adding the same number four times and then doing the multiplication by four. Then with another number added to itself five times, and multiplying by five. Even though you seem to be doing something completely different, it works every time. I had to try out some other cases I made up myself.

Finally he showed me how to multiply by ten, you just move everything over one place and put a zero at the end.

"Try doing that with your Roman Numerals," he said.

We had to make some changes to the production line for the ox shoes, but it wasn't much different. The biggest problem was that we ended up with different numbers of left and right sides until Tenobius had us producing only one type for a time, then switching to the other side for a time.

After we got a satisfactory number made, we had them bring in the horses or the oxen in a group. We brought in Fulvius or Caractacus for the actual shoeing, but one of us had to do the fitting for the hooves. Again, fine work wasn't the best thing for the two apprentices, but Corticus turned out to be very good at it.

~ * ~

The business moved ahead, and after a few days Tenobius brought me with him to have a talk with Marcus. I had no idea why.

Tenobius started off by asking him how the business was doing, and how many shoes we sold. Marcus didn't want to say, at first, but Tenobius said he had a real reason for asking, he was getting a portion of each sale, so he wanted to know how many there were. Marcus said he didn't have to worry about getting his share, but Tenobius said that wasn't the point.

It turned out that we'd sold eight sets of horse shoes, and fifteen sets of ox shoes. Tenobius asked to see the accounting for it. Marcus asked what that meant. Tenobius said he wanted to see the account book where it was written down.

"Written down?" asked Marcus. "Do I look like a scribe? I keep it here," and pointed to his head.

That struck Tenobius a telling blow. He couldn't believe anyone would try to run a business without writing down his accounts somewhere.

Marcus countered he wasn't going to waste good money on papyrus when he could just remember it. Tenobius asked him how he could keep track of the money amounts. If we were charging twelve denarii for a set of shoes for horses, then how would he know how much to charge? Marcus said he'd figure it out with his tally sticks. Tenobius was surprised again, I think. What were tally sticks? He asked.

Marcus didn't want to show him, at first. I think it was a secret that shopkeepers keep to themselves, but Tenobius insisted so much that he finally gave in, showing how he used a set of shaped sticks to add twelve to itself eight times, getting ninety-six. Tenobius mumbled something about an abacus in stick form.

He told Marcus that there was a faster way to figure this out, and that he had trained me in it. He then had me show how I could represent 'twelve' with my symbols, and either add these eight times, or I could multiply twelve by eight, getting ninety-six both times.

I think Tenobius was hoping Marcus would be impressed, that he would see this demonstration as the wonderful thing that I did, and would agree to hire me as a number-writer for the shop. I could have told him that wouldn't work. Marcus is not me. He didn't care for the numbers, didn't understand my symbols, and didn't understand how the *mathematics*, Tenobius' word, worked.

Why, he asked, would he want to entrust his livelihood to a lowly apprentice using marks that only he understood, when he could use his tally sticks and his memory as his father and his uncles had? He told Tenobius to never say anything about it again.

I could see Tenobius was crushed, the way he had been after the mice ate his Islanding. It wasn't until then that I realized what he was doing, he was hoping to find me a job, something to, in his words, get me 'off the street', and he'd failed. Worse, there was no way to pull himself back up. This wasn't one of his technical problems, where he just had to think of another way to do something. He'd put all his hopes on this, and they were dashed.

I told him it was all right. I didn't care. I was happy to learn how to multiply. I'm not sure he heard me.

~ * ~

Tenobius was still feeling sad the next day. He wasn't really trying to hammer out parts, and finally Marcus had to tell him to move aside and let Arnicus take over on the line. I was still finishing up at the end, so I couldn't go over to him. He just sat at his table in the back, not even working on his trinkets.

He would come out of it eventually, if the past was any guide. Some idea would be stewing in the back of his head while he fretted. When it bubbled up, like the water when he boiled the leather scraps, he would rush off to do something strange and unexpected. For now, he was quiet. He'd pulled out a sheet of paper and a stylus, and every now and then he'd scribble something on it.

About the middle of the day he disappeared. He simply left without saying anything. No one knew where he went. We didn't see him for the rest of the day.

He was gone the next day as well.

When he returned the following day, Marcus went after him. You could hear his yelling down the street. Where had Tenobius been? How could he simply take off like that, without leaving word? If he, Marcus, hadn't organized the workers, nothing would have gotten done. Was he sick, or injured? If not. Marcus would make sure he *was* injured. And so on.

Tenobius didn't care. He went back to work as if the past three days hadn't happened, and Marcus hadn't blistered him with words. He asked Marcus what orders were needed, and wrote them out on his paper and nailed it up, with the numbers written in both regular Roman style and my numeral system. Once he finished, he got everyone in line and started the production going. We made a record number of Ox shoes that day.

At the end of it, Tenobius seemed like his old self. He even started something weird.

"I need to find glass," he told me. "Clear glass, like for a vase or a goblet."

I rarely saw glass. It was expensive and meant for wealthy people. The glass I did see was mostly broken, full of bubbles, and not clear, usually. I told Tenobius this.

"We'll have to scour the market," he said. "I think we'll have to try the Big Forum."

We finally found a large stall filled with glass vessels. They were colored blue and yellow and were wonderfully clear. They were also very expensive. The shopkeeper blocked our way in. I think he was afraid Tenobius was some stupid servant and I was a stupid kid. Tenobius argued with him for an hour before he'd even let him stay near the shop. It wasn't until he emptied his purse into his hand and let the shopkeeper see what he had that the shopkeeper finally melted a bit. He let Tenobius, but not me, come closer. He still wouldn't let Tenobius even touch the pieces. He'd hold them up for him and let him look.

Neither of them were happy. Tenobius didn't seem to see what he was looking for, and the shopkeeper saw he probably wasn't going to make a sale. He tried to interest Tenobius in a gaudy, rough piece of what even I could see was cheap glass.

Now it was Tenobius' turn to get mad, and he did. I almost never saw him shout at shopkeepers, but he was reaching his limit. He flat-out asked if he was the artisan who made these pieces. The shopkeeper hemmed and hawed. Finally, Tenobius gave him money for, well, nothing, it seemed to me. It made the keeper happy, so I guess that's what counted. With money in his hand he unbent a little more and answered Tenobius' questions. No, he wasn't the glassmaster. Could Tenobius talk to him? Maybe. Tenobius wanted to commission a special piece. The Master didn't like making special pieces, the keeper said. Tenobius said he'd make it worth his while. Do you have any idea what that would cost, the keeper asked. Do you, said Tenobius, right back at him. He didn't, as it turned out.

Tenobius wanted to talk to the artist, but the stall keeper wanted more money. Nothing happened until Tenobius threatened to go to another glass dealer. Even then, the keeper didn't believe him until Tenobius picked out another stall by eye and started walking there. The glassmaker would be back, but not for another three days. Tenobius said he'd be back in three days, and would pay the Keeper then, if the glassmaker was there.

After we got around a corner and out of sight and hearing, Tenobius laughed, and offered to buy me something to eat.

"How can you eat?" I asked. "I can barely swallow. I thought you were going to hit him, or something."

"I almost did. You'll learn you have to keep your head when you're negotiating. If I'd hit him, I'd feel a lot better. I also wouldn't be seeing the glassmaker in three days."

We found a dealer in nuts and figs. They didn't look too badly eaten by insects, so we bought some.

"What now?" I asked, hoping we'd go home.

"Who puts out fires around here?" asked Tenobius.

I knew we were off on another chase.

I didn't know of anyone who put out fires. If you caught it when it was small, you put it out yourself. If a fire caught an entire house, you ran away. The idea of trying to put out an entire burning house sounded crazy to me. As I found out by following Tenobius around, that's just because I wasn't rich. If you had enough money, you could hire people that would try to squelch a burning house. It took a while to find these people, because they didn't let you know about them, if you had a big enough house, they came to you.

Tenobius approached it in a roundabout way. He asked around among the laborers and the people who handled fire to try to find what he called the *firemen*, the ones who actually put out the fires. That took the rest of the day, but he finally located one. He was a porter in the Forum, with a regular station. After much talking, and giving him some money, he finally agreed to tell us where we could talk to one of those running the business.

It wasn't a stall, or even a shop. The place he sent us to was a private house, and in a good district, too. I would've been afraid to even go near it, but Tenobius on the hunt isn't afraid of anything.

The House Servant didn't want to tell us anything, and tried to get us to leave, but Tenobius insisted, and said he wouldn't leave until he talked with the master of the house. Eventually, the doorman said he'd ask, but he still wouldn't let us in. I thought this was just a trick to make us wait at the door forever, with no one ever answering, but they surprised me. An official-looking man in a toga actually came to the door, and listened impatiently as Tenobius explained himself.

No, he said, he wasn't there to *insure* a house—that was the word they used. He simply wanted to know where they purchased their equipment. Why? Asked Mr. Toga, so they could set up their own business and compete? What else would you want the equipment for? Tenobius explained he was a craftsman, a goldsmith and ironworker, who was trying to use the equipment to build something. Toga wavered for a second, but finally said he wasn't interested, and if he wanted to know where he got his equipment, he could go talk to Vulcan. After that he went in and had the doorman slam it on us.

I was so used to seeing Tenobius get what he wanted, by talking to people, or lately by paying for it, that I was surprised he failed. Here was someone who wouldn't listen, and was too wealthy to be bribed.

"What do we do now?" I finally asked him, as we looked at the shut door.

"We do something else," said Tenobius, easily. "What would you do?"

"I don't know what I'd do. I don't know what you're even looking for."

"Fair enough. You know I'm looking for information about fire fighting equipment."

"Yes."

"So, we need to find someone who knows about fire fighting equipment."

"You found him," I said, and pointed at the door, "and you can't buy him."

Tenobius smiled.

"That's true. We need someone who knows where we can find fire fighting equipment, and who *needs* the money. Where can we find someone like that?"

"Well, I don't know. The only..." I stopped as I realized the answer. "The porter!"

"Yes. We shouldn't have left him to come here. I thought the Head Man would know more. I hadn't thought that he might not even talk to us. Back to the Forum."

Fortunately, the porter was still there. When Tenobius asked him where they got their pumps from, he told him easily enough, and Tenobius rewarded him with some more coins.

The sign over the shop read *Munitor*, which Tenobius said meant a builder, and people acted as if that really was his name. It was a fixed shop, not a stall, and it reminded me of Marcus' forge, only it wasn't set up for iron and steel. This shop made things out of leather, copper, and bronze.

Tenobius asked to speak to the owner, and explained himself. He was surprised to learn that Munitor already knew of him, or at least of his horse shoes. They talked about them for a while, with Munitor telling him he did not have to worry about competition, he wasn't set up to work in iron and had no wish to. Tenobius explained that he needed a piece of equipment, and would be willing to buy it, rather than trying to make it himself. He described it, using words I hadn't heard before. Munitor nodded, went back into the shop and returned with what looked like an enormous candle made of bronze. It must have been over three feet long, and as big around as my arm.

I must have been looking at it puzzled, because Munitor looked at me and asked "You don't know what it is, do you?"

When I didn't answer, Tenobius spoke.

"If you want to put out a fire, but you don't want to get close to the flames to throw your bucket of water on them, what would you do?"

I didn't say anything, because I had no idea. Munitor took the bronze candle over to a basin of water used to cool down soldered work, stuck the pointed tip in, and then pulled back the bottom of the 'candle'. To my surprise, it pulled back, leaving the rest still sticking in the water. Below the end, the part he pulled out was thinner than the rest of the candle. He drew back perhaps a foot of it, and after he did so, I saw that the level of water in the basin had gone down.

He tilted the pointed end up and walked to the front of the shop.

"Foronius the Dyer is always stinking up the neighborhood with his foul brews," said Munitor. "I can always use an excuse to complain about him."

With that he raised the candle, pointed the end at the Dyer's shop across the way, and pushed in the base of the 'candle'. A thick stream of water shot out and across the street, arcing across and going neatly in through a window. As Munitor finished squirting the water, we heard a loud voice start to yell and curse, calling Munitor by name.

"Do your damned dying at night, and stop driving my customers away!" yelled Munitor, in reply.

"*That's* how you put out a fire without getting close," explained Tenobius to me. "Use something like that to soak the base of the flame from far off. Firemen get to be good aims with those things, shooting right in the window, like Munitor here."

"I used to be chief of my company," Munitor said, proudly. "These days I'd rather make and sell the equipment."

Tenobius took him aside, and explained he'd like to place a special order, a device like this, but with special features. He'd pay, he said. Half in advance, and showed him the money. After some haggling and discussion, Munitor said he'd have it in a week.

~ * ~

After that day, we had work to catch up on. Tenobius said he liked to alternate working on his Dreamship with work in the forge. You could get lost in the work at the forge, he claimed, and come back to the tough problems refreshed. I don't know. To me it's all tough work, aside from working with numbers. We turned out a lot of shoes and nails that day.

The next day we were able to wrap up our 'legitimate' work early, and turn to other things. We could take it easy, and we had visitors.

Publius Marcurius, The Runt, wanted to see what Tenobius was doing, or so he said. I showed him the horse shoes and the ox shoes, and told him about our adventures in the forum. I showed him my number system, and some of the number tricks Tenobius had shown me. The Runt got interested, and I was surprised at how fast he picked it up. I could tell there was something bothering The Runt.

For his part, Tenobius was working with the wire-pulling machine. He'd used it to make some fine silver wire, and was now making very coarse bronze rods. As a guest, he had Lillia, who was watching him use the lever to draw the bronze through. She brought a bowl of some bready stuff, and the kitten NexMuris.

Publius tried to pet NexMuris, but the cat wasn't interested. It was hunting again.

~ * ~

"How do you know how to build all these things?" Lillia asked Tenobius. "Were you apprentice to a master craftsman?"

Tenobius only hesitated a little before he said, "Yes," but I noticed. However he learned his skills, it wasn't as an ordinary apprentice. I knew that now. It was easier for him to just agree. Even so, I knew Tenobius thought it a lie, and he hated lying.

He seemed to think it wasn't enough, or else he didn't want the silence to go on. So, he talked.

"It wasn't just that," he went on. "I wanted to know how to make things. When you live in a…city. Like this. You start to rely on other people. You get your bread from the baker, and your wine from the wine seller, and your jars from the potter. What if you had to make all those things yourself? What if you lived way out in the country, where you couldn't buy things from other people, and had to make it yourself? Could you do it?

"I knew that I couldn't. We have a book, a story, back in my land. It's about a man named Crusoe whose ship sinks, and he ends up alone on an island. Not like the seven people I told you about before, this is a serious story. He has to do everything himself. He has no *Professor* to help him. He saves what he can from his ship, but he still has to find shelter, find food, make clothes. He had run a plantation before this, so he wasn't used to it. Forced to survive on his own, he learned by trying things and by hard work. Eventually, he was able to raise his own wheat, separate the grain from the chaff, grind it, and make bread. I didn't know how to do all that. So, I started to pay attention to the way things were done. I learned how to do many of the things I took for granted, even though I didn't think I'd ever have to use that knowledge.

"Look at these bits of apple in this bowl you brought over. Where do apples come from?"

"Where do they come from?" asked Lillia. "They grow on trees."

"And where do the trees come from?"

"Seeds, I guess. Like everything else."

"If I plant the seeds from your apples, they won't grow up into trees that make apples like these. Usually they make smaller apples, and they don't always taste good."

"No!"

"Really. There's a trick to raising good apples, or olives. Freshly picked ones are bitter. The ones you buy in the market taste good because they have been fermented. Wild almonds are poisonous. I can go to the Little Forum and get fine apples, olives, and almonds, but if I tried to pick the wild fruit off wild trees, I'd starve. There are so many other things like that. Most city people don't know how to butcher an animal, for instance."

"I know how to butcher anything."

"Well, that's a point in your favor. It's because you used to live in the country, so you would know that. Most people don't know which parts of an animal are good to eat. They also don't know which plants you can eat, and which are better than others. If you haven't done it, it's foolish to pick and eat wild mushrooms, because some can kill you."

Lillia gestured around the shop, at what they were doing.

"None of this looks like food."

"Well, that was just an example. The same kind of knowledge goes for things you make in a shop. Marcus buys his iron from iron makers, and he probably doesn't know how to make it himself. You need to mix together three kinds of stone in a special furnace to make iron. Even then, if you don't treat it right, it's not a hard-black metal you can use to make pots and hooks and things, but a bubbly brittle mess. This bronze here is made from copper and tin, but you have to make both of those from rocks, treated with heat and flux. After that, you have to blend them in the right proportions, like making this apple stuff you made, or you don't get proper bronze."

"Did your *Crusus* on his island know how to make bronze?"

"I don't think he ever tried. He knew how to butcher, though, and how to cure hides, and how to raise wheat and grind it and make bread. He also knew how to make medicine out of tobacco."

"What is *tobacco*?"

"Ah, I keep forgetting. You don't have it here. It's a plant we have. Some people like to chew it or...well, they like the smell. It's not really good for you."

"Maybe he took it as medicine to make him throw up."

"Something like that. He was just one example of the kind of character I try to follow. We have stories about lots of them: *William Robinson, Hank Morgan, Martin Padway, Cyrus Harding, Kit Draper, Mark Watney.* They're all made-up stories about people who never existed, but there were real-life examples, too."

"So how does this help you fix your Dreamship?" Lillia asked, holding up one of the bronze rods.

"It replaces a part that was broken in my ship. I hope. This part is going to be one of the most difficult to replace." Tenobius carefully took it from Lillia and wiped it with a cloth. "I'm trying to keep it very clean. Even the oils from your fingers, and the juices from the cut-up apples might not be good for it." He held up a bottle. "*Spiritu vini*, Spirits of Wine. I felt sure I could find distilled liquids in Rome. I got this from Speculus, the same doctor who sold me the *saccharum*. I could have made my own, if I had to, but this saved me having to find a potter who would throw an *alembic* for me."

"What is it?" asked Lillia.

"It's the fiery part of wine, the part that makes you drunk, concentrated down. It's not good for drinking, although some people would disagree. It's good for cleaning, though. I'm going to clean these rods and the silver wire with it, when I'm finished with them."

"Why?"

"Because I'm going to put them in a glass full of nothing, and I'd like it to stay that way."

He went back to work, taking some of the Spirits and using it to wipe down the rods with a very clean cloth. He whistled while he did this, some strange music from his home, I guess. I don't know anyone in Rome who whistles as he does. Lillia looked at him strangely.

Tenobius cleaned the rods carefully, then placed a section near the end on top of a small anvil that had been covered with his soft leather. He covered this with another piece of soft leather, and a piece of flat metal, then began carefully hammering it. After hammering for a time, he took it all apart and examined the rod, now flattened at one point, turned it over, put the stack together again, and hammered again. He repeated this many times, with three rods, until he was satisfied with the result. He had three rods that looked as if a powerful set of fingers had pinched them flat at one point, as if a baker had rolled out dough for a round loaf and flattened it at one point. Lastly, he cleaned them again with the spirits from the bottle and stored them in a cloth bag.

NexMuris jumped up on the table. She had something in her mouth, which she dropped in front of Tenobius. It was a mouse, still moving a little.

"She brought it to you," said Lillia. "She likes you."

"I'm flattered", said Tenobius, who didn't make a move toward it.

"If you don't take it, she'll think you don't like her."

Tenobius looked at her, then back at the mouse.

"Well," he said, "I've put the clean rods away already." He took the mouse by the tail and picked it up.

"*Gratias*," he said to the cat.

Lillia took the now-empty dish back inside, and NexMuris followed her in. Tenobius put away his things, saying that was enough for one day.

"The day after tomorrow I'm going to see the glassmaster, I hope," he said. "Publius, I don't think I've seen you here before."

"I don't want to get caught down in a workplace," he said. "My father says that I need to cultivate my mind."

"Does he think you can't do that in a place like this? Artisans and workers have to think, too. Look at what you're learning from Argus, here."

"Oh, but this isn't a typical shop. You're different."

"Well, that's flattering to hear, but I'm not sure how true it is."

"Where else would I find something like this?" he said, indicating the paper with our figurings on it.

"Well, do you think a carpenter doesn't have to figure out how big to make things, or a potter making a measuring jug? There are other kinds of knowledge besides what you learn at home. People in the shops remember stories that haven't been written down, and proverbs about everything from when to pick grapes to how to predict weather. They aren't just empty vessels producing goods to sell you. They have their own lives. How are you going to be a Senator like your father if you can't understand and talk to the people? "

"I talk to Argus, and to you."

"That's a start, but we're not Rome. How did you start talking to Argus?"

"I saw him playing a game on the steps of the temple, and kept watching him. So, he invited me to play."

"Yes, and took all the nuts he had," I added.

"That's true but you showed me how to play. Nobody else in the Little Forum would even talk to me. I learned how to play from you, and even started winning."

Well, I'd let him win, so he'd have something to eat, but it was better not to tell him now.

"So, you do the same thing with other people, only you have to speak first. Don't let other people do all the work. Try to remember names and faces. That's the best tool for a Senator. People like when you remember their names and something about them. Do you still go to sit in Tullius' tree?"

"Sometimes. He still charges me money for it, though. Sometimes he tells me I have to give him money even when we're not in the tree, just out on the street."

"What? Why?"

"He says it's payment in advance for the next time I want to go up in his tree. Even so, he still wants money every time I go up."

"That's not right. He's...extorting money from you."

"Yes. I know."

"So, do something about it. Say 'no' to him."

"I want to, but I just can't."

"Publius, if you don't tell him 'no' then he's just going to keep asking, now that he knows he can. He's being what we call a *bully*."

"But..."

"But what?"

"I don't think I can."

"Look, don't think that he's going to stop being your friend. He's going to do that if you let him keep taking your money. Go to his tree tomorrow afternoon and tell him that you already paid."

"I don't think..."

"Go ahead and do it. Let me know what happens."

After Publius left, I went over to Tenobius. I was worried.

"If The Runt goes to Tullius and says he's not going to pay, then I can tell you what's going to happen."

"What?"

"He'll be lucky if Tullius just pushes him out of the tree. He'll probably get beaten up. And you told him to do it."

"If Publius doesn't stand up to Tullius, then the *bully* is just going to keep asking for more and more. If it goes on for a long time, it'll be bad all around."

"So? What did you think was going to happen when he does say 'no' to Tullius?"

"I'll tell you what I have in mind. Tullius knows he can get money from Publius because his father's important, and rich. But he hasn't thought it through."

"What?"

"Well, his father's a senator. He IS important. If he doesn't buy leather from Tullius' father, his constituents probably do. If Publius gets beaten up, that's an offense to the Senator. He might take direct action against Tullius' father. He just might make sure everyone takes their business elsewhere. If that happens Tullius' father will get mad, and punish Tullius."

"Huh. You're right. That'd teach him."

"Yes, but it would be a little late. Publius would already be beaten up, and Tullius' father's business would already be hurt. We shouldn't let two people suffer because Tullius can't think far enough ahead."

"So, what do we do?"

"It would be very unbecoming if Publius himself told Tullius this. That's why I didn't suggest it. It would make him look arrogant and proud. There's no reason *you* couldn't have a talk with Tullius tomorrow morning, and point all this out to him."

"Me? Tomorrow morning?"

"That's why I told him to talk to Tullius tomorrow afternoon. Can you do that for me, for The Runt, Tullius' dad, and Tullius himself, for that matter. Just lay out the facts, like I did. Don't make it sound like a threat. Don't tell The Runt, either. We want to build up his confidence."

~ * ~

I went to see Tullius in his place in the tree the next morning. I brought him a bit of Tenobius' silver wire to buy my way in, and we spent a lot of time talking about what he was making now. We talked about the goings-on in the Little Forum, and the girls he was watching. I finally got to talking to him about The Runt, and tried to work it that I was giving him advice for his own good. Tullius is very sharp about some things, and knows what's going on in the market, 'On the street', as Tenobius likes to say. He can also be real stupid about other things, and I had to tell him about Publius and his father more than once. I had to explain it in detail before he understood at last what I was trying to say.

Even then he resented it, even if he saw the reason. I suggested he might let him come up in the tree a few timers without paying, even if he was alone. He might loan him the magic color square he got from Tenobius, as long as he got it back.

Because I was with Tullius, I missed Tenobius' visit to the glassmaker's stall. The glass master was there, he told me, and he was an angry little man.

"He wasn't interested at first," said Tenobius, "but when he saw the money I had, he was persuaded. He didn't want to show me his shop, but I talked him into it. He has a lot of samples of his work there, and it's exactly the kind of strong, thick-walled glass I need. I tried to explain what I wanted by drawing it on paper, but he couldn't understand the drawings. I'm going to have to make it with him, a step at a time, I think. It takes quite a bit of fuel to get his furnaces going hot enough, so I offered to buy the charcoal he'll need for the next run. That won't be just for me, though. I'm sure he'll have his apprentices working out of the furnace at the same time. It got me in his good graces. If he has them."

~ * ~

Over the next few days, between fine repairs on jewelry, a visit for fitting horseshoes, and general tasks, Tenobius readied his parts for the glassmaking. He also visited Munitor to get the bronze candle-pump. Munitor insisted on coming back, so I was surprised to look up from the bellows I was pumping to see him walk in. I couldn't leave my work, but I could steal glances over at them to see Tenobius showing off his work to Munitor, who seemed interested in everything.

It wasn't until I was relieved at the bellows that I got a chance to get a close look at the thing, and by that time Munitor had gone.

It was an impressive thing. It was about four feet long, and it was clean and spotless and gleamed in the sun. There were neat solder joints everywhere, neater even than the ones Tenobius has learned to do.

It wasn't just a single large tube with a conical spout at the end. There was a second, smaller tube parallel to the main one, and attached at each end with sections that curved into the main one. There were rods and plates that went with it, as well. The end opposite the cone wasn't soldered, as with the others at Munitor's shop, but unscrewed. The top lay off now, and it was clear that it had been partially disassembled. The rod that pushed the plunger had teeth made into the side. Sitting by itself, having been removed, was a gear assembly that I could see matched the teeth, although I couldn't figure out how it all went together. Some parts were made of copper, I guess. The contrast between the rosy pink of the copper and the yellow-orange bronze made it pretty. It was an awesome but puzzling piece of work.

~ * ~

Tenobius spent the rest of the day taking the thing apart, measuring parts, and cleaning it out with cleaned cloths dipped in the Spirits of Wine on the end of a long stick with a cleft end. He then put together some forms out of wood before he settled in for the night.

The next day, as soon as he could, he went to see Corvus, the glass master. This time he let me come along, although he told me to stay out of sight at first.

Corvus' shop was at the edge of the houses, in a large building with a huge pile of charcoal piled outside. I could feel a blast of heat from the door, even hotter than Marcus' shop when we're running hard. There was a big furnace in the center. It was round, with several openings around the outside, and workers going to and from each. Most of them seemed to be making thick-walled cups and bowls, a lot cruder than the delicate glasses we saw in the shop. Corvus obviously made different grades of work for different customers.

I stayed far back, outside, actually, so I couldn't hear what Tenobius said to the old, squinting Corvus. he was showing Corvus the drawings, which Corvus clearly didn't understand. Tenobius pulled out the rods he'd prepared and showed him using those. Corvus immediately took those carefully cleaned rods and examined him with his dirty hands. Tenobius winced at this, but said nothing. They moved into the shop, and Corvus gathered what must have been the things he needed.

He got a long rod and placed it in the furnace to heat up. After a time, he gathered up a glob of something from the furnace. I guess it was hot glass but it glowed orange and flowed like bread dough at Madame Nux' shop. He spun it around, back, then reversed the spin again, constantly twirling it with speed I wouldn't associate with an older man. The glass spun itself into a short, thick disc. Corvus kept going until he liked the size and thickness of it. He showed it to Tenobius, who nodded. After getting Tenobius' approval, he stuck it in the furnace again, spinning it all the while. He removed it. Tenobius took his rod and lined it up with the rod in Corvus' hand pressing it in toward the center, cutting into the edge of the

156

glass with the flattened part of the bronze rod as if it was a knife. He did the same on the other side, using two rods this time, and they put some spacers in and wound a cord around the whole thing to keep the rods in place. Corvus began rotating the rod again, then stuck it into the furnace, still spinning it. After it had been in there, he took it out and examined the end. Tenobius studied it, too. They evidently liked what they saw. Corvus gave it to Tenobius to spin against a board, then went away.

I figured this was a good time to see Tenobius, so I walked in. Tenobius saw me.

"What do you think?" he asked. "That's our work for today."

"This? This is it?"

"It's enough for one day. After the glass cools enough, I have to clean the rods and do some work on them."

"I could see you didn't like the way he touched them with his dirty hands. Especially after you spent all that time cleaning them."

"I can clean them again. Anyway, we got this far. I think the rest will be easy."

~ * ~

When we finally returned to the shop, Tenobius started up a pot of boiling water to make his 'island' stuff. While he was waiting, he carefully cleaned off the bronze rods, made the silver wire into a coil, threaded the ends through small holes in the bronze rods, and used solder to cover the ends. Finally, he cleaned it all again.

He made up an extra-thick mixture with the hide, honey, and other stuff, but left out the powder Lillia gave him for keeping mice away. He poured it into the molds, which was difficult because it was so thick, and covered them. When he finished, he went to bed.

~ * ~

Marcus wouldn't let me go with Tenobius the next day when he went to Corvus' shop, saying one of us needed to put in a full day's work. So, I pumped bellows, hammered out nails, and cleaned up things in the shop.

Maybe it was just as well. Tenobius was disgusted when he returned, but he had his glass thing with him, and he was proud of it.

It WAS interesting-looking. It was mostly a cylinder of thick glass, topped off at each end by the pieces they'd made a couple of days before. A long snout of hollow glass led off the side. You could put it on a table for people to admire or wonder over, if you wanted, and they would. I had no more idea how it was supposed to work than I had about his other things, but I had to admit it had a kind of beauty to it.

The glass was so thick he could probably have thrown it to the ground without harm, but he handled it as if it was one of those thin-walled goblets we saw in the Forum. He took it out back and shut it up in his cabinet. With it securely in the cabinet he took out the pieces he cast, took them out of their molds, examined them, and fit them to their nests in the bronze construction he got from Munitor. He carefully trimmed them, washed them with his spirits, and put them together. He stuck one piece of his 'islanding' stuff to the bottom of a beam with some nails, then he called me over.

"Hold this for me," he said, giving me the finished device from Munitor. His *pump*, he called it. I'd held it before, and it was just as heavy now. The addition of the pieces of Islanding must have made it a bit heavier, but not so you'd notice. He took it back.

"Now watch. This is both my pump and my Magdeburg Half-A-Sphere."

I have no idea what he meant by that. It was nothing like a half of a sphere. Tenobius was just talking to himself, through me.

He stuck the tip of the pump against the disk he'd nailed to the beam, then pulled the handle back, slowly. When he couldn't pull any further, he made an odd movement with his hand, and a mechanical assembly rotated into place beside the handle. A gear, Tenobius called it a *worm gear*, engaged with a row of teeth made into the side of the shaft beneath the handle. It kept the handle from being pulled back into the pump, as I knew it could be. He started to turn a handle, and it pulled the handle even further out, bit by bit, as the gear turned against the row of teeth. At first it was easy to turn, but it slowly became harder to do, and he stopped.

"Watch this," he said. He let go of the pump.

I *know* that it was heavy, because I'd just held it. I know all he did was press the end against the disc. Now the entire heavy pump was hanging from the tip as if there was a hook up there and an eyelet to swing it from. I had to stare.

"What's holding it up?"

"Nothing. Literally nothing. My countrymen would call it a *vacuum*. It's the worldly equivalent of our *zero*."

He looked satisfied with himself as he looked at his hanging pump, then back at me. "It means the pump works. So does my thicker 'islanding' stuff. Grab hold of it again. It doesn't weigh down on you, right? Well, hold on tight. It's going to get heavy again."

He reached over to the stopcock on the second tube and opened it. There was a loud hissing sound, as if a hundred serpents were suddenly in the yard, and I could feel the *pump* getting heavier. The sound stopped, and it weighed as much as before.

"We're almost set," he said. "A couple of days more work on this, and we'll be able to finish the Tube. "

"The glass thing you made? What will happen then?"

"What then? If everything works, I can put this in my Dreamship and go home."

~ * ~

Could that be true? After all this time, Tenobius was almost ready to complete his Dreamship and leave? That was crazy. Despite all I saw him do, it wasn't believable that he really had some craft that would carry him away. I'd never seen it, and didn't know where he'd docked it. And could a collection of wires, pottery, glass, and paper, all covered in boiled cowhide and honey actually take anyone anyplace? I was torn, as so many times before, between believing the proven magician and the crazy man.

If thought he was going to be leaving, I might as well treat it as true. I decided to go see people and tell them about it. I went to see Publius. I hadn't seen him since my talk with Tullius in the tree, anyway, and wanted to see how that came out.

The Runt was at home, and answered when I called at his window. He told me about how Tullius treated him well, inviting him up into the tree, and even lending him the little square rainbow thing he'd gotten from Tenobius. He didn't seem aware I was responsible for Tullius' change of mind. I told him not to abuse Tullius' kindness, and suggested he give Tullius a gift in return. That would cement their friendship.

I went to see Lillia, and told her about Tenobius' claim to be leaving soon. As I expected, she didn't believe it at all.

"What," she said, "Is he going to sail away on a ship made of wire and paper?"

I told her that, no matter what she thought, Tenobius believed this. Even if he didn't depart by Dreamship, he might be leaving soon by some other method. I told her I would let her know.

When I got back, Tenobius said he had been looking for me. Everything was ready, and he needed my help *now!*

He had made a small lamp, fueled, he said, by the spirits of wine. There was a rolled metal tube near the flame, which he demonstrated he could blow into to increase the flame, just like pumping the bellows would fire up the forge's charcoal fire. He'd used this to somehow attach his big pump to the thing he'd made with Corvus. He tied things down so they wouldn't move, but there was a lot to do at the same time, and he needed 'another pair of hands', as he put it.

I was ready for anything Tenobius set up, even if it might mean his leaving. We set to work.

He had me put a sort of basket over my face, and put one over his.

"I don't think anything is going to break here. The glass is pretty thick and the metal is sound. Just in case, this will keep any flying things out of our faces and our eyes."

That made me stop and think. Before I could protest, Tenobius turned away and was starting to do something. He went to the handle of his pump, checked it, and started to draw the handle back.

"Hold onto the tube," he said, indicating the glass thing from Corvus. "It's tied down, but I don't want it to move or to twist. We can't stress the connection between it and the pump." He indicated where he meant.

He began pulling the pump handle back. He was able to pull it all the way to the end, unlike the other day. I guess it was because it was attached to the 'tube' this time, instead of just ending in a disc. He worked the valves he'd built in, pushed the handle all the way back in. The pump hissed. When it was all the way in, he worked them again, then started to pull out the handle. He only got part way before it became hard to pull. As he did the other day, he swung the gear assembly into place and started to turn the crank, slowly pulling the handle further out. Tenobius' arms had gotten stronger during his time at the forge, and he could probably have pulled that old wire maker with his bare arms now, as Marcus had. He still preferred to use his clever machines to do the hard work. I saw now that his gear thing was like the lever, he used in wire pulling. It made it easier to pull the handle back, and kept it from being pulled back itself.

He cranked as far as he could, and worked his valves again, pushed the handle back in, even though he hadn't got it all the way out. The hissing, if it was there, was too quiet to hear.

Now he didn't even try to pull the handle by hand. He used the gear right from the start, cranking hard against the resistance of...well, against the *nothing*. Against the *zero*. Slowly, the pump handle was pulled backward, until he could get it to move no more, and he deiced it was finished.

"I'd like to have done this a couple more times," he said, "I'm not sure how far to trust my piston. Better to have an imperfect *vacuum* than none at all. I'd really have liked to use a *turbomolecular pump* or a *diffusion pump*, but there's no way I could have built one of those." He was talking, I think, to reassure himself, and to brace himself for the next step.

Finally, he roused himself.

"Now to seal it off," he said.

He placed a stool near the tube that attached the glass thing to the pump and placed his lamp with its pipe atop it. He adjusted things until the flame sat just to the side of the tube. That was when he turned to me.

"*Okay*," he said, using that barbarian word he often said when he was getting ready to do something. "I'm going to blow into this pipe and direct the flame at the glass. It's going to melt the glass. As it does so, the glass will get soft and glow, like it did at Corvus' We're going to pull this and twist it to seal off this opening. We're going to pinch it closed, like Mama Nux pinches off her pastries from the dispenser. You understand?"

I said I did, and we started. I think it took a lot longer than Tenobius thought it would. Eventually the glass turned orange and softened. It didn't want to stretch out, but he was able to twist it away and close off the end. He couldn't pull away the end with the pump, but he let it cool off like that, and then he broke the glass attached to the pump. By then he was out of breath from constantly blowing on the pipe. It seemed like more work than the pumping had been. Finally, he looked at the glass thing and smiled.

"It's ugly," he said, "But it ought to work."

I didn't think it was ugly. It was strange, though. Probably the strangest-looking thing Tenobius made, and that made it sort of pretty.

"My God," he said, "I can't believe it's over. I'll let this set a while, then test it. He set it carefully inside his cabinet.

We went for a little celebration at Catella's Taberna.

~ * ~

That evening we sat in the backyard at the shop. Tenobius had the glass thing sitting on the table and was using his magic box with the needle to decide if it worked. He kept doing things over and over and frowning, which I know is a bad sign. As he started again, I decided to ask him.

"Well, does it work?"

"Yes and no. It's on the edge. This is the trickiest piece to make. I don't really trust the vacuum pump I made. I wish I could have put a *getter* inside, or something."

"Could you make another piece?"

"I could, but I don't see the point. This is as good as I could make it. The pump has been used once and it's already deteriorating. I'd have to cast new pads for it. If *outgassing* is my problem, that won't fix it. "

"So, if this is as good as you can make it, why not use it? Worrying about it won't help."

"That's true."

"You said that the other parts could only last so long. You should use this while it's still fresh."

"You're quoting my own words at me."

"Were you wrong before?"

"No. It's just that...that I'm afraid it might not work."

"So? If it doesn't work, you'll think of something else to try."

"Not this time. If this doesn't work, I don't know what I'll do." He looked at me. "*That's* what I'm afraid of."

"Is there anything else you can do?"

"No." He sighed, deeply. "This really is it. I'll have to put this in place and...just try it."

"And then what?"

"If it works, I'll just go home."

"If that's what you're going to do, you'd better say goodbye, in case it works."

"You're making fun of me."

"I am not. I'll bring Lillia to see you off. If it works."

"Tomorrow. We'll do it in daylight. I'll need the light to hook this up, anyway."

~ * ~

Early the next morning I found Lillia getting water for her house and told her Tenobius was going to be leaving. She didn't take it seriously at all, but I finally got her to realize, even if she didn't think he was leaving, he was convinced he was. If she didn't come to see him try to leave, he would be disappointed.

I don't think she truly understood Tenobius really thought he would be going away. To her, it was like a big game of 'pretend'. She finally decided, if he thought he was going, she would have to be there. She could always comfort him when he failed.

I didn't tell anyone else. Tenobius didn't want anyone else to know.

~ * ~

We waited until mid-morning. By then the sun had risen enough to give good light, and people were about their business. Tenobius did not say goodbye to Marcus. When I asked him what to say if Marcus asked why Tenobius was no longer around, he said to tell him whatever I wanted.

"Tell him I went back home," Tenobius said. "He'll believe that."

He gathered up the glass thing and some tools he said he'd need. I ran and got Lillia, and we were off.

Tenobius whistled again. He did that when he was happy. Lillia asked about the whistling, and I explained it. People in Rome only whistled as a signal, to other people or to animals. Tenobius was the only person I met who whistled a song. He said back where he was from, lots of people did it. Lillia asked what the song was, thinking it was some religious thing.

"It's called *Yesterday*," said Tenobius. "It seems appropriate. For lots of reasons."

~ * ~

I never knew where Tenobius kept his Dreamship. He took us to a wall built into the side of an earth bank, as if the wall was holding up the bank. It was made of bricks laid in diagonally. There was what appeared to be a large rock in the wall, but when we got close, I saw it was a cloth heavily stained and stiffened with earth and clay, so it looked like a rock. Tenobius pulled this away, revealing a closely-fitted door in a jamb. The door was secured with a carefully knotted rope.

"One of the annoying things is that I haven't been able to find a proper lock anywhere in Rome," said Tenobius. "I had to fall back on the old practice of tying an elaborate knot, so I'd know if anyone ever broke in. Of course, someone could always cut the knot."

He started to untie the big knot.

"I ended up using the knot I use for my *gi*, followed by the way my mother used to tie my shoes, double knotted. I doubt if anyone in this city ever tied either of those knots." It was taking him some time to undo the complicated knot.

"Maybe we could just cut the rope," I suggested. "You don't think you're going to have to tie it again."

"Thanks for the vote of confidence, but I'd rather not. You're like

Alexander and the Gordian knot."

"Who?"

"Alexander the Great. They named Alexandria in Egypt after him. He conquered almost all the known world before he died. He was thirty-three. Anyway, when he started out, he was confronted with a famous knot, way more complicated than this. I think they said that the man who undid it could rule the world, or something. So, he took his sword and just cut it apart. Now most people who tell that story think they're talking about his unorthodox and straightforward way of solving problems, but I think the real point, meant by the people who owned the knot, was that Alexander didn't respect the rules and property. Instead of trying to figure the knot out, and not damaging things, he just cut it to pieces, and proved he was just another barbarian. Maybe that's what you need to conquer the world, and here I've finished my knot, proving I'm not an uncultured barbarian. So now you'll finally be able to see my Dreamship."

Tenobius drew the rope through the holes in the door, then grabbed the doors and thrust them open.

As I said, I think that, until then, I didn't really believe Tenobius and his wild story, not deep down inside. I know Lillia didn't. With my first sight of his Dreamship, I knew Tenobius was what he said. He was real, strange, and came from somewhere that you couldn't explain. What followed afterward made certain I believed, but actually seeing the Dreamship convinced me. I was in the presence of an awful reality.

It was big enough to hold a man inside, and was half constructed of metal and half of what I first thought was glass. When I felt it, though, it didn't feel like glass. It was something...else. Not hard and brittle and cold like glass. It was several different colors. It was a piece of handicraft that went beyond anything I ever saw in Rome. Far beyond the wares in the shops in the Big Forum, or the chariots of the army, or the litters of the wealthy, or even the palaces and temples. Everything was made so very well, so much better than Tenobius did, or Marcus, or any of the artisans I'd met. It was all *curved*, and everything fitted together perfectly. This was something from Somewhere Else. I looked over at Lillia, and her eyes were wide open. So was her mouth. I realized I looked the same way, the glass-like stuff acted as a mirror, and I could see myself, distorted.

I don't know what I expected. Maybe a big box made of rough pieces of wood put together, with wheels. Maybe a boat-shaped thing, hammered together out of rough planks, and with Tenobius' strange little pieces attached to it. Perhaps a scaled-up version of a boat or chariot built by a child. Just what you'd think a mad man would do, but not this. This was a professional piece of work done by a hundred Tenobiuses, with all the time they needed. The metal was smooth and polished and perfect. Tenobius didn't put this together in moments away from us. He traveled here, somehow, from his own country in this Thing that had no wheels, prow, oars or sail.

I couldn't speak. I had no idea what to say. What Tenobius did next, natural as could be, as if it was nothing special, utterly stunned me. Stunned us. Lillia didn't fully appreciate perfect craftsmanship, but she knew this was something unnatural.

There was a door of some sort I hadn't even realized was there. Tenobius opened it, and the side of the Thing opened up. The inside was as perfect as the outside, filled with toggles and knobs sticking out of flat surfaces. He did something, and one of these opened up. There inside was where he had been working.

There were big sheets of some green stuff. It looked and felt, when I got a chance to touch it, like horn, but it was covered with little attached cylinders and metal. One of these green sheets was blackened and discolored. I think there had been a fire there. It smelled like, well, if metal was left outside in a hot sun until it spoiled, it would smell like that. It didn't look neat, as the other sheets did. Tenobius removed many of the cylinders and replaced them, I saw, with the things he had been making. There was the necklace I'd worn when we first met. He had taken the beads and strung them on wire. I remember he showed me that, and I thought it was a poor necklace. Only now I saw that it was not supposed to be one. It was replacing one of those metal paths that had been on the sheet before, with the beads taking the place of the 'islanding' stuff he later made. Tenobius followed my gaze.

"Yes. That's one of the first repairs I made. I needed the beads as *insulation*. It looks clumsy, and it took up too much space, which is why we had to use the stuff made from cow hide and honey. But I'm glad I put the beads in there and never replaced them. That wire carries a lot of *current*."

I could see the honey-roll things hanging from the sheets in places, the ceramic tubes covered with burned paper, dipped in the 'islanding', and the tubes wrapped with wire. Over there was the horseshoe the apprentices ruined, now with many turns of wire wrapped around it.

Other things I did not recognize. It looked as if Tenobius took them from elsewhere in the ship. Little black things that looked like bugs and tiny hornlike things in many colors. Some things were suspended on strings, or on little wooden platforms he made. It was on one such platform he placed the Glass Thing he'd brought. He connected it using pieces of wire I had not seen before, which ended in little jaws with teeth that clasped the ends of the bronze rods like hungry mouths.

"I decided to save my only sets of *alligator clips* for last," said Tenobius. "Saves me the hassle of trying to solder this in place"

He folded down a different sheet elsewhere, and it became a seat. Tenobius sat down on it.

"Okay. I'm going to start my Dreamship with this panel open, and the main door open. That should be all right. I want the two of you to stand back from this about the distance that a man is tall. Go on, move!"

Lillia and I did, reluctantly. Tenobius did something that made us jump back. He reached for the biggest toggle and moved it.

Instantly lights appeared in the Dreamship. Many of those hanging, hornlike things lit up, and all together. It was like looking through one of those walls set with bits of colored glass or stone when the sun comes up behind it, only there was no sun here. Tenobius made these things light up without sun or flame. No wonder there had been a fire. There were sounds, too. I heard sounds like wheels turning, and sounds like crickets now and then. The entire inside of the Dreamship seemed to come alive. Lights appeared on the walls in places I didn't know they could be, and they moved and changed. Lillia and I jumped back at the first indication of this. We must have looked terrified, because Tenobius spoke.

"Don't be afraid! Don't be afraid! This is how it's supposed to work! He looked at all of the lights and inspected them. He pulled out his Magic Box and used it on several of the things in his Dreamship, especially the Glass Thing. He seemed satisfied.

"I'm going to start the sequence now. Whatever you see, don't move, and don't touch me or the Dreamship."

"Which way is it going to go?" I asked. I wanted to get out of its way.

"In the direction you can't point!" he answered, grinning. "*Perpendicular* to everything else!" His fingers worked more of the toggles. Different lights lit up, and some went out. The Dreamship didn't catch fire.

Things began to feel strange. The air and sky seemed to be darker, and I got a sense of the wind. It was hard to see more than a little distance away. The Dreamship made strange noises.

The sound of rushing wind got louder, and I got the impression we were in the center of a great rotation. It felt like when my mother pulled the plug at the bottom of a basin when doing a large wash and let it drain into the street. The water formed a funnel-like whirlpool. This felt like that. The whirlpool was getting stronger and louder and we were inside it. It got very dark and gray, and directly overhead it began to dimple upwards, as if the funnel was forming there. Tenobius looked up, and his mouth opened in a gape that turned into a smile. It was working. Despite what Tenobius said, it looked as if his ship was going to go UP into that whirlpool.

Instantly, there was a bright flash! It came from the Glass Thing on its wooden shelf. Tenobius' face told me what I needed to know, something was wrong. It wasn't supposed to do that. There came another flash, and all of the lights went out. The noises stopped. Very quickly the gray whirlpool around us evaporated.

Tenobius screamed! He worked the toggles in different combinations. He was silent a moment, then started to shout things in his barbarian tongue. I couldn't understand what he said, but I knew what he was saying.

Some of the lights came back on, and the noises returned, but the whirlpool didn't. Tenobius finally picked up the Glass Thing and looked at it. The wire that had been stretched across it was broken, and there was a big splotch of black on one side of the Glass Thing. I don't know what it did, or how. I gathered that it couldn't do it with the wire broken.

"No. no. no. no. no. no. no. no. no. no. no. NO!" screamed Tenobius.

He took the Glass Thing and threw it as far away as he could. He got up and stumped slowly away. He made no effort to close things up or hide his Dreamship. I came back and did that later. Right now, Lillia and I got out of his way. Tenobius had shown himself The Great Magician. Our Crazy Man, the local Mad Man had shown he was the Master of Weather and Lightning, and we had new awe and respect for him. Who knew what else he could do? He was a kindly teacher who made horseshoes and paper and fixed jewelry, but he could command the Cosmos. We were frightened of him, and let him stalk away in grief in private.

When we got back to the forge, after shutting up the Dreamship, we found the backyard in a mess. Tenobius' things had been thrown around, many of them broken. That magnificent pump was a twisted wreck, the handle torn off and the barrel battered against something, probably the anvil.

Tenobius himself was sitting out back, off on the side, facing the wall. We hadn't seen him at first, because he was perfectly still. We went up to him and spoke, quietly at first. He didn't notice us. He didn't see us or hear us. He was closed off from everything. It was worse than when he tried to get Marcus to hire me to keep track of numbers. He stayed that way, unmoving, not seeing or hearing anything, no eating or drinking, for days.

I felt very guilty about it, because I was the one who encouraged him to try out the Glass Thing, even though Tenobius wasn't sure about it. If only I hadn't done that. If only he had a chance to redo it, or rethink it, the Dreamship might have worked. I apologized to him, over and over. Even though he didn't hear. I said I would rebuild the parts, if only I knew how. Knowing Tenobius was the only one who could do that.

Lillia made him a soup, and tried to get him to eat. She went as far as to try to force the spoon into his mouth. Tenobius, without looking at her, raised his hand and pushed her away. It was an action, at least, but it didn't rouse any faith or excitement in us.

"He won't react," I said to Lillia. "He won't notice us."

"We thought he was crazy, and we found out he wasn't," she replied. "This is how some crazy people act. When they find out they're wrong about the world, something inside dies. They just sit and stare. Ssometimes they mumble to themselves."

"Lucky us," I said. "He really is a wizard, but he couldn't get his ship to work, and it ends up the same way. We have to do something."

Lillia thought a while.

"Leave him like this, for now. He has to get over this. In the meantime, he has to eat sometime." She turned to me. "Talk to him. Just don't apologize. Remind him of who he is and what he'd done. Make him remember how great he can be."

She got up, went over to Tenobius, and rubbed his shoulders, then went back into the house.

Tenobius sat like a statue. After a long time, I went over to him and spoke about how we'd met, how he made the wire, how he tried and failed to make paper, and to make the islanding stuff. About how the mice ate it, and all the rest. Nothing changed. He didn't move, and there was no spark in his eyes.

~ * ~

Marcus saw Tenobius sitting there the next day, and came over to yell at him. He called him a lazy bastard, and asked why he wasn't working, and did he expect everyone else to do things for him? Tenobius didn't react. Marcus went as far as to hit Tenobius' back and slap his face. When Tenobius didn't react, Marcus turned to me with a worried look on his face. What happened, he wanted to know. I explained to him about the Dreamship, without giving details. Marcus, who hadn't seen the Dreamship, and never believed in it, nodded his head knowingly. I could tell that he thought Tenobius finally went completely over the edge. He brought a shawl and covered Tenobius with it. I don't know if Tenobius was cold, or if Marcus thought he was, but he felt, I think, he had to do *something*.

Tenobius made no effort to remove the shawl. He sat there with it the whole day, and through the night.

I tried to get him to eat, then talked to him again about all he had done. I thanked him for showing me how to read and helping me with numbers, but he didn't respond.

Lillia came in and asked me about him. She brought NexMuris, the kitten, with her, and put him by Tenobius. The kitten ignored Tenobius at first, walking around and looking at things. At last it came over to him and purred. It licked his hand. Even this got no reaction from Tenobius. He sat still as a lump of lead.

I sat down next to him, and NexMuris slunk over to me. She sniffed at my hands, then abruptly turned and sniffed my face, licking my nose. Despite the situation, I laughed. The cat couldn't rouse Tenobius from his gloom, but she cheered me up.

"Stop," I said "Your whiskers are tickling me."

Suddenly NexMuris leapt from my lap. It was so sudden and so desperate her claws dug into my thighs and made a long cut. Before I could react to this, I saw what it was that had startled her.

Tenobius was standing up! His eyes no longer had that shrouded look, but were staring at something far away, visible only to him. I saw that look before. As I watched, his lips curled into a slight smile, and he spoke. At first in a whisper, then louder.

"Cat's whiskers," he said. "Tickling with cat's whiskers. Cat's whiskers!" He looked over and saw me, saw *something*, for the first time in days. "That's how we'll do it! I've been stupid! Cat's whiskers!"

I looked over at Nex Muris, now licking her paw, and tried not to feel the pain in my leg.

"You're not going to need *all* of them, are you?" I asked.

~ * ~

As Tenobius explained, 'cat's whisker' was just slang, a term used for one of those wizard devices of his. I wouldn't have thought of wizards having their own slang. If soldiers, washerwomen and blacksmiths have their own argot, I suppose wizards would, too.

When Lillia saw that Tenobius was up and around again, she insisted on making him something to eat. It had, after all, been three days. He said he wasn't hungry, but when she brought a plate of something I didn't recognize, he ate it without even asking what it was.

It was as if the days and nights of his being shut off from the world hadn't happened. We were so glad to have him back we almost overlooked the way he controlled things we couldn't understand. Almost. He spoke and acted like the old Tenobius. Having decided what to do, he sped off to do something about it, disappearing out the front of the forge right past Marcus without saying a word to him. For his part, Marcus was annoyed, and thought Tenobius should at least have greeted him after being practically dead. With Tenobius not around to yell at, he yelled at me.

It was late when Tenobius returned, carrying an extra pouch, besides his money purse, which he emptied onto his work bench. It was filled with rings and lockets and loose gems. The jewelry was set with gems, as well. All of the same type, ugly ones. I would have expected diamonds or brightly colored emeralds or rubies, but the gems he brought back, from the same jewelers who sent him so much work over the past year, were all grayish-blue, somewhat shiny stones with squared-off fractures. They were interesting, at least, but not beautiful. I told him so.

"I don't care what they look like," he said, "As long as they do what I want."

"What do you want them to do?" I asked, knowing it was actually pointless to ask.

Tenobius could have told me he wanted the stones for imprisoning tiny demons, and I'd believe him. I'd have no choice, since I had no idea what any of his things did. I understood his answer, a little.

"I want it to do the same thing the Glass Thing did."

"Are we going to have to build another pump?" I asked, thinking about the magnificent one he'd bent into shapelessness.

"No." he replied. "I should have known I'd never get the kind of *vacuum* I'd need with the materials I had. Nobody built a practical *light bulb* until they'd come up with a decent *vacuum* pump. I could spend my entire life trying to do that. That project was doomed from the start. On the other hand, I'd never be able to grow a decent *semiconductor* crystal, either, even if Myles Cabot could do it. So, I'm going to cheat, and use natural crystals. Instead of engineering my own devices, I'm going to search for defects that will do what I want."

He looked over the gems he'd brought, one at a time, cleaning them off and examining them.

"What do they look like, these things you're looking for?" I asked.

"Eh? Oh, you can't see them. They're too small. I'll have to use my *multi-*, uh, my 'Magic Box' but first I'll have to build some things."

"Can I help?"

"I'm counting on it."

So, I helped. We made a clamp out of pure gold, with just enough alloy in it to give it some strength. We built a stiff wire mounted to some fine screws that let him position it carefully, and we built a wooden fixture to hold it all.

When it was finished, it didn't look like much. It was neat, but you wouldn't think it could do anything. It wasn't like the original work on his Dreamship. If it could make that work again, it would be impressive.

To make his tests, Tenobius used a collection of parts he'd made of the kind I saw in the Dreamship, which he arranged with his Magic Box. He called it a *circuit*, and I recognized the world for *circle* in that. He said I was correct. The *electrons* flowed from part to part in a circle, as if that meant something to me.

He took one of the gems and placed it in the clamp, screwing it down to hold it securely, then brought over the wire on its mount at placed it against the face of the gem. "You see, he said, the wire is like a cat's whisker, and moving it around is like 'tickling' the gem. I have to find just the right spot."

"The right spot for what?"

"To make this needle move the right way."

He didn't look at me, and did things with his Magic Box. Then he moved the wire over a little, and started over again. He did this over, and over, and over again. It got boring after a while.

"What are you looking for?"

"I want the needle to swing over when I do *this*, but not when I do *this*," Tenobius said, demonstrating.

Most of the time the needle either swung on both occasions, or didn't swing for either. Sometimes it looked as if he found a spot, but when he tried it again, the needle swung instead of staying still. It was a long and drawn-out task.

"Of course, this really isn't the best way to do this," Tenobius suddenly said. "What I should be doing is wearing a pair of *headphones* and listening for a *radio* throwing-of-the-seeds. Except that nobody in Rome has a *radio*."

"What's a *radio*?" I asked, knowing he wanted me to.

"It's a way we have of sending music through the air. You can't hear it unless you have a proper receiver, and a crystal like this used to be the way to make one. That's what Rome needs, a *Radio* station. We could call it SPQR. All Roman Music, All The Time. What music would we play? What would people listen to? Not that awful stuff from the funerals, or from the religious processions. What popular songs do you like?"

"Fromius plays his *cithara* down at the marketplace and sings old army songs. Since he lost his leg, he can't do much else. People throw him coppers."

"With a *radio* he'd be a star," said Tenobius.

"A star?"

"An important performer. He wouldn't have to beg. People would pay money to listen to him, and he could afford to build a *villa*."

Tenobius started singing to himself, making up things for his Roman *radio*. I don't think anyone would pay to hear him sing, but some of the things he said were funny. Even when he spoke in barbarian words, he spoke in a funny voice.

"You're listening to SPQR, the Voice of Rome. Try Drinka Jara Wineaday. It pays for the sand in the arena." It was so silly, I had to laugh.

"Of course," said Tenobius, "If it worked with a crystal set, it'd have to be *AM radio*. I think even in Ancient Rome nobody listens to *AM radio* anymore. All you get are political orators and chariot commercials."

After that, he stopped talking, but it had been interesting for a little bit. He went back to the monotonous business of looking for the spot he wanted on his crystal.

~ * ~

It took days. After Tenobius exhausted one face of a crystal, he'd turn to another and start the same thing all over again. He showed me what to do, and I tried for a while, but he took it back again. He didn't trust me to do it right, and he was afraid I might find a good spot and not realize it, so he ended up doing almost all of the searching.

To break up the monotony, he made up what he called *programs* on his Roman *radio station* SPQR. I gathered that these were like little comic plays, like the ones about the seven people on the island. Once I realized that, I helped make some up. He made up plays about the seven castaways, and about the three idiots Larri, Curli, and Mo. I suggested ways that different shops in the little Forum might sell their wares. Lillia came over to see what we were laughing at. We had a good time, but we were getting very frustrated. Tenobius was starting to think he might have gotten something wrong with his whisker device.

He finally found a spot that *almost* did what he wanted. The needle moved when he had his *circuit* one way, and almost didn't react when he did it the other. Almost. After being still at first, the needle slowly moved. Tenobius wasn't discouraged. He said this showed we had the right kind of crystal. We just didn't have the right spot. Maybe the whisker was too big.

Tenobius filed and sanded the end of the wire smaller and started looking again, step by slow step across the face of the crystal. Twice more he thought he had it, but the needle eventually moved.

It wasn't until he had flipped the crystal to another side that he found what he wanted, a spot where he got a response one way and not the other. He jiggled the entire mount holding the crystal, clamp, and whisker, but the response remained the same. He put a lid on the box and fastened it so nothing could disturb it.

"I'm tempted," Tenobius said, "To make another one of these, in case this goes bad. Unfortunately, it took too damned long. This one might fail if I leave it too long."

"Don't," I said. "We'll take this to the Dreamship and put it in place."

"Where's Lillia?" Tenobius asked. "I want her to be there."

"I'll get her," I said. "You stay with that thing and get it safely there."

Tenobius agreed, and finished securing the lid. I ran out to get Lillia, and found she wasn't at home. I was told that she probably went out for water, so I ran out to the public fountain.

As I ran, I passed something that made me stop. It was a troop of soldiers. Nothing odd about that. I'd seen them all my life, and plenty in the streets of Rome. There was something different about these.

They were clean and neat. Soldiers always try to appear clean for their commanders, but these were different. They were *immaculate*. Their links in their armor were oiled, and everything was perfectly polished, and they were marching in tight formation. That is something you do not see all the time in a small Roman street. This was an official elite company. These were soldiers far above the level of my father, of Mopsus, or even Quintus, who'd bought the horse shoes.

They were going back along the direction I'd just come. I suddenly had a terror that something bad was about to happen, and I ran back to the shop.

Sure enough, they had pulled up in formation in front of Marcus, with the commander in front. Three of them went in, but I could hear what they said, it was loud enough.

"Is there one here who is called Tenobius? You are to come with us at once."

~ * ~

I kept back as they marched Tenobius out, surrounding him with a square formation. Tenobius kept trying to ask where they were taking him and why, but I knew that set to a soldier's jaw, they were Doing Their Job, and nothing but. I kept back far enough to not be seen, but to keep them in sight. I'd done that so often in the streets I could do it in my sleep.

After a little while I had an idea of where they might be taking him. I recognized the way. We were going to the home of The Runt. His father was a Senator, someone who would have the clout to order an elite troop of soldiers to do something for him. I ran ahead of the group down a side street and stationed myself where I could watch the front entrance, and dart in the back if I had to.

They swung around the corner, marching swiftly up to the house and coming to a halt in front. The leader walked up to the front door and kicked at the front door plate, the way soldiers are ordered to. At that I went around to Publius' room, hoping he would be home. He was, but I had to explain to him three times what was going on.

"They're bringing him *here*? Why?"

I told him I didn't know, but could he get me in so I could listen to what was going on. He hesitated then said that he could, but I'd have to keep it a secret. A Big Secret. I clambered in and followed him.

"They'll take him in to see my father, and they'll almost certainly go to his hall. It's private, and no one can get in or listen in."

"How are we..." I started.

"When they repaired it a few years ago I pried open one of the joints in the Marble so I could see in. My father doesn't know," he whispered.

He took me to a place where a panel closed off a section of wall, and he pried it open. There was a very small, very tight space inside. It would hold two boys, barely. We worked our way in and tried to be quiet, and Publius pulled the panel shut with a handle he'd attached to it. I hadn't thought him capable of such skullduggery, but my mother always said that it's the quiet ones you have to watch out for. Although I think she meant me.

Once inside, we arranged ourselves with me above Publius, both looking through the same gap. We could see the entire room. His father, who I'd only rarely seen, entered and sat on a big chair that rested on a slightly raised platform. The door opened and the leader of the troop led Tenobius in. Publius' father thanked the soldier, and said he should wait outside. The soldier left and closed a door.

A door! Doors were for the outside Nobody I knew had a door inside their house. You had a curtain you could draw, if anything. This room could be completely closed off for privacy. My first thought was that this showed real wealth, although later I realized Senators must have to keep secrets. It was also the cleanest room I had ever seen, with marble floors and lower walls, and with clean wood and paintings on the upper walls. There were several lamps on brass stands, so that even though the room had no windows to the outside, it was well-lit. There were openings high up for ventilation, but they were useless for light, or eavesdropping.

Publius' father sat motionless in his chair, looking at Tenobius. Tenobius sat. His eyes darted around, his restless hands moved in his lap, but he didn't look guilty. That was probably a good thing. I don't know what made the Senator bring him in, but looking guilty would only have made it worse.

"I'm not sure what to do with you," the Senator said at last. "I tell you frankly this is a new experience, and there is no precedent to fall back on."

"Perhaps..." said Tenobius, and his voice caught.

I think his throat was dry, and who could blame him?

He started again "Perhaps you could begin by telling me who you are, and why you asked me to come."

"Yes. That would be best. You are polite, considering the way I summoned you. I hope you will forgive that. It was necessary. Even so, I would like you to be at ease."

He lifted up his voice to call, "Donatus!"

The door opened immediately and a middle-aged man looked in.

"Bring us two cups of wine," he said, and Donatus disappeared.

"I can tell that your throat is dry. Mine will be, as well. We have much talking to do."

Donatus was back with two cups, proper cups. He gave one to Tenobius and one to the Senator.

"You are looking at the cup strangely. I assure you it is not poisoned," said the Senator.

To prove it, he swallowed from his own.

"I didn't think that it was," answered Tenobius. "It's just been a long time since I drank wine from a cup."

"Ah, you've been to the wine shops in the Little Forum. They must use pots and bowls. You are a refined man, are you not?"

"It's not that. They always use cups where I come from."

"Indeed. Are where are you from? Don't answer that yet. I will tell you that I am Caius Marcurius, and I am a Senator. Do you know what that is?"

"I do."

"Then you should know that I have a responsibility for the safety and welfare of the people I represent. They are under my protection If there is anything unusual, I want to know about it and understand it, and see if it poses a danger to my people. Please don't be offended when I say that you are...not usual.

"Your name, I am told, is Tenobius. No one knows where you come from. You work at the blacksmith shop of Marcus not far from the Little Forum. When you came, you spoke very little, and to very few people, but now you speak Latin quite well. You have distinguished yourself by doing fine work with metals, by making excellent wire, by contriving footwear for horses and for oxen, which you have been selling to our army. You also go about looking for strange items.

"I have many people who gather information and who tell me things. Some of them think that you may be a spy. You come from an unknown place and you interfere with our army. They would like to see me arrest you and question you. How do you feel about that?"

"That I am happy you want me to be at ease," said Tenobius. "If you did not tell me that, I would be frightened."

"Well answered. Now, perhaps, you can tell me where you do come from, and why you are doing these things."

"I'm not sure that I can explain where I'm from. It's a land your people are not familiar with."

"Oh, we know many things, many more than I think you are aware of. If you think I have not seen people with eyes like yours, you are mistaken. A senator sees many strange things, and I have talked with people who come from far in the north and east of here, beyond the *Pontus Euxinus*."

"I could lie and say that is where I am from, but I am not."

"Then perhaps this will surprise you, I believe you when you say that you are not from there, and that you might not be able to tell me where you are from. So. How did you get here?"

"In a ship, which foundered. All my efforts have been to repair it and go home."

"If I were to offer you a ship, and to have it take you in whichever direction you wished to go, would you accept my offer?"

"I think it's more generous than you can really grant."

"You're right. What have you learned of Rome? Can you name our Emperor?"

Tenobius talked about the City he knew, and about the markets, and buying things. He named the Emperor. I don't know if he was right, all the emperors are called *Caesar*, and about making wire and horseshoes. The Senator let him talk, and had more wine brought in. Finally, he stopped Tenobius.

"Enough. I tell you, Tenobius, that I do not think you are a spy. I have spoken to my officers and seen these contraptions you made for horses and oxen, and they look like improvements. I do believe that you have been seeking the funds and parts you need to repair your...ship. You are clearly an intelligent man, and if you were intending to be a spy, you have done a poor job of it. You have made yourself conspicuous, which a spy should not be.

"I have been more concerned because you know and have spoken with my son, Publius. They call him 'The Runt', did you know that? Apparently, I have you to thank for advice you have given him. If you were a spy, that would be a very foolish thing to do. It drew too much attention from someone like me. I considered that perhaps you were trying to worm your way into my family, perhaps to attack me. But then I realized I had overlooked something I ought to have known from the first."

The Senator seemed to be speaking to himself.

"We never see things that are right before our eyes, and recognize them for what they truly are. I should have known what you were, but you were living right here in the city, talking with my son, working in my town. I was expecting something, forgive me, even stranger than you. *This* is what made me realize my mistake."

He held out his hand, and it sparkled with all the colors of the rainbow as he moved it about. Tenobius realized, as I did, that he was holding the square of rainbow stuff, the twin of my rainbow disc, the one he had given to Tullius, and which Tullius had loaned to Publius. I looked at Publius, who shook his head. He had no idea his father had it, or even knew about it.

"I have taken this to many of the wise men of the Court. No one can tell me what this is. Like you, it is unique, and from somewhere else. Two of the emperors you have named have not sat in the Throne. Not yet, at any rate. What convinced me was your name. You have made it into a Latin form, but that is not its original form, is it? That is what confused me for so long. Your name is really *Wah-Tah-Nah-Bay*, is it not? *Watanabe* becomes 'Tenobius' in the mouths of the Roman people. I've been expecting Watanabe for years, but with a name like that, I thought you would be Egyptian. I think you are not only a man out of your Place, but a man out of your Time."

I stared through the gap in the wall at Tenobius, and I was finally beginning, I think, to understand where he came from. Tenobius, for his part, looked at the Senator with confusion written on his face. Finally, he came to a decision, and I knew what it must be. He was thinking the Senator was someone come back in a Dreamship to rescue him, or knew someone who did.

Tenobius said something long and rapid in his barbarian tongue, hoping the Senator would understand. I could see from his face the Senator did not. I think he had no idea what sort of language Tenobius, Watanabe, was even speaking. If not that, then how did the Senator know about him? Tenobius' face showed he had the same question.

The Senator raised his hand.

"Enough. I do not understand your language. I think no one in Rome does. I believe you are shipwrecked here, as you say. The question I have is, why have you come? What have you brought us?"

"I do not understand," said Tenobius, "Possibly you don't. I haven't come to bring anything. I came to see Rome. I came to see if I *could* see Rome."

The senator regarded him in silence for a time.

"I don't know if you are being honest, lying, or simply testing me. We hoped that you would provide some new revelations."

"Revelations?"

"You seem to be a strange blend of knowledge and ignorance. Is it possible you do not know of your predecessor?"

"No. I'm afraid I do not know what you are speaking about."

"Your predictions of the names of the future emperors. I know that they are correct, and your naming them, along with your name, prove your identity. The reason I know those names, and a select group of senators knows them, is because we have the books." He gestured toward a table, which had some scrolls placed in careful arrangement on it.

"The *Libri Sibillini*, the Sibylline Books. They were obtained by Tarquinius Superbus, the last king of Rome, half a millennium ago. In them are written the history of Rome, before it happened. The predictions have rarely been incorrect. All the prominent men, the coming of the emperors, the important wars, all are in there. Even you are in there, mentioned by name, *Watanabe*. You were long looked for, and we hoped you would add to the knowledge in those books."

Tenobius looked over at the scrolls, and then back at Caius.

"What do the scrolls say about me?"

"You don't know, then?"

"No. Your words are the first I heard of these. The Sibylline books were, will be lost, destroyed. Some say deliberately."

"That is a pity. The books only go so far, and only say so much. Of you they only say you will be seen in Rome at this time, and you are another protected oracle. It says something about controlling the lightning, but the passage is garbled."

Tenobius was staring, his mouth open as mine had been when his Dreamship came to life.

"Where did these books come from? How can they possibly know about me?"

"You really do not know? You, an oracle, according to the books themselves? You really don't know their story?"

"No. I am sorry if I disappoint, but...no."

"Well, then. I don't understand that, either. It's as if Jove did not know of the existence of Hera. I will tell you the story, and perhaps you will remember, or maybe understand.

"These books were said to be handed down from the Sibyls and prophetesses of Greece. The Cumaean Sibyl came to Tarquinius Superbus, King of Rome, and offered to sell him nine books of prophecies. Tarquinius of honored memory refused to buy them, even though they offered to foretell the future. The Cumean Sibyl had been proven time and again to be accurate, because the price she demanded was too high. So, she tossed three of the books into the sacrificial fire and offered to sell him the remaining six books, but at the same price. Again, he refused. She tossed three more books into the fire, obliterating them and all their knowledge for all time. That was when she offered to sell the last three to the King for the same price that she offered for all nine. This time, rather than see the remaining three books go into the fire, he relented, and paid for the books.

"I have often wished, with many others, Our Father Tarquinius had bought all nine books, rather than only the remaining three. They have directed us through our development, and Rome is now the Master of the World because of them. Now what do you have to say?"

To my utter surprise and amazement, Tenobius suddenly had that faraway look in his eye, stayed that way for a few seconds, before he started to laugh.

~ * ~

"Sibyl!" he shouted. "Sibyl! Our own Emily Sibyl Watkins! She was, is, the Cumean Sibyl! My gods! My gods!" He sat back in his chair, open mouthed and wide-eyed, and breathed heavily. He was, I could tell, thinking and deducing. I don't know if the Senator understood all that Tenobius said next, but I was beginning to. I think.

"There was a flaw, a defect, in *her* Dreamship, too. There must have been. Mine was not the only one to fail! Emily Sibyl went to the time of Tarquinius and found herself stranded there! Emily doesn't know a damned thing about *electronics*, and it would have been harder to build technical things five hundred years ago, anyway, so she was stuck. She needed a way to live, to get by. She knew people, and organizations, and, more important, she knew the history of Rome. She became a prophetess, and a good one. She must have needed a lot of money at one point, so she wrote out a series of scrolls and went to Tarquinius with them. So, she bargained. She *could* bargain, I have purchased things from her. I've seen her beat people down for prices. That way of burning the scrolls to scare Tarquinius into paying her price for the scrolls, that's *just* what she would do. She must have set down every fact and detail of Roman history she knew in those three scrolls. If it is any consolation to you, I don't think there was anything important in the six scrolls she burned. They were probably blank."

"Blank?" asked the Senator.

"Yes, of course. They were only *bargaining chips*, and she *knew* the outcome, so it wasn't really much of a gamble. Dear gods, dear gods. So much for the *Prime Directive*. Well, I can't complain too much. I introduced paper and horseshoes because I needed money."

"Why does she name you in these books?"

"Because she knew I was coming, and when. Perhaps it was to give me some protection by declaring me an oracle. I don't think I can give you or tell you anything. Emily Sibyl knew much more Roman history than I. She has already told you more than I could. I have given you horseshoes and ox shoes and better wire pulling, but I think those things will not last. Don't ask me for other things. As the people I have worked with can tell you, it takes a long time to build anything, and the road is paved with failed attempts. If I were to try to build some kind of weapon for you, I'd probably end up killing myself. All that I want is what the Sibyl herself wanted, to go home."

The Senator was silent for a long time as he regarded Tenobius. He took a swallow of wine from his own cup.

"I did not know what I expected from this meeting, but I did not expect this. You say that the giving of our sacred Sibyl's books was a mercenary act, and you have nothing to add."

"I did not mean to dirty the memory of the Sibyl. Can you account for her actions in any other way? She was bargaining, pure and simple."

The Senator gave a short bark of a laugh.

"We thought she was chiding him for his hesitation and his tight-fistedness. You may be correct. Especially if you knew her, though how you do, when she lived hundreds of years ago, I cannot understand."

"We have stories of people who have fallen asleep and wake up after many, many years have passed. Do you tell stories of this sort?" asked

Tenobius. "We are like that, the Sibyl and I, only when we wake up, it is earlier than when we went to sleep. I've been trying to figure out a way to explain what we do, but that is probably the best way. Only after we awoke, we found we could not fall asleep and awake in our own time. Sibyl is stuck, was stuck, in the time of Tarquinius, and I am here now. We owe our knowledge of what will happen to our memories of times gone by, or from what we have been told of them. The Sibyl knew and remembered more of your kings and rulers than I ever knew."

"It is said," remarked the Senator, "That we learn from our mistakes. That, after a thing has happened, it is easy to see what to do. Even if you do not recall the names of emperors and rulers, what do you advise us to do?"

"That is a difficult question to answer, even if you know the future. All paths may run badly, and I only know how one of them turns out. One is afraid of...changing history."

"Take this opportunity, then, knowing what you know. How would you...change history?"

Tenobius drew in a deep breath and slowly let it out.

"You are ruled by emperors. Some have been wise, others have been extremely bad. You know this, I am sure."

"Yes."

"You *could* have a Republic again. I know that it has been tried. You could break the power of the Praetorian Guard, overthrow the rule of a single man, and re-instate the system of the Consuls, supported by the Senate."

The Senator considered this.

"Yes, we could. It is a daunting prospect, as I'm sure you realize. It has, as you say, been tried. The plots have always been revealed, and the plotters executed. Besides...we already *know* who the next emperor is to be. And the next. And the next. It's written down, in the Sibylline books."

"I see. I see. Those books are what my people call a 'two-edged sword'. They have given you hundreds of years of stability and growth. Now they have dictated your future under rulers you know might be bad, and you can't change from that path. The Sibyl might possibly have given you the ability to become the world's greatest empire, but now you cannot control your own future. Maybe it would have been better if she'd burned the last three books, as well. Maybe this is why the Sybilline books don't survive until my time. Who can tell?"

~ * ~

There was another long silence. Finally, the Senator spoke.

"So, what do we do with you?" he asked.

Tenobius shrugged. It was a very non-Roman gesture. I don't think he realized this, or even knew he did it.

"I'm no danger to you. I don't think there's anything useful I can tell you, aside from the advice I just gave you. I have told you I cannot return to my home. I work in the forge of Marcus, and can be easily found."

Caius considered this.

"Others of the Senators might wish to speak with you. It is true that the Sibyl's words offer you some protection. I do not know if it will be enough. Some of my compatriots are still convinced you are a spy, and might suggest severe methods. Do you understand? You might not be able to go home, but you can surely go somewhere."

"I understand. Can I ask a favor of you?"

"You can ask."

"Your son, Publius. He must surely have mentioned another boy who is a friend of his. The boy is named Argus."

"Yes, he has. I have inquired about him. The son of a soldier of the lowest order, and thrown out of his own house. I have forbidden him to associate with the boy, but I think he still does. What about him?"

"Inquire further about him. He has helped your son in dealing with other boys on the streets, and has taught him some strength. He was also my apprentice at the forge, and has learned many skills. Among other things, he has devised his own system of numbers."

"Numbers?" The Senator showed the first sign of interest.

"He devised his own way of counting, adding, and multiplying numbers, far better than the system in common use. I have helped him with this, adding a little of my own knowledge. I approve of what he has done. It can give more rapid results, with less likelihood of mistakes, than what your shopkeepers and clerks now use. I have not been able to persuade any to enlist his services, but you could be an active patron of his."

"I would want to know more about this. I've long thought our mathematics could be improved, and could show us to be superior to the Greeks. You approve of this mode?"

"Yes. The boy understands it perfectly."

"Why should you care what happens to him?"

"Because he helped me when I first came here and had trouble making myself understood. Because I have seen where he comes from, and what future awaits him if he remains living as he is. His life is not recalled in our histories, but I don't need to read it to know what his future would be. He has intelligence, perseverance, and a good heart. He has helped me, and your son. You can now help him, and be rewarded for this in the new system of numbers."

"I will look into this. I can promise nothing. Now, you should perhaps go. There is no need for an escort, unless you do not know the way back."

"I know my way well enough."

"Good, then. Remember what I have told you."

"Thank you. You should remember, as well, what you have heard."

"Donatus!" called the Senator.

The servant came, and showed Tenobius out.

~ * ~

Publius and I moved as quickly as we could out of the hiding place while keeping quiet, replaced the panel, and I snuck out of the house in time to come around the front to see Tenobius walk out and down the front steps.

No one took any notice of him, which was probably just as well, since he didn't seem to notice anything around him. His eyes were focused far away as he thought, but somehow, he managed to avoid obstacles. I thought he might like some assistance, so I ran over to him.

He didn't seem surprised by me. He still didn't seem to be in the world at all.

"Argus," he said, dreamily, "I've been talking with The Runt's father."

"I know," I said, quickly. "We were watching."

That roused him.

"You saw?" he asked. "You heard?"

"I did. Tenobius, I never really understood you before."

"I'm still absorbing it. There's something I still don't understand."

"Tenobius, we have to get you back to your Dreamship before something else happens."

"Not yet. I have to figure this out. Let's sit on those steps for a minute."

We went over and sat. No one paid any attention to us. Tenobius was staring at the ground, thinking. Finally, without shifting his gaze, he spoke to me.

"You heard everything in there?"

"Yes. I never heard of these books before."

"I have. I thought they were just a legend, or maybe a collection of vague predictions that could be about anything. I never thought they'd be a set of accurate predictions about Rome. Here all this time I've been trying to avoid changing history! I could have just taught you modern mathematics straight out! Now I know it's better that you came up with it yourself."

"So, what is troubling you?"

"Sybil. *The* Sybil, I guess. I know her, knew her, will know her. De Camp was right. *Time travel* messes up your grammar. I've seen her picture somewhere in Rome."

"Here? Where?"

"That's what I'm trying to remember. I'm trying to remember everywhere I've been since I arrived here, and I can't place it." He was silent as he stared at the ground, searching his memory, I guess. Suddenly he looked up.

"I have it! It's not in a building that's here *now*. The building doesn't exist yet. There's a painting of the Sybil in the Sistine Temple. I can remember, can see it in my mind's eye. The only one of the Sybils to be facing out, and it's her face. It's Emily Sybil. I could swear it is. That's over a thousand years from now..." He frowned and stared out again.

"Oh, my gods," he said. "What if it wasn't just my Dreamship and Sybil's that failed, but *all* of them? A *common mode* failure. All four had the same defect. Leonard Vincent was travelling to about the right time. He could have been around when Michael the Messenger was painting the Sistine, if he lived long enough. *He* knew what Sybil looked like, and he was a superb artist. He could've drawn her picture for Michael. He could have..." And he stopped speaking again.

"Nooooo. Leonard was a superb artist and mechanical engineer, but...No. It couldn't be." He turned to me, with an odd expression. "Maybe Heinlein was right. It *was* easier in those days to hide your traces and fabricate your life. Oh, Argus. You and I are only passing through history. Sybil and Leonard, they *are* history."

I had no idea what he meant, he was really talking to himself again. I saw something he left out.

"You said there was a fourth dreamship. What about that?"

"Oh, yes. That was Ashok. He was the most brilliant of us. He was going to a time when there might not even have been people in Rome. If anyone could build a *Time Machine*, a Dreamship, out of stone knives and bearskins, it would be him. I don't know. Perhaps his ship did not fail. If it did, I don't know how to find out, short of going back and looking for him. I think Sybil and Leonard were stranded, and not able to repair their ships. I should probably leave now, before something else happens to mine."

Another odd look came over his face.

"Argus, when I was arrested, the box with the cat's whisker was still on the table. Did you put it away?"

"No. I was away from the shop. When I saw what was happening, I directly followed you."

"Come on!" he shouted, and started running back to Marcus' smithy.

~ * ~

We found that the box had been swept off the work bench and onto the ground, but who did it or why, no one there could tell us. It might have been one of the soldiers, or one of the workers in the shop, who needed the space. It didn't appear to be a deliberate attempt to break it, because we fond all the parts readily enough. Unfortunately, the careful positioning of the whisker had been lost, and Tenobius had to go through it all again.

He was not as bothered by this as I would have thought. He knew he found the spot once before with this same crystal, and could do it again, especially if he could set the crystal the right way up in his clamp. Still, it took him the better part of the day to do it.

I had a haunting suspicion that kept bubbling up in my mind as I watched Tenobius work. Could it have been Lillia? Finally, I had to ask Tenobius. He said no, how could she possibly know what this piece did. I said nothing, but the box was pretty clearly Tenobius' handiwork, and she knew what his creations were for, now. She might simply have swept the box from the table in frustration, or it might have been a weak attempt to keep him from going. I don't know if he would believe that.

No one could have been happier than Tenobius when he finally got his crystal working. He double-checked he connection, tried out shaking the box to make sure it could stand handling, Satisfied, he shut up the box and took his other things from the table. He stood up and looked over the table and the shop, as if for the last time. I realized that it *was* the last time. Tenobius had all he needed. He was going home.

"I'm going to do what I should have done before. I am going to say 'farewell' to Marcus. He's been good to me for these past months, and deserves not to be walked out on. Can you see if Lillia is around?"

"I'm not sure she'll want to come," I said.

"Hm? Why not?" he asked, as oblivious as ever.

I think I saw a light dawn in his eyes.

"Ah. Ask her anyway."

So Tenobius went, box clasped protectively under his arm, to find Marcus, and I shuffled next door to see if Lillia would come to say goodbye. I found her sitting in a corner, mechanically cleaning something. At first, she didn't want to come, but I persuaded her, saying it might be her last chance to see Tenobius. She finally agreed, but her heart wasn't in it.

We met Tenobius in the courtyard. He was alone, and said Marcus obviously didn't believe he was going anywhere. That the crazy man with the strange plans that worked out would think he was going home in his imaginary ship, and would just come back in the morning. I think the three of us, with the possible exceptions of Senator Caius Marcurius and his son, were the only ones who believed Tenobius would really be going away. We started walking to where Tenobius stored his Dreamship.

"I will miss you all," said Tenobius as we walked. "I'll miss the Little Forum, and Mama Nux's pastries. I'll miss the fish pies they sell. Who would have thought I would ever develop a taste for *those*? I have changed in my time here. Do you know that I've lost weight? I can tell from how I had to change the way I tie my cincture. I've probably eaten a healthier diet since I got here. I know my arm muscles are stronger. I'll probably deteriorate after I get back."

"So, Tenobius, is your name really...Watanabe?"

"Yes. I was shocked when the Senator said that. I never told anyone here my real name after the first few people I spoke with turned it into 'Tenobius'. It's my family name. My family was originally from a land far, far to the East of here. They called it the Land of the Rising Sun, in fact. Later some of them went to another land far to the west of here, beyond the sea, which is where I was born."

"From far to the East to far in the West? Why would they do that?"

"It's too complicated to explain now. It wasn't as far as you might think. The East and the West come together on the other side of the world. The world is round, you see."

"What?"

I couldn't tell if he was joking or not. He might be telling me another one of his strange truths. You couldn't tell, except that Tenobius didn't make that sort of joke very often, so it was probably for real. He might even have wanted me to ask him about it, but I wouldn't give him the satisfaction.

I decided to ask him something else, instead.

"All this time, as long as I've known you, then, I've been calling you by your family name,? Not your personal name? The one your mother called you by?"

"Yes, I guess so."

"You guess so. You've been calling me by my real name. What's yours?"

"I didn't want to tell anybody."

"Why not? Are you a sorcerer, or something?"

I heard once that sorcerors keep their real names hidden. I already knew that Tenobius was a wizard, but as he an evil sorcerer, with secrets to hide?

"I didn't want to confuse people. My given name is *Mark*. Don't tell Marcus."

"Marcus Tenobius," I mused. "Mark Watanabe."

~ * ~

We reached the room in the wall where the Dreamship was stored. The doors were shut, and the complicated knot I'd tied was still in place, so no one had been at the thing since we left it. I had to untie the knot, since I was the one who tied it. It took a long time, and I suggested he might want to cut it, like Alexander had. Tenobius said he didn't want to imitate the Conqueror that way. Besides, none of us had a sword.

It was finally undone. Tenobius set the box on one of the shelves he'd built to hold parts. *'strain relief'*, he called it. He did some sort of test with his Magic Box, and declared it ready to go.

"This is it, for real and for always, now. Goodbye, my friends. Thank you for everything you've done. I owe you my life and my sanity. I can't repay you as you deserve, but here's what I can give you."

"Argus, you can have any of my manufactured tools you can take away from Marcus' shop before he notices. Don't take any of his tools, but he has no claim on the things I bought and made. You have knowledge, too, of making paper, *insulation*, horseshoes, ox shoes, and that system of numbers. Now, this is important, at the end of my meeting with the Senator, I asked him to employ you. He wants to know how those numbers work."

"I know," I said. "I was listening through the gap in the wall."

"That's right, you told me. Do this. Work for him. Even if you leave his employ, your name will be known, and you can refer back to him. You won't have to spend the rest of your life sleeping on a sand bank and eating boiled leather soup. I wish I could have done more, but now you have a shot at a real job."

"Lillia, thank you for bringing me back to life, for comforting me and feeding me."

"So," she said, "You're just going to leave me, after all that?"

She slapped his face and stepped back.

"Lillia, understand, can't take you with me. They wouldn't allow it, in the first place. Although now that I know what Sibyl and Leonard did, this seems like *small potatoes*. More important, though, the Dreamship can only carry one person. This was a test. Even if you sat on my lap, it couldn't take you. I can't stay. I really do have a duty to my fellow travelers. I have to report back on what went wrong. I wish that I could stay with both of you if I could simply run back and forth between home and here. Even if I get back, I don't think that will happen. You may be angry with me, but please wish me farewell. I want to give you this."

He held something out. Lillia didn't want to look at first, but he finally persuaded her. It was a large gem. A diamond, maybe, although I can't tell one clear stone from another. It was beautiful, and sparkled with colors almost as bright as the ones in my disc. He also gave her his purse, with the rest of his money.

"Take these, and think well of me, if you can. I may perhaps be able to do something for you yet, but I don't know for certain."

"Now, it's time for me to go. You two should stand back further."

Tenobius sat down in his Dreamship, and it was like before. He worked the toggles, and the Dreamship came to life, with a whirring of wind, the cheeping like crickets, and all those wonderful lights without flame starting up. He moved other toggles, and the lights changed and the crickets chirped. The whirring got louder, and the world around us started to darken and the sensation of swirling began. The whirlpool formed and the dark point of the funnel formed directly overhead, then began to descend...

~ * ~

The Chrono Displacement Module started up under its jury-rigged control mechanism. Fortunately, the heart of the spacetime reactor had not been damaged by the short-circuit fusing that destroyed one entire panel. Mark Watanabe's clever cannibalizing of unneeded components, the re-purposing of operational amplifiers to new tasks and of indicator LEDs as functioning diodes in the control circuits was a successful gamble. The burned-paper carbon-film resistors did not fail when called upon, nor did the hand-wound inductors, nor the hand-rolled capacitors, all made from hand-pulled wire coated with horsehide glue mixed with honey, chalk, and aconite to dissuade vermin. The acceptance criteria of the oscillators were broad enough that the variation of time constants due to the fortuitous values of resistance, capacitance, and inductance did not matter. His hand-wound transformer functioned well enough, and the cat's whisker diode, replacing the failed vacuum diode, which in turn replaced the one big damaged component he could find no substitute for, functioned without fail this time. The Temporal Vortex formed, and the control circuits properly guided its formation and positioning. After that, they were no longer needed, and if they failed again, Watanabe would still be able to return to his own time, properly identify it, and stop. The CDM, the Dreamship, lifted off in its temporal dimension, and vanished from Ancient Rome.

Epilogue

The funnel descended on us and everything was lost, as if in a fog. At last the fog slowly vanished, and the Dreamship and Tenobius were gone. We looked at where it had been, then we looked around. Everything was the same, except for Tenobius and his Dreamship being gone. We would never see him again. I think that Lillia realized it at the same time I did, and she started to cry. After a moment, I did, too.

We walked home together, and she went into her house. I went into the forge and started gathering up Tenobius' things. I would take them back to where the Dreamship had been stored, and put them in there for now. After I did that, I didn't feel like doing anything.

~ * ~

I went to see Publius the next day and asked him to introduce me to his father. Deep down, I really didn't believe he would do what Tenobius said. The Senator called both of us into his room and talked with us a long time. He asked me many questions about Tenobius, where he was from, and where he went. After we discussed him, I told him about the things Tenobius made, and how he went around finding things. I explained my numbers to him, and showed them how they worked. The Senator said he would pay Marcus for my services, so he would not suffer from the loss of an apprentice.

After that, he asked me where I lived. I tried not to answer, but he got it out of me anyway. He told me I could have a room to myself in the servant's quarters, and he would arrange for me to work with the clerks. It took some time to convince Donatus and the other servants I wasn't just another houseboy, brought in to sweep out rooms and clean the privies, but I convinced them.

The day after Caius Marcurius took me in, I went back to Marcus and told him Tenobius really had gone for good, and I was leaving, too. He was happier about getting the money from the Senator than he would be from my continued service. I didn't miss working in Marcus' Shop.

That was the beginning of my new life. After the Senator found he could trust my numbers, and I showed him I could both read and write, I got the special assignments. I was soon his leading private secretary. As the years went by, I rose in his service, going off to oversee his businesses abroad. I made my own contacts with men in business as well as in the government, and set aside money. I used the lessons of finding things in the markets that Tenobius taught me. When the Senator fell out of favor with the Emperor, was imprisoned, and later executed, I was able to set out on my own.

I helped my mother and my brothers and sisters when I could. My father disappeared somewhere with the army. I never saw him again. I married, and had children of my own, and built a good house.

Marcus kept turning out horse shoes and ox shoes for a while after Tenobius left, but he did not hustle after business as Tenobius had. Eventually the product line died as fewer and fewer customers came for them. Marcus always expected business to come to him, and didn't see the point of going after it. I think that without Tenobius there to keep the standard up, the quality started to decline, as well. That made sales drop, too. Marcus still used Tenobius' wire-making machine, but otherwise, it was as if he had never been there.

I saw Lillia less and less after I left the shop. Sometimes I'd swing around to look at the shop, I brought Marcus some business myself, since I knew his shop best. Sometimes I would see her, say hello, or just wave. As time went by I stopped seeing her altogether. I learned the old couple who owned the house died, and some other relative moved in. Lillia must have gone back to her family in the country, or gone elsewhere.

Tullius' father died, and Tullius took over the leather business. I purchased hides from him now and then. His own son took over the tree in the Little Forum.

Publius grew quite a bit as he got older, a Runt no more. His father got him into politics, and he got to be very good at it, showing confidence he lacked when I first knew him. He avoided the consequences of his father's fall, making himself inconspicuous until the times were favorable, and eventually became a Senator himself.

~ * ~

It was some thirty years after Tenobius left I heard something strange in the Forum, the Big one, not the Little Forum. I was searching for items I could put together and sell, much the way Tenobius had, although my creations were not as far-fetched and strange as his had been. I was, in fact, remembering Tenobius, when I heard someone *whistling*. Aside from trainers whistling at their dogs or horses, or people signaling across the Forum, I hadn't heard much whistling at all. This wasn't a short call, like a signal to a person or an animal. It was an extended whistling of music, just like Tenobius did. No, it was *exactly* as Tenobius did. I think it might even have been the same music he whistled. I turned to see who was whistling.

It was Tenobius.

He was dressed as he always had been before, and he looked exactly the same as the day he left. My face must have shown my surprise, because his face broke into a broad smile, and he laughed. I ran to see him, and we embraced.

"*Edepol*! Tenobius, it's you! It's really you! I never thought I would see you again! I thought you couldn't come back!" A sudden deep suspicion crossed my mind. "Did your Dreamship break? Did it stop here and strand you?"

He laughed again.

"You always were fast in figuring things out, Argus. No, I made it all the way back to my home. It took a lot of arguing with them to let me come back and see you. I had to do it, and to let you know. Come with me. I've arranged a private place for us to talk."

He took me to a small house nearby, and we entered into a villa with a small, cool Peristylum, filled with flowering plants and a pool of clear water. Tenobius got two goblets and jar of wine. There were couches for reclining, and no other ears to hear.

"I have rented this, just for our meeting. I can only stay a little while, but I wanted to see you again, to see how things worked out, and to tell you what I have done. This visit is also a test, like my first one. We are fine-tuning our calibrations."

"I cannot believe how good you look, Tenobius," I said. "It's been over thirty years, but you look exactly the same"

"Well, not exactly. It has been a few years for me, but not as many as for you. I can see that you've done well. The Senator took you into his service, then?"

I answered that he had, and told him everything that happened since.

Tenobius told me about his homecoming. They were surprised when he showed them his Dreamship, and explained how he repaired it himself. The people who sent him out were amazed he could do that.

"I told them I had help. They were very impressed with what I told them about you."

"You told them I could pump bellows very well?"

"They were more impressed with your independently inventing *Hindu-Arabic* numerals, with a little help from me. When I told them about that, the horse shoes, the ox shoes and the paper, they *went ballistic*. I mean, they got very upset," he said, explaining his barbarian words. "They were all convinced I brought down ruin on their heads with *temporal paradoxes*. At least, until I told them what Sybil and Leonard did. That was when they got VERY upset and angry. It was a long time before I could calm them down."

"They *did* calm down, eventually. Some of them said it was a confirmation of the *Novikov Self-Consistency Principle*. In any event, it's clear that, when something is done, it is most certainly done. No one wanted to go back and try to undo what those two did, for fear of somehow making things worse. Because they believed that it would necessarily be impossible to change."

"They learned from this. We now have much improved methods of probing the past to learn things without actually having to visit. We use *unmanned probes*. So, we can get the answers we are looking for without making more disturbances, and if we travel back, we aren't flying blind anymore. That's why we were able to know how to prepare this room for our meeting."

"We learned that all four of the Dreamships did fail, and in exactly the same way. Since there was little that Ashok could have done to make a lasting impact, we went back to get him. He hadn't started repairing his Dreamship with stone knives and bear skins. He had set up a very comfortable dwelling. He was happy to see the rescue team."

"As for Sybil, I convinced them we could go to see her after she sold her books to Tarquinius Superbus. No one knows what happened to the Sybil after that, she vanished. So, she did, because we brought her back. Leonard was a more difficult case. We couldn't bring him back, he was too well-known, and his life was recorded right up until his death. He didn't want to come back with us, anyway. Why would he want to be a relatively unknown mechanical engineer and undiscovered artist, when he could be one of the Greatest Minds in History? He stayed where he was and lived out, is living out, his life. There was only one thing he wanted. He gave us some plans, and insists that we cast his Giant Bronze Horse. I think the government of Rome has agreed to pay for it."

"As for me, I didn't make much of a splash. I'm not cut out for greatness, I guess. We've followed the progress of Marcus' forge, and we know the horse shoe business declined and died. What happened with your numbers?"

"After the Senator was taken," I said, "no one else was interested in them. I still use them for my business, but I have to translate everything into proper Roman numeral for everyone else to understand."

"You see the extent of my impact on history," said Tenobius. "I could give you a good life, make some extra money for Marcus and a few other people. I understand my horse shoes are forgotten, even now."

"I don't know what happened to Lillia," I told him, explaining what I knew.

"That's no problem," he responded. "As I said, we have much improved abilities to monitor the past. We could follow her progress."

"You know?" I asked, excited. "What happened to her? Did she go back to her family?"

"There is a cost in energy to transfer a person from the past to the future, or from the future to the past. You can reclaim that energy when you transfer that person or thing back, it's a sort of *Temporal Conservation of Energy* law. Don't worry about what that means exactly. Think of it as a fare you have to pay to ride the Dreamship. If it's a round trip, it costs a lot less than a one-way trip. It hurt some people to consider the cost of leaving Leonard in the past, but what could they do? The alternative was to change history,"

"Why are you telling me this?"

"Because I managed to persuade the *Research Board* to pay that sum a second time, to bring back a *biological specimen*, a person, for study. The *biologists* want to know about the illnesses and the parasites of this Rome, and the best way to do it is to have our doctors examine them in their own offices. The person you bring back can never return, he or she picks up knowledge of the future, and although it's unlikely this will alter history, why take the chance? Lillia was the specimen I persuaded them to choose. We brought her back to my home, and she's been living there with me."

"You came back for Lillia?" I was excited and happy for her.

"Yes. That's why you didn't see her around anymore. I owed it to her. I was worried about what would happen to her after Rufus Placidus and Alena died."

"That's not the only reason you came back for her!"

"No. I guess the *Chronic Argonaut* has to come back and rescue his *Weena*."

"Whenever something gets too close to you, you always try to hide it with these barbarian words of yours. Why can't you just say that you love her?"

"Because I can't, I guess. It's the way I am."

"How does she like it, back where you are from?"

"She loves some things. She doesn't have to carry water back from a well, build a wood fire, or go to the market every day. She insists on cooking. She has much greater variety to choose from, but she misses the familiar things. We call it *Culture Shock*. She can't get the things she's used to from our markets, and she complains that much of the food isn't fresh enough. She misses the Temples, the Little Forum and a thousand things she's used to. I did find a group of people who worship the Roman gods, no easy thing. She keeps telling them all the things they have wrong. She's re-instituted many of the festivals, and teaching people the Old Ways keeps her happy. She tried to make a worshipper of me, but I think she's given up on that now. We're happy."

"My Dreamship has been preserved in a *museum*, now. They show it off as an example of Creative Thinking in a Crisis. The new ships don't fail, and I've made sure there are *redundant circuits* in them to prevent any more accidents. Is there anything else I can tell you?"

"Everything is good with you, then? They're no longer angry with you?"

"Oh, no. I'm important now. I have more practical experience with Dreamships than anyone else, so they're keeping me around. That's what they call them now, *Dreamships*. They didn't think people took them seriously when they called them *Time Machines*. How about you? Is your life good? Is there anything you need?"

"I'm happy enough. I have my wife and my children. I have interesting work to do. Nothing threatens my life. What more could I want? I wouldn't mind seeing your home, though."

"I can't," said Tenobius. "It was hard enough arranging this meeting. All *Temporal Exploration* now is done through viewers and remote devices. It's only because of my reputation that I could make this trip. They'd never approve the energy cost to bring you forward, even if they get much of it back on rebound. Just take my word for it, we are happy, too. What more could you ask?"

"Well, I can ask this, can I see your new Dreamship? All I saw was the wreck of your old one."

Tenobius laughed at that, and took me to a room in the villa that held his new Dreamship. It looked different from the old one. When he showed me the panels, none were fire-scorched or smelled bad. There were no hand-made wires coated with ox hide *insulation*, strung with beads, or with wooden shelves holding his hand-made parts. It was much cleaner and neater. At the same time, it lacked the personality of his other one. Tenobius poured several months of his life and his soul into his shattered Dreamship.

This one was just a superb piece of handiwork, with no flaws or faults.

    We embraced again, and said our farewells for the last time. I stayed to watch him leave. Tenobius closed the door and started up his Dreamship, with its lights and noises. It generated the same whirlwind, and disappeared into the funnel and the mist. After it cleared, I was alone in the empty villa. I left the house, and walked out into the rest of my life.

About the Author

Stephen R. Wilk gas always been interested in Unusual Things. His first publication was "The Physics of Karate" in *Scientific American*. He has written on History, Mythology, Physics, Optics, and Popular Culture, including two books from Oxford University Press: *Medusa: Solving the Mystery of the Gorgon* and *How the Ray Gun Got Its Zap!*. Steve's published fiction includes Science Fiction, Fantasy, Horror, and Mysteries. *The Traveler* is his first published novel.

**VISIT OUR WEBSITE
FOR THE FULL INVENTORY
OF QUALITY BOOKS**:

http://www.roguephoenixpress.com

Rogue Phoenix Press

Representing Excellence in Publishing

Quality trade paperbacks and downloads

in multiple formats,

in genres ranging from historical to contemporary romance, mystery and science fiction.

Visit the website then bookmark it.

We add new titles each month!

www.ingramcontent.com/pod-product-compliance
Lightning Source LLC
Chambersburg PA
CBHW021036130626
46552CB00005B/1869